IN THIS LIGHT

Also by Melanie Rae Thon

IN THIS LIGHT

NEW AND SELECTED STORIES

Melanie Rae Thon

GRAYWOLF PRESS

This publication is made possible by funding provided in part by a grant from the Minnesota State Arts Board, through an appropriation by the Minnesota State Legislature, a grant from the National Endowment for the Arts, and private funders. Significant support has also been provided by Target; the McKnight Foundation; and other generous contributions from foundations, corporations, and individuals. To these organizations and individuals we offer our heartfelt thanks.

Published by Graywolf Press
250 Third Avenue North, Suite 600
Minneapolis, Minnesota 55401

www.graywolfpress.org

Published in the United States of America

ISBN 978-1-55597-585-2

2 4 6 8 9 7 5 3 1
First Graywolf Printing, 2011

Library of Congress Control Number: 2011922712

Cover design: Christa Schoenbrodt, Studio Haus

Cover photo: *Boarded Window*. Photo © Bradford Dunlop, www.bradforddunlop.com.

for my mother and brother and sisters
for our beautiful children
for the ones who have joined us by marriage
and for all who shall come in the future
for our father who loved this life—and who taught us to love one another

Does the light descend from the sky or rise out of us? That instant of trapped light . . . reveals to us what is unseen, what is seen but unnoticed. . . . It shows us that concealed within the pain of living and the tragedy of dying there is a potent magic, a luminous mystery that redeems the human adventure in the world.

—Eduardo Galeano,
from the introduction to *An Uncertain Grace:
Photographs by Sebastião Salgado*

Contents

IN THIS LIGHT

FROM *Girls in the Grass*
(1991)

Iona Moon

WILLY HAMILTON NEVER DID LIKE Iona Moon. He said country girls always had shit on their shoes and he could smell her after she'd been in his car. Jay Tyler said his choice of women was nobody's business, and if Willy didn't like it, he should keep his back doors locked.

Choice of women, Jay said that so nice. He thought Iona was a woman because the first night they were together he put his hand under her shirt and she didn't stop kissing him. He inched his fingers under her brassiere, like some five-legged animal, until elastic caught his wrist and squished his hand against her breast. She said, "Here, baby, let me help you," and she reached around behind her back and released the hooks. One hand on each breast, Jay Tyler whistled through his teeth. "Sweet Jesus," he said, and unbuttoned her blouse, his fingers clumsy and stiff with the fear that she might change her mind. Jay Tyler had known plenty of girls, girls who let him do whatever he wanted as long as he could take what he was after without any assistance on their part, without ever saying, "Yes, Jay," the way Iona did, just a murmur, "yes," soft as snow on water.

In the moonlight, her skin was pale, her breasts small but warm, something a boy couldn't resist. Jay cupped them in his palms, touching the nipples with the very tips of his fingers, as if they were precious and alive, something separate from the girl, something that could still be frightened and disappear. He pressed his lips to the hard bones of Iona Moon's chest, rested his head in the hollow between her breasts and whispered words no boy had ever spoken to her.

"Thank you, oh, God, thank you," his voice hushed and amazed, the voice of a drowning man just pulled from the river. As his mouth found her nipple, Jay Tyler closed his eyes tight, as if he wanted to be blind, and Iona Moon almost laughed to see his sweet face wrinkle that way; she couldn't help thinking of the newborn pigs, their little eyes glued shut, scrambling for a place at their mother's teats.

Iona supposed Willy Hamilton was right about her shoes, but she was past noticing it herself. Every morning, she got up early to milk the four cows. Mama had always done it before Iona and her brothers were awake. Even in winter, Hannah Moon trudged to the barn while it was still dark, slogged through the mud and slush, wearing her rubber boots and Daddy's fur-lined coat that she could have wrapped around herself twice. Waves of blue snow across the fields fluttered, each drift a breast heaving, giving up its last breath.

Mama said she liked starting the day that way, in the lightless peace God made before he made the day, sitting with your cheek pressed against the cow's warm flank, your hands on her udder, understanding your pull has to be strong and steady but not too hard, knowing she likes you there and she feels grateful in the way cows do, so she makes a sleepy sound like a moan or a hum, the same sound Iona heard herself make at the edge of a dream.

Willy had a girl, Belinda Beller. She wore braces, and after gym class, Iona saw her stuff her bra with toilet paper. Willy and Belinda, Iona and Jay, parked down by the river in Willy's Chevy. Belinda kept saying, "No, honey, please, I don't want to." Jay panted over Iona, licking her neck, slipping his tongue as far in her ear as it would go; her bare back stuck to the vinyl seat, and Willy said, "I'm sorry," his voice serious and small, "sorry."

He thought of his father handcuffing that boy who stole the floodlights from the funeral home. Willy was twelve and liked cruising with his dad, pretending they might get lucky and find some trouble. They caught up with the boy down by the old Miller Creek bridge. His white face rose like a moon above his dark clothes, eyes enchanted to stone by the twin beams of the headlights.

Horton Hamilton climbed out of the patrol car, one hand on his hip. The thick fingers unsnapped the leather band that held the pistol safe in the holster. Willy's father said, "Don't you be gettin' any ideas of makin' like a jackrabbit, boy; I got a gun." He padded toward the skittery, long-legged kid, talking all the time, using the low rumble of his voice to hold the boy in one place, like a farmer trying to mesmerize a dog that's gone mad, so he can put a bullet through its head.

Willy recognized the kid. His name was Matt Fry and he lived out west of town on the Kila Flats, a country boy. Horton Hamilton believed you could scare the mischief out of a child. He cuffed Matt Fry as if he were a grown man who'd done a lot worse. He said stealing those lights was no petty crime: they were worth a lot of money, enough to make the theft a felony even though Matt Fry was only fifteen years old.

A policeman didn't get much action in White Falls, Idaho, so Horton Hamilton took what business he had seriously. He'd drawn his gun any number of times, or put his hand on it at least, but he'd had cause to shoot only once in nineteen years, and that was to kill a badger that had taken up residence on poor Mrs. Griswold's porch and refused to be driven away by more peaceable means.

Fear of God, fear of the devil, that was good for a boy, but Willy heard later that Matt Fry's parents had had enough of his shenanigans and that a felony was the limit, the very limit. They told the county judge they'd lost control of their boy and it would be best for everyone to lock him up and set him straight. Until then, Willy didn't know that if you did a bad enough thing, your parents could decide they didn't want you anymore.

When Matt Fry came back from the boys' home, he smelled like he forgot sometimes and pissed his own pants; he didn't look at you if you saw him on the street and said, "Hey." His parents still wouldn't let him come home and he slept in a burned-out barn down in the gully. People said Matt Fry got caught fighting his first day at the state home. They threw him in the hole for eighteen days, all by himself, without any light, and when they dragged him out he was like this: lame in one foot, mumbling syllables that didn't add up to words, skinny as a coyote at the end of winter.

Willy stopped pawing at Belinda and sat with his hands in his lap until she leaned over to peck his cheek and say, "It's all right now, honey." Iona Moon had no sympathy for Belinda Beller's point of view. What sense was there in saving everything up for some special occasion that might not ever come? How do you hold a boy back if it feels good when he slides his knee between your legs? How do you say no when his tongue in your ear makes you arch your back and grab his hair?

Willy liked nice girls, girls who accidentally brushed their hands against a guy's crotch, girls who wiggled their butts when they walked past you in the hall, threw their shoulders back and almost closed their eyes when they said hello. Girls who could pull you right up to the edge and still always, always say no.

Iona thought, you hang on to something too long, you start to think it's worth more than it is. She was never that way on account of having three brothers and being the youngest. When she was nine, her oldest brother gave her a penny to dance for him. Before long, they made it regular. Night after night Iona twirled around the barn for Leon, spun in the circle of light from the lantern hanging off the rafter. Dale and Rafe started coming too; she earned three cents a night from her brothers and saved every penny till she had more than four dollars. Later they gave her nickels for lifting her shirt and letting them touch the buds that weren't breasts yet. And one time, when Leon and Iona were alone in the loft, he paid her a dime for lying down and letting him rub against her. She was scared, all that grunting and groaning, and when she looked down she saw that his little prick wasn't little anymore: it was swollen and dark and she yelled, "You're hurting yourself." He clamped his dirty hand over her mouth and hissed. Finally he made a terrible sound, like the wail a cow makes when her calf is halfway out of her; his mouth twisted and his face turned red, as if Iona had choked him. But she hadn't; her arms were flung straight out from her sides; her hands clutched fistfuls of straw. Leon collapsed on his sister like a dead man, and she lay there wondering how she was going to explain to Mama and Daddy that she'd killed her brother. He crushed the breath out of her; sweat from his face trickled onto hers, and she felt something damp and sticky soaking through her jeans. When she tried to wriggle out from under him, he sprang back to life. He pinched her face with one hand. Squeezing her cheeks with his big fingers, he said, "Don't you ever tell, Iona. Mama will hate you if you ever tell."

After that her brothers stopped paying her to dance for them, and Leon made Rafe and Dale cut their thumbs with his hunting knife and swear by their own blood that they'd never tell anyone what they did in the barn that year.

·   ·   ·

You can't make my brothers do much of anything unless you force them to swear in blood, Iona thought.

One morning after a storm, she tramped out to the barn to do her milking. The wind howled, cutting through her jeans. Snow had drifted against the door; she bent over and dug like a dog. The first stall was empty. She ran to the next, shining her flashlight in every corner, trying to believe a cow could hide in a shadow like a cat, but she knew, even as she ran in circles, she knew that all four cows were out in the fields, that her brothers had just assumed an animal will head for shelter on its own. They didn't know cows the way Iona and her mama did. A cow's hardly any smarter than a chicken; a cow has half the brains of a pig; a cow's like an overgrown child, like the Wilkerson boy, who grew tall and fat but never got smart.

She heard them. As she ran across the fields, stumbling in the snow, falling on her face more than once and snorting ice through her nose, she heard them crying like old women. The four of them huddled together, standing up past their knees in the drifts. Snow had piled in ridges down their backs; they hadn't moved all night. They let out that sound, that awful wail, as if their souls were being torn out of them. Iona had to whip them with her belt to get them going; that's how cows are: they'll drop to their knees and freeze to death with their eyes wide open and the barn door barely a hundred feet in front of them.

Later, Iona took Mama her aspirin and hot milk, sat on the edge of her bed and moaned like the cows, closing her eyes and stretching her mouth wide as it would go.

Mama breathed deep with laughter, holding her stomach; the milk sloshed in the cup and Iona had to hold it. Mama had a bad time holding on to things. Her fingers were stiff and twisted, and that winter, her knees swelled up so big she couldn't walk.

Iona Moon told Jay Tyler how it was in the winter on the Kila Flats, how the wind had nothing to stand in its way, how the water froze in the pipes and you had to use the outhouse, how you held it just as long as you could because the snow didn't fall, it blew straight in your face; splinters of ice pierced your skin and you could go blind or lose your way just walking to that little hut twenty-five yards behind the house. She told him she kept a thunder mug under her bed in case she had to pee in the night. But she didn't tell him her mama had to use a bedpan all the time, and Iona was the one who slid it under her bony butt because Mama said it wasn't right for the man you love to see you that way.

Mama knew Iona had a guy. She made Iona tell her that Jay Tyler was on the diving team in the summer. He could fly off the high board backward, do two somersaults and half a twist; he seemed to open the water with his hands, and his body made a sound like a flat stone you spin sideways so it cuts without a splash: blurp, that's all. Mama worked the rest of it out of Iona too. Jay's father was a dentist with a pointed gray beard and no hair. Jay was going to college so he could come back to White Falls and go into business with his dad. Iona said it as if she was proud, but Mama

shook her head and blinked hard at her gnarled hands, trying to make something go away. She said, "If I was a strong
woman, Iona, I'd lock you in this house till you got over
that boy. I'd rather have you hate me than see your heart
be broke."

"Jay's not like that," Iona said.

"Every boy's like that in the end. Dentists don't marry
the daughters of potato farmers. He'll be lookin' for a girl
with an education." She didn't talk that way to be mean.
Iona knew Mama loved her more than anyone alive.

Willy thought that just listening to Jay Tyler and his father might be dangerous, a bad thing that made his stomach thump like a second heart. Horton Hamilton had
raised his son to believe there was one way that was right
and one way that was wrong and nothing, absolutely
nothing, in between. Willy said, "What if someone steals
food because he's hungry?" And his father said, "Stealing's
wrong." Willy said, "If a man's dying, if he feels his whole
body filling up with pain, would the Lord blame him for
taking his own life?" Horton Hamilton rubbed his chin.
"The Lord would *forgive* him, Willy, because that's the
good Lord's way, but no man has the right to choose his
time of death, or any other man's time of death." Willy
thought he had him now: "Why do you carry a gun?" His
father said his gun was to warn and to wound, but only if
there was no other way. He liked talking better.

Willy remembered the way his father talked to Matt
Fry. He saw Matt Fry hobbling down the middle of the

street, his head bobbing, his pants crusted with dirt, smelling of piss. He thought maybe Matt Fry would have been better off if his father had shot him dead at Miller Creek. And he bowed his head with the shame of letting himself imagine it.

Jay Tyler's dad wanted to be a lawyer but became a dentist like his own father instead. He taught Jay to argue both sides of every question with equal passion. When Willy told him there was one right and one wrong and all you had to do was look in the Bible to see which was which, Andrew Johnson Tyler scratched his bald head and said, "Well, Willy, I tell you, it's hard for a *medical man* to believe in God." Willy couldn't figure out why, but there was something about the way Dr. Tyler said "medical man," some secret reverence, that made Willy afraid to question him.

Jay's mother floated across the veranda, her footsteps so soft that Willy glanced at her feet to be sure they touched wood. The folds of her speckled dress fell forward and back; Willy saw the outline of her thighs and had to look away. "All this talk, all this talk," she said. "How about some lemonade? I'm so dry I could choke." Everything about her was pale: her cheeks, flushed from the heat; the sweep of yellow hair, wound in a bun but not too tight; a few blond tendrils swirling at the nape of her neck, damp with her own sweat; the white dress with tiny pink roses, cut low in front so that when she leaned forward and said, "Why don't you help me, Willy," he saw the curve of her breasts.

In the kitchen she brushed his hair from his eyes, touched his hand, almost as if she didn't mean to do it, but he knew. He scurried out to the porch with the lemonade on a tray, ice rattling against glass. From the cool shadows of the house, he swore he heard a woman holding her laughter in her throat.

Willy lost his way on the Kila Flats. All those dirt roads looked the same. Jay told him: "Turn left, turn right, take another right at the fork"; he sent Willy halfway around the county so he'd have time in the backseat with Iona Moon, time to unhook her bra, time to unzip his pants. Willy kept looking in the rearview mirror; he'd dropped Belinda Beller off hours ago. He imagined his father cruising Main and Woodvale Park, looking for him. He imagined his mother at the window, parting the drapes with one hand, pressing her nose to the glass. She worried. She saw a metal bumper twisted around a tree, a wheel spinning a foot above the ground, headlights blasting into the black woods. She washed the blood off the faces of the four teenagers, combed their hair, dabbed their bruises with flesh-colored powder, painted their blue lips a fresh, bright pink. That was back in '57, but she saw their open eyes and surprised mouths every time Willy was late. "Forgive me, Lord, for not trusting you. I know my thoughts are a curse. I know he's safe with you, Lord, and he's a good boy, a careful boy, but I can't help my worrying, Lord: he's my only son. I love my girls, but he's special, you see, in that way." She unlaced her fingers and hissed, "I'll thrash his hide when he walks in that door." She said it out loud because God only listened to prayers and silence. He was too busy to pay attention to all the clatter of words spoken in ordinary tones.

Jay said, "Shit, Willy, you took the wrong turn back there. I told you *right* at the fork." And Willy said he did go right, and Jay answered, "We'd be in front of Iona's house if you went right." There was something in Jay's voice, a creak or a gurgle in the throat, that gave him away. Willy slammed the brakes; his Chevy did a quarter spin that threw Jay and Iona against the door.

"What the hell?" said Jay.

"Get out," Willy said.

"What?"

"You heard me. Get out of my car."

Jay zipped his pants and opened the door; Iona started to climb out after him. "Just Jay," Willy said, and he got out too. The front window was cracked open enough for Iona to hear Willy say, "You're gonna get me grounded because you wanna fool around with that little slut." Jay shoved Willy over the hood of the car, and Iona watched the dust curl in the streams of yellow light, waiting for the blow. But Jay didn't hit him; he held him there, leaning on top of him, ten seconds, twenty; and when he let Willy up, Jay clapped him on the shoulder, said, "Sorry, buddy, I'll make it up to you."

Jay stood on the diving board, lean and tan, unbeatable. Willy was almost as good, some days better; but next to Jay he was pale and scrawny, unconvincing. Jay rolled off the balls of his feet, muscles flexing from his calves to his thighs. He threw an easy one first, a single somersault in layout position. As he opened up above the water, Iona gasped, expecting him to swoop back into the air.

Willy did the same dive, nearly as well. All day they went on this way, first one, then the other; Jay led Willy by a point and a half; the rest of the field dropped by ten.

Jay saved the backward double somersault with a twist for last. He climbed the ladder slowly, as if he had to think about the dive rung by rung. His buttocks bunched up tight, clenched like fists. On the board, he rolled his shoulders, shook his hands, his feet. He strutted to the end, raised his arms, and spun on his toes. Every muscle frozen, he gritted his teeth and leaped, clamped his knees to his chest and heaved head over heel, once, twice, opened up and twisted, limbs straight as a drill.

But in that last moment, Jay Tyler's concentration snapped. By some fluke, some sudden weakness, his knees bent and his feet slapped the water.

Iona thought she'd see Jay spit with disgust as he gripped the gutter of the pool, but he came up grinning, flashing his straight, white teeth, his father's best work. Willy offered his hand. "I threw it too hard, buddy," Jay said. *Buddy.* Iona stood outside the chain-link fence; she barely heard it, but it made her think of that dusty road; stars flung in the cool black sky by a careless hand; Willy pinned to the hood of the car; and Jay saying: *Sorry, buddy, I'll make it up to you.* Only this way, Willy would never know. It was just like Jay not to give a damn about blame or forgiveness.

Willy's dive was easier, two somersaults without a twist, but flawless. He crept ahead of Jay and no one else touched their scores. They sauntered to the bathhouse with their arms around each other's shoulders, knowing they'd won the day.

Standing in the dappled light beneath an oak, Jay Tyler's mother hugged Willy and Jay, and his father pumped their hands. Willy wished his parents could have seen him, this day above all others, but his father was on duty; and old lady Griswold had died, so his mother was busy making her look prettier than she ever was.

Iona Moon shuffled toward them, head down, eyes on the ground. Willy nudged Jay. In a single motion, graceful as the dive he almost hit, Jay turned, smiled, winked, and flicked his wrist near his thigh, a wave that said everything: go away, Iona; can't you see I'm with *my parents?* Willy felt the empty pit of his stomach, a throb of blood in his temples that made him dizzy, as if he were the one shooed away, as if he slunk in the shadows and disappeared behind the thick trunk of the tired tree, its limbs drooping with their own weight.

He was ashamed, like the small boy squinting under the fluorescent lights of the bathroom. His mother stripped his flannel pajamas off him with quick, hard strokes and said, "You're *soaked*, Willy; you're absolutely *drowned*."

Upstairs the air was still and hot, but Hannah Moon couldn't stand the noise of the fan and told Iona, no, please, don't turn it on. Iona said, "I'm going to town tonight, Mama. You want anything?"

"Why don't you just stay here and read to me till I fall asleep? What are you planning in town?"

"Nothing, nothing at all in particular. I get this desire, you know. It's so dark out here at night, just our little lights and the black fields and the blacker hills. I want to see a whole blaze of lights, all the streetlamps going on at once, all the houses burning—like something's about to happen. You have to believe something's going to happen."

"Don't you go looking for him," Mama said. "Don't you go looking for that boy. I know he hasn't called you once since school got out. Bad enough what he did, but don't you go making it worse by being a fool."

"He's nothing to me, Mama. You want a treat or something, maybe a magazine?"

"Take a dollar from my jewelry box and get me as much chocolate as that'll buy. And don't you tell your daddy, promise?"

"Promise."

"He thinks it's not good for me; I think I've got to have some pleasure."

Daddy sat on the porch with Leon and Rafe and Dale. They rocked in the great silence of men, each with his pipe, each with the same tilt of the head as if a single thought wove through their minds. A breeze high in the pines made the tops sway so the limbs rubbed up against one another. The sound they made was less than a breath, a whisper in a dream or the last thing your mother said before she kissed you good night. You were too small to understand the words, but you knew from her voice that you were loved and safe; the kiss on your forehead was a whisper too, a promise no one could keep.

Iona buzzed up and down Main, feeling strong riding up high in the cab of Daddy's red truck, looking down on cars and rumbling over potholes too fast. Daddy kept a coil of rope, a hacksaw, and a rifle in the back behind the seat. She had no intention, no intention at all, but she swung down Willow Glen Road, past Jay Tyler's house. She honked her horn at imaginary children in the street, stomped on her brakes, and laid rubber to avoid a cat that wasn't there; but all that noise didn't lure anyone out of the Tyler house, and no lights popped on upstairs or down. In the green light of dusk, the house looked gray and cool, a huge lifeless thing waiting to crumble.

She sped toward Seventh, Willy Hamilton's street. She might just happen to roll by, and maybe in the course of conversation she'd say, "Are the Tylers out of town?" Not that she cared; she was only mildly curious. "The house looks absolutely deserted," she'd say. "I don't know why any-one would want to live in that big old thing."

Sure enough, Willy stood in the driveway, hosing down his sky-blue Chevrolet. Iona leaned out the window. "Hey, Willy," she said. He wrinkled up his forehead and didn't say anything. Iona was undaunted. "You wanna go get an ice cream with me?" she said. The spray from the hose made a clear arc before it spattered on the cement and trickled toward the gutter in thick muddy rivulets.

Willy was feeling sorry for her in a way. But he still didn't like her, and he didn't think he could stand the smell of her truck. He told himself to be brave; it wouldn't last long, and it was such a small thing to do, such a small, kind

gesture; then he felt very proud, overcome with the realiza-
tion that he was going to do this good thing.

He was still thinking how generous he was when they
finished their cones and Iona jolted out along the river
road instead of heading toward his house. He said, "Where
are you going?" And she said, "The river." He told her he
needed to get home; it was almost dark. Iona said, "I know."
He told her he meant it, but his voice was feeble, and she
kept plowing through the haze of dusk, faster and faster,
till the whole seat was shaking.

She swerved down to the bank of the river, where all the
kids came to park; but it was too early for that, so they were
alone. Willy stared at the water, at the beer bottles bobbing near the shore, and the torn-off limb of a tree being
dragged downstream. "I'm sorry about Jay," he said.

"Why're you sorry? He's not dead."

"He didn't treat you right."

Iona slid across the seat so her thigh pressed against
Willy's thigh. "Would you treat me right?" she said. He
tried to inch away, but there was nowhere to go. Iona's
hand rested on his knee, then started moving up his leg,
real slow. Willy swatted it away. "You still think I'm a slut?"
Iona said. She touched his thigh again, lightly, higher than
before. "I'm not a slut, Willy; I'm just more *generous* than
most girls you know." She clutched his wrist and tried to
pull his closed hand to her breast. "Don't be afraid," she
said. "You won't be fingering Kleenex when you get a grip
on me." Willy looked so confused that Iona blew a snort
of laughter out her nose, right in his face. "You don't know,

do you, sweetheart? You don't know Belinda Beller's tits are made of paper."

"I don't want to hear you say her name," Willy said.

"Fine," said Iona, breathing in his ear. "I don't wanna talk about her either."

Willy felt the pressure in his crotch, his penis rising against his will. He thought of his mother putting lipstick and rouge on old Mrs. Griswold after she died, but even that didn't help this time.

Iona Moon pounced on top of him, kissing his mouth and locking the door at the same time. She fumbled with his belt, clawed at his zipper. He mumbled *no*, but she smothered the word, swallowed it up in her own mouth.

When Willy wrestled his sisters, his father told him to be careful: the strong have to look out for the weak, he said. It didn't matter that his sisters were older. Even if they jumped him two at a time, Willy was the one who had to go easy. He wasn't strong enough to win a fight without hurting them, without kicking and wrenching and taking a few blind swings, so he had to hold back. Most times he was lucky just to get away.

Willy clamped Iona's arms, but she twisted free. "You know you want it, Willy," she said. "Everybody wants it." But he didn't, not like this, not with Iona Moon. She bit at his lips and his ears, sharp little nips; her fingers between his legs cupped his balls dangerously tight.

With his hands on her shoulders, he shoved her back, flung her against the dashboard so hard it stunned her, and he had time to unlock the door, leap, and flee. But he didn't get far before he heard the unmistakable sputter of tires in mud, an engine revving, going nowhere. Slowing to a trot, he listened: rock it, he thought, first to reverse, first to reverse.

He heard her grind through the gears, imagined her slamming the stick, stamping the clutch, thought that by now tears streamed down her hot cheeks. Finally he heard the engine idle down, a pitiful, defeated sound in the near darkness.

Slowly he turned, knowing what he had to do, hearing his father's voice: *A gentleman always helps a lady in distress.* She's no lady. *Who are you to judge?*

He found small dead branches and laid them under the tires in two-foot rows. One steady push, his feet braced against a tree, one more, almost, third time's charm, and the front tires caught the sticks, spun, spat up mud all the way to his mouth, and heaved the truck backward onto solid ground. He wiped his hands on his jeans and clumped toward the road.

"Hey," said Iona. "Don't you want a ride?" He kept marching. "Hey, Willy, get in. I won't bite." She pulled up right beside him. "It'll take you more than an hour to get home. Your mama will skin you. Now get in. I won't lay a hand on you." He didn't dare look at her. His face felt swollen, about to explode. "What I did before, I didn't mean anything by it. I never would have tried anything if I thought you wouldn't like it. Willy?" He glanced up at her; she seemed no bigger than a child, hanging on to that huge steering wheel. "Willy, I got a gun. Right here behind the seat, I got my daddy's gun." *Don't you be gettin' any ideas of makin' like a jackrabbit, boy.* Willy didn't know if Iona meant it as a warning or a threat, but he knew there was nothing real behind her words, no reason not to get in the truck, no reason except his pride, and that seemed like a small thing when he weighed it against the five-mile trek along the winding road, his mother's pinched face, and the spot of grease from her nose on the windowpane.

White Falls sat in a hollow, a fearful cluster of lights drawn up in a circle for the night, a town closed in on itself. Iona said, "I almost died once. My brother Leon and I started back from town in a storm that turned to a blizzard. Everything was white, like there was nothing in the world besides us and the inside of this truck. Leon drove straight into a six-foot drift; it looked just the same as the sky and the road. We had to get out and walk, or sit there and freeze like the damn cows. We stumbled, breaking the wind with our hands; then we crawled because the gusts were less wild near the ground. I saw the shadows of houses wavering in the snow, right in front of us, but they were never there. A sheet of ice built up around my cheek and chin, and I kept stopping to shatter it with my fist, but it took too long; Leon said, leave it, it will stop the wind. I thought they'd find me that way, the girl in glass, and they'd keep me frozen in a special truck, take me from town to town along with the nineteen-inch man and the two-headed calf. But Leon, Leon never thought for a minute we were going to die on that road. When I dropped to my belly and said I was warm now, he swatted my butt. Not this way, he said, not this way, God. And then I wondered if he'd whispered it or if I heard what he was thinking. Leon talking to God, I thought; that was more of a miracle than surviving, and I scrambled back to my knees and lunged forward.

"Just like a dog, Leon knew his way. I forgave him for everything. I swore in my heart I'd never hold a harsh thought against him, not for anything in the past or anything he might do later on, because right there in that moment, he was saving our lives.

"When Mama wrapped my hands in warm rags and Daddy pulled off my boots to rub my toes as hard as he could, I knew that nothing, nothing in the world was ever going to matter so much again." She punched the clutch and shifted into fourth. "Do you know why I'm telling you this?" Willy nodded, but he didn't know; he didn't know at all.

It wasn't until Iona Moon eased into her driveway and shut off the engine that she remembered her mother's chocolate and the ragged dollar bill still crumpled in her pocket. *I think I've got to have some pleasure*, that was the last thing Mama said. She rested her head on the steering wheel. A single sob erupted, burst from between her ribs as if someone had pounded his fist against her chest. She fought her own cry, choked it dry, and was silent.

Punishment

IN 1858, THE SLAVE CALLED LIZE WAS HANGED in Louisville, Georgia, for the murder of her master's son. I was twelve that day, and now I'm ninety, but I still see her bare feet, scratched and dusty from being dragged down the road. Those feet dangle among leaves so green they writhe like flames. I stand in the garden. The perfume of gardenias makes me dizzy enough to faint.

From where I hang, I see a woman thrown from a ship because her child don' come. She screams too loud and long. The others lift her over the rail, let her fall. They all touch her. They all say: I'm not the one. I see the mother of my mother, standing naked on a beach. The men look her over, burn a mark on her thigh. She squats in a cage for fifteen days. Flies land on her face. She don' swat them away. I see the bodies chained in the holds of ships. Each man got less room than he got in the grave. They panic, break their own ankles, smother in their own waste. They jump if they get the chance. Black sea swallow a black man. Nobody stop to find him. On the distant shore, I see a runaway stripped of his own skin like a rabbit, torn limb from limb. To teach the others. I see Abe's head. I crawl on

my hands and knees, look for his ears. But Walkerman takes
them. Did you see how long a man bleeds? Did you see how his
head festers in the heat? No way to clean those wounds though
I wash him morning and night.

Mama died of a five-day fever we couldn't break with wet
towels and ice baths. She left her baby squalling with hunger. That's why Father brought Lize to the house, to keep
Seth alive. My brother, four months old, still wrinkled and
nearly hairless, was going to have a full-grown woman slave
of his own.

Mama would not have abided seeing Lize close to her
boy. Father owned more than thirty Negroes, but Mama
kept an Irish girl, Martha Parnell, to brush her hair and
make her bed, to wipe the vomit off the floor during the
weeks when her belly first began to swell, to rock the baby
during the days when she lay dying. Mama wouldn't have
no nigger woman upstairs, touching her child, fondling the
silver-handled mirror on her dresser or cleaning the long,
light hair out of her comb. She said they were dirty, first
of all, and they had appetites dangerous to men; she didn't
want Seth getting used to the smell of them. Only Beulah,
the cook, two hundred and twenty pounds and fifty-seven
years old, was allowed to stay in the house while Mama
was living. And Beulah was allowed to care for me, to wash
the blood from my scraped knees when I fell in the yard, to
lay cool rags on my head when my temperature flared, to
cradle me in her huge arms when I shook with chills.

Every day, Mama sat for hours listening to me read

from the Bible, making me repeat a verse a dozen times, until every pause was perfect and every consonant clipped. She smiled and closed her eyes, her patience endless: *Again, Selina.* But she couldn't bear my small wounds or mild afflictions. She had no tolerance for suffering; my whimpering drove her from the room and made her call for Beulah to come with her root cures. And I was not permitted to hold the precious mirror or brush my mama's hair either. She said I was too rough, too clumsy—seven years' bad luck—I brushed too fast, only Martha Parnell did it right: *Yes, Martha, that feels nice.* I hid in the shadows of the doorway. *Yes, like that, good girl, Martha, just another hundred strokes.* Mama's honey hair caught the light, shot back a thousand sparks of gold fire. Martha said, "My mam told me the angels have yellow hair, Missus." She stopped to press the silken strands to her mouth and nose, forgetting Mama could see her in the mirror. "Stop that," Mama said. "I don't have time for such silliness." Martha raised the brush, gripped it like the stick she'd used to beat the stray dog in the yard, but she brought it down gently, brushing again—a hundred strokes, just like Mama said—before she coiled that angel hair into two thick braids and pinned them tight, high on Mama's head.

Martha couldn't make Seth take the bottle after Mama died. She was a spinster at twenty, a girl who never ripened, hips narrow as a boy's and bone-hard, breasts already shriveled before they'd blossomed. Her body offered no comfort to man or child. Father cursed the sight of her, abused her

for the foolish way she cooed at the baby, making him cry
harder till he was too hoarse to wail and only squeaked. She
dipped her finger in warm milk, but Seth was not fooled.
Only Beulah could soothe him, holding him on the great
pillow of her lap, quieting him with hands so fat and smooth
she seemed to have no bones. She gave him a bit of cloth
soaked with sugar water. He suckled and slept. Still, my father's only son was starving; that's what drove him down to
the slaves' quarters, looking for Lize.

*The man come to the shack. He say, my boy's hungry. He pulls
my dress apart at the neck, looks at my breasts like I'm some
cow. He say, looks like you got plenty to spare.*

Secretly I was glad to hear my father rail at Martha Parnell,
calling her a worthless dried-up bit of ground, threaten-
ing to send her scrawny ass back to Ireland if she didn't
find some way to make herself useful. At my mother's funeral, she tugged on my braids and hissed in my ear, "Looks
like you're no better'n me now, Miss Selina. Nothin' but a
motherless child with no one but the devil to keep her safe
from her daddy. Don't I know. Eight of us. Mama and the
ninth dead and me the oldest. Just you watch yourself, little
girl, and lock your door at night." My lack of understanding made her laugh out loud. People turned to stare. When
Father caught my eye, my face burned, blood rising in my
cheeks as if I'd just been slapped.

Martha's only pleasure was bringing sorrow to others.
Her lies cost Abe his ears. Mama was nearing her sixth

month when it happened. She yelled when a door slammed
too hard, fretted when the heat got too heavy—she was a
walking misery, despising her own bloated body, its strange
new weight, its hard curves. When Martha claimed Abe
cuffed her jaw and shoved her down, Mama's judgment was
swift and cruel. He was going to be an example. "Can't let
these boys get above themselves," she said.

I pleaded for mercy. Martha was always calling Abe,
telling him to fetch her some water, fetch her some eggs.
One day she'd say, "Help me move this rockin' chair, Abe."
And the next day, she'd make him move it back to where
it had always been. She ran her fingers through her dry,
colorless hair; she batted her stubby eyelashes and never
thanked him.

I knew she led him into the grove, looking for mush-
rooms, she said; but as soon as the trees hid them, she
grabbed his wrist and pushed her face against his, mouth
wet and open for the kiss he would not give. Scorned
gentleman, proper husband of another woman, he knocked
the girl to the ground and fled.

Spitting blood from her bitten lip, Martha came com-
plaining to Mama. False and fearful, she whispered she was
lucky to have her virtue intact. "Just think what he might'a
done if I hadn't kicked him and run."

No one truly believed her, not even Mama, and least of
all my father. Still, the orders were given. Three other slaves
held Abe down in the barn, and old Walkerman, Father's
overseer, took a knife to Abe's head. His howls filled the
yard. The green twilight pulsed with the throb of his veins.

I sat on the porch, racked by dry sobs. Mama said, "Quit that fussing. It's for your own good. If he thinks he can get away with slapping Martha, maybe he'll go after me next—or you. Slaves must be obedient to their masters on earth, with fear and trembling, just as we are obedient to the Lord," she said. "I want you to find that passage and memorize it for tomorrow's lesson."

Father gave me a swat to the back of the head. He said, "What would people think if they heard you crying over some nigger boy, Selina?"

In the barn, a man lay facedown in his own sticky pool of blood. On the veranda, Father kissed Mother's radiant hair, sat down beside her and laid his hand on her belly. "My son," he said.

"I can't make that promise," Mama told him.

That night I stood at my window and saw my father run toward the grove, a bundle in his arms. His high black boots caught the moonlight, flashed in the dark. I followed him deep in the trees. Limbs snagged my hair; shrubs tore at my dress. I saw the girl-child, naked on the ground, saw him raise the shovel, heard the dull crack, metal on bone, a pumpkin cleaved open to spill the seed. My father dug a shallow grave for my sister. She was small enough to hold in his two broad hands, but he let her drop, unwanted runt, the shoat that will starve because it's weaker than the rest, so you kill it and call yourself merciful.

When I woke, the image hovered between dream and memory. I too prayed my mother's child would be a son.

I saw Abe chopping cotton in the fields, skin so black it blazed blue at noonday. For weeks he wore a bandage around his head, and I pretended his ears were growing back, that when he unwrapped himself in the evening, he could feel the first nubs, and soon, very soon, the whorls would bloom to full size, firm in the curves and fleshy at the lobes, perfect ears. I touched them in my sleep, peeled away the crust of dried blood, pressed my lips to the fine lines of his scars until they disappeared. I clambered to the edge of sleep to wake hot and tangled in my sheets, my hair damp with sweat, my chest pounding. *Yes, I was the one he hit; yes, I was the one who told.*

After Lize came, my brother ate day and night. He shrieked if she set him down. She couldn't go to the toilet alone or wash her face without bouncing him on one hip. If she tried to talk to Beulah while she nursed, he'd start to whine and then to wail. He needed every inch of her and every breath. Mama hadn't had enough milk for him. After months of hunger, he was determined never to want for anything again. He seemed to know his power already, four-month-old master, king, little man. Green-eyed Lize, flesh full from cheek to thigh, gave him her body and did not complain.

Lize, I do not believe you loathed my brother. You showed a certain kindness toward him, and fed him well. Soon he grew fat. His fine white hair fell out in patches and the hair that grew in its place was coarse and dark, glossy as my father's hair.

Sounds new to me rose out of the night air. Whip-poor-wills repeated their own names, a sleepless dirge; the wings of insects clicked and buzzed, a swarm in the yard, hissing in the dirt. Even the earth carried a sound, a distant stamping, a thunderous herd of wild horses.

Abe call at my window. I say, go away. I say, havin' no ears ain't bad enough? You want to die too? But he keep callin' so I go down. He tell me, the boy don' eat. He say, won' take no milk-wet finger. Your own baby gon' die, Lize, and you lettin' some white man's child suck you dry. He cryin' there in the bushes like some fool. I say, what you want me to do? I say, that white boy shake the house with his screamin' if I go. Your baby get one good meal 'fore we all dead.

Later, there were other sounds. One night, before I learned to hide, before I learned to pull the blankets over my head and press my palms against my ears, I heard a muffled cry in the kitchen and crept down the back stairs, shadow of myself.

The man pushed me up on the table. He slap me when I yell. One smack break my nose. Nobody notice bruises on a black-skinned woman, that's what he think. He say, why fight? I never knew no nigger woman who didn't like a white man better'n her own kind. I close my eyes. He don't take too long.

I stood mute, though I saw her skirt bunched up around her waist, and my father's pants dropped to his knees. His black boots were dull and brutal in the dim light, but the pale globes of his buttocks made him ridiculous, a child caught pissing in the woods, his tender flesh exposed.

I remembered my mother's caution, her voice in my skull: *A nigger woman's appetites are dangerous to men.* And I believed, because she spoke to me so rarely. *God is light. In Him there is no darkness.* Still I was afraid, hearing Martha Parnell whisper: *Nothin' but a motherless child with no one but the devil to keep her safe from her daddy.* The son of Noah saw his father drunk and naked and did not turn away. So Ham was cursed, forced to be a slave of slaves to his brothers—because his brothers were good, because his brothers walked backward to their father and covered his nakedness without looking. *Read it again,* Mama said. *Slowly, Selina, open your vowels.*

The morning I woke with blood on my sheets, I wept half the day, until Beulah came to me, held my hand between her two soft hands, and explained the life of a woman to me. Later she laughed with Lize in the kitchen, shaking over the joke of me, mouth wide, pink tongue clicking: *Silly white girl, cryin' over a bit of blood,* and then, the terrible words again: *Motherless child don' know nothin'.*

Fool or not, I stole a knife from the kitchen, hid it under my pillow, slept with one eye open.

I heard the table scrape across the floor, heard my father cuss. No one was laughing now. I scuttled down to the bottom of my bed and buried myself beneath the heavy blankets. I almost wished to smother, to have him find me there in the morning and repent.

Abe came to me that hot night. I was blue-veined and pale. In the grove, I knelt beside him and touched his dark back, making his muscles mine. I laid my hands on his chest, drained him until my skin was black and he turned white and woman in my hands.

They bury my boy 'fore I know. I go down to the shack. Don' wake nobody. Don' want to see the husband all weepy eye, ear place bloody I know 'cause he pick the scabs when he not thinking. I find the heap of ground. I dig in the loose dirt. Don' take me long, he not bury deep. I hold my baby next to my naked breast. Eat, I say. I wipe the dirt from his eyes, dig it out of his nose and ears, pull a clot from his mouth. He smell bad and I cry and cry but I don' make no sound. I say, God, You ain't nothin' but a dark horse stamping on my soul.

My brother's tiny coffin had flowers enough to drown him: gardenias and orchids, lilies so white I was afraid to stare, afraid my gaze would stain them. The gravestone was twice the size of Seth, its four carved names too great a burden for a six-month-old boy to bear.

When they come lookin' for me, I don' tell no lies. I say, I smothered him between my own breasts. He beat and beat at me with those tiny fists, but I hold him tight till he go limp in my arms. I hold him tight, then I put him in his basket, rock him all night.

Lize, I condemned you for the murder of my brother, execrated you for your bold confession when lies might have kept you alive. You were dangerous to men in ways my mother never dreamed. *What fellowship has light with darkness?* Devil in a woman's shape, you kept me pure, but I thought you deserved to hang, unnatural woman, I'll say it plain: death for death, justice simple and swift.

I never risked my father's curse, never spoke of the ring of bruises on your wrists the day you died or the scratches on my father's face, though I knew well what these signs meant.

At dusk, Abe cut her down, lifted her in his powerful arms as if she weighed no more than a child. Beulah followed, her face a map of sorrow, rivers of blood in the lines of her cheeks, broad forehead a desert to march, bodies laid out in the sun, mountains to rot behind her eyes.

In the shack, the women washed the body in silence, no sound but the wringing of rags and drip of water. They rubbed her until her skin shone, until her feet were beautiful and clean, toes dark as polished stones. They dressed her in white, wrapped her hair in gauze, folded her hands across her chest.

At nightfall the keening of women rose from the shack. Their moans raised Lize up to the arms of God and He took her, begged *her* for forgiveness—poor, betrayed murderer.

The cicadas screamed in the heat of day, the buzz of their wings a wild cry. A constant, rising hum and hiss swelled in waves, a torrent surging through the endless days of summer. In the morning, I'd find their shells belly-up on the steps, a horde that had tried to invade the house each night, and each night failed.

The cotton fields steamed. All day the Negroes chopped, backs stooped, knees bent. All day they coughed, choking on cotton dust. When they stood to clear their lungs, Walkerman cracked his whip, crippled them with a shout. Even the women with bellies bulged enough to burst worked until the sun struck them down and they had to be carried to the shade. Walkerman waved salts under their noses. If they woke, he put them back to chopping until they fell again.

My father festered, grew foul with self-pity. The best part of him, his beloved son, was dead. The sound of his boots on the porch scattered us like mice, sent us all skittering to separate corners of the house. At night, he paced the hallway, and I tossed, gripping the knife whenever his shadow darkened the line of light at the bottom of my closed door.

Martha Parnell still owed Father five years for her passage to America, but in August he sold her time to Walkerman for a single dollar. In the first month, she lost three teeth to his fists, paying at last for Abe's ears. By the fifth month she was swollen up like a spider, her great load teetering on spindly legs. As soon as one child stopped suckling, another began to grow. Her third pushed at her dress when the war started and Walkerman and my father went off to fight.

Walkerman never did come home. Even his body disappeared, was buried with a dozen others in a common grave or left to rot on the road, bloated and black with worms. Martha was free but had no money and nowhere to go.

She stayed long enough to see my father's fields scorched, long enough to see the fine house fill with dust and start to crumble. One day she told me she was going to find Walkerman. I imagined she felt some misguided sense of devotion and wanted the father of her children to have a Christian burial. But I was mistaken. "Have to be sure the bastard's really dead," she told me.

My father lost his legs and his mind in that war. I nursed him for ten years, saw his nakedness daily and could not turn away as the good sons of Noah had. His chest shrank, his eyes fell back in his skull, his hair turned white and fine as a child's. Only his hands were spared. Huge and gnarled, they flailed at the air, cuffed me when I came too near, clutched me in his fits of grief. When he wept, he did not call to Seth or my mother. No, he mourned only for his own legs, kept asking where they were, as if I might know, as if I had hidden them.

Though I knew he could not stand, sometimes I saw him at my bedroom door. His boots gleamed. "Touch me," he wheezed. "I'm cold."

To save what little money I could for train fare to Chicago, I buried him in a four-foot box and marked his grave with a wooden cross. The big man fit in a boy's coffin, and I believed I had nothing left to fear.

I fled the South to take a job as a teacher at a Catholic school. Father would have detested me for that: tasting their bread, drinking their wine, letting it turn to body and blood in my mouth. My constant sins were the lies I told, pretending to be Catholic. Mornings I woke at five to pray. At each station of the cross I murmured: *Hail Mary, full of grace. The Lord is with thee. Blessed art thou among women. And blessed is the fruit of thy womb, Jesus.*

In the chill of those lightless winter mornings, I almost believed in this God who could change Himself to human flesh and die for me. But alone, in my room, the prayers that rose in my heart called out to another god. There were no crosses, only the leafless trees beyond my window.

All these years I have lived in one room, cramped and dim, a place I chose because it did not burden me with spaces to fill. There were no hallways to swarm with drunken soldiers, no parlors to become hospital rooms for the one-armed men, no banisters to polish, no crystal to explode against the wall when my father raged, no trees near enough to scrape the glass with frenzied hands, no scent of gardenia in the spring to make me sick with memory.

Still, there was room enough for my father, withered in my daydreams, spitting gruel back in my face when I tried to feed him, but tall and thick through the chest at night, stamping with impatience, his boots loud as hooves on bare wood. There was room for my brother, his puling cries when he was hungry, and then, his unbearable silence. And there was always room for you, Lize. For seventy-eight years I have watched you hang.

My brother and I were the last of my father's line. Your blood spilled on the ground and flowed like a river to the sea. Ours dried in my veins. You died for my silence.

Untouched by a man, unloved by a child, I never mourned the slow death of my body, but now I see this is your just revenge.

All day she sways in the wind, her body light with age. By night she roams the streets. Her bare feet leave no mark in snow. I have seen her often and prayed she would not know me. Tonight I duck into an alley. Garbage is piled high; the shadows are alive, crawling with rats. Lize follows. She has no age, but I am a fleshless woman, bones in a bag of skin. *Murderer,* she whispers. I am too frail to flee. *I see you watchin' your daddy and me.* She pins me to the wall. *You don' say nothin'.* Her knee jabs my brittle pelvis; the bones of my back feel as if they'll snap. *You kill me, and my child too.* She holds my arms, outstretched. I dangle in her grasp, toes barely touching the ground, legs weak as clay pocked by rain. *You take Abe's ears,* she says. *I can't find them.*

"No, Walkerman tacked them to his wall," I say.

You cry to your mama, tell your lies.

"No, that was Martha."

Whitewoman, you all look the same to me. You all kill us with desire.

I crumple to my knees, alone in the alley. "I never touched him," I say. "Only in a dream." The wind whistles down the canyon of brick, repeating Lize's last word. I sob between two garbage cans. The smell is sweet and foul, gardenias rotting in the heat, but I am cold, so cold.

I curl into a ball, tight as a fist, small as an ear. The snow is falling. Rats sniff my ankles and scurry away. I am not even food enough for them. Voices hover. Hands stroke my face, hands softer than my mother's hands, fingers tender as Beulah's—Mother never touched me that way. Soon enough the voice is human. The hands shake my shoulder, call me back from the dead.

"Honey, what you doin' in this alley? You lose your way?" The woman's dark face is close to mine, her breath warm with whiskey. "Let Ruthie help you, honey," she says. "Tell Ruthie where you live."

At first I am afraid, Lize. I think it is you in disguise, come back fat as Beulah to torture me again. But no, this woman knows nothing of my crimes. She is condescending and kind. In her eyes I am harmless, my white skin too withered to despise. She helps me find my way home, half carries me up the stairs, sets me in my chair by the window and covers my legs with a blanket. She asks if she can heat some soup, but I say, "No, please go."

From where I hang, I see all the brown-skinned children. You think your death can save them? Your father's blood runs dark in the veins of my children. Your father's blood clots in the heart, bursts in the brain. Your father's blood destroys us all again and again.

"Forgive me," I whisper. The fog of my breath turns to frost on the windowpane. Chill has turned to fever. I cannot kneel or stand, so I sit at my window and wait.

Listen, Lize, I am a desiccated shell of a woman, a cicada

you could crush with one step. Put your weight on me, and be done with it. I am old enough and prepared to die.

She does not answer. Her eyes are always open, bulged and blind. She never looks at me. At dusk, Abe comes and cuts her down. I follow her all night, calling her name down unlit alleys. I hear her breath when she stops to rest. But she is a cruel god, she who becomes flesh only to be crucified again and again. At dawn, I am still alive. At dawn, Walkerman ties a noose. Everywhere the silent snow is falling, melting on bare trees until their bark is black and shiny as wet skin. Soon, the men will drag Lize down the road, haul her up, and let her fall. I will see her wrists tied, her blouse torn; I will see her bruised and battered feet. And I will sit, just as I do now, mute witness to her endless death.

FROM *First, Body*
(1997)

Nobody's Daughters

I. IN THESE WOODS

I WAITED FOR YOU IN THE RAIN. My tongue hurt. I'd been telling lies all day. Lies to the four Christian teenagers who thought they could save me. My first ride, Albany to Oneonta—they sang the whole way. More lies to the jittery pink-skinned man who took me north. He offered tiny blue pills and fat black ones. He said, *It's safe—don't worry—I'm a nurse*. He said, *I'll make you feel good*.

I think I had a sister once. Everywhere I go she's been before me. There's no getting out of it.

When the pink nurse stopped to piss, my sister Clare whispered, *Look at him—he'll kill you if he can*. I hid in the woods by the lake full of stumps. I didn't move. I let the sky pour through me. He called the name I'd said was mine. Sometimes I heard branches breaking. Sometimes only rain. Finally he yelled at me, at who he thought I was. He said, *No more games*. He said, *Fine, freeze your ass*. His voice cracked. I could have chosen him instead of you, but Clare breathed on my hands. She said, *He doesn't have anything you want*.

You were driving toward me, your blue truck still hours away. Cold rain, cars whipping water—only my faith made me wait. I swear I knew you, your soft beard, how it would be. But you never imagined us together. You never meant to stop for me.

This I won't tell. This you'll never know. Mick says I'm fourteen going on forty. I've got that dusty skin, dry, my eyes kind of yellowish where they're supposed to be white. It's the rum I drink, and maybe my kidneys never did work that well. Mick, who is my mother's husband now, says I'll be living on the street at sixteen, dead at twenty. He says this to me, when we're alone. Once I paid two dollars, let Mama Rosa read my palm to see if he was right, and she told me I was going to outlive everyone I love.

I know I'm strange. I drift. Maybe I'm smoking a cigarette, leaning on the bricks. Somebody's talking. Then I'm not there. I'm a window breaking. I'm pieces of myself falling on the ground. Later I wake up in my own body and my fingers are burned.

Clare says, *Just stand up.*

She's careless, my sister. She gets drunk. She puts other people's blood in her veins. Her skin's hot. She goes out in the cold without her coat and waits for her lover to come. Wind drives snow in her face. Ice needles her bare arms. Some night she'll lie down in the woods and he won't find her. Some night she'll lie down in the road.

It's November. I know because there are Halloween men rotting in all the yards, snagged on fences, skewered on poles. Pumpkin heads scooped hollow—they stink of their own spoiled selves. One boy's stuck in a tree. His head's a purple cabbage. You could peel him down to his brainless core.

I know some men downtown, Halloween men trying to walk on stuffed legs. Rags on sticks, pants full of straw, foul wind blowing through them to scare the crows. I think they made themselves. They have those eyes. Carved. Candles guttering inside their soft skulls.

They live in a brick house you can't blow down—boards instead of windows, nails in the doors. They tell me, *Come alone.*

They have dusted joints and I have seven dollars. They have pockets full of pills and I have pennies I found in the snow. I know how easy it is to go down the steps to the basement, to stand shivering against the wall. Nothing hurts me. Earl says, *Pain is just a feeling like any other feeling.* He should know. *Knife, slap, kiss, flame.* He says, *Forget their names and they pass through you.* Earl has wooden arms and metal hands. His left ear's a hole, his nose a bulb of flesh from somewhere else. He sits in the corner and smokes. He holds the joint in his silver claw. His long feet are always bare. When he whispers in his half-voice, everything stops.

No money the night before I found you. One of the Halloween men said, *Come with me.* He had pink hearts and poppers. He knew I'd need them. He said, *It's danger-ous to sleep.* I looked at Earl. I thought his lips moved. I thought he said, *Nothing lasts too long.*

This speedboy with poppers was the whitest man I ever saw. When I closed my eyes he was a white dog bounding through streets of snow. I tried not to think of his skin, all of it, how bright it was, how his body exposed would blind me, how his white palms blazed against my hips. I thought of Earl instead, smooth arms, cool hands, Earl who only burned himself, hair flaming around soft ears, holy angel, face melting into bone.

Clare said, *Nobody will find you.*

The whiteman was in me, close enough to hear; he said, *Not even God.*

God doesn't like to watch little girls pressed against basement walls. God doesn't like little girls who swallow pills and drink rum. God's too old to get down on his hands and knees and peer through the slats of boards. Glass broken long ago but shards still on the ground. He might cut his palms. If he ever thinks of me, maybe he'll send his son.

I never slept with the whiteman.

I mean, I never lay down and closed my eyes.

Clare said, There's no reason to go home. She made me remember the trailer in December, a ring of Christmas lights blinking its outline, red and green and gold, the wet snow the first winter she was gone. She made me remember the white ruffled curtains on the windows and the three plastic swans in the yard. She said she hitched two hundred miles once to stand outside, to watch us inside, the fog of our breath on the glass. She said our mother had a new husband and two sons. She said we were nobody's daughters. She said, They all want you to go.

Singing Christians, pink nurse, rain—I waited, saw your blue truck at last. I had a dream once of your body, damp hair of your chest, my fingers in it. As soon as you stopped,

I remembered the hunting cap on the seat between us, the rabbit fur inside your gloves.

I surprised you. I'm the living proof: unknown father's daughter. Tall bony Nadine. Dark-eyed Nadine. Girl from the lake of stumps. Water swirling in a mother's dream. His face rising toward her. Shadow of a hand making the sign of the cross.

I pulled the blanket from my head and you saw the holes in my ear—you counted the tarnished hoops, nine, cartilage to lobe.

Later I'll show you: the holes in my ear never hurt like the hole in my tongue.

You were amazed by the space I filled—long legs, muddy boots; you had no reason to let the wet-wool, black-hair smell of me into your warm truck. Moments before, I looked small and helpless, a child on the road, no bigger than your own daughter, ten years old, her impossibly thin arms, all her fragile breakable bones.

I closed my eyes so you wouldn't be afraid. I was just a girl again, alone, but the smell—it filled the cab; you breathed me; I was in your lungs. I was your boyself, the bad child, the one who ran away from you, the one you never found.

Later there was fog and dark, the rain, heavy. You didn't know where we were going. You didn't know where to stop. The lights of cars coming toward us exploded in mist, blinding you. I said, *Pull over.* I said, *We can wait it out.*

And it was there, in the fog, in the rain, in the terrifying light of cars still coming, that I kissed you the first time. It was there parked on the soft gravel shoulder that I stuck my pierced tongue in your mouth and you put your hands under my shirt to feel my ribs, the first time. It was there that you said, *Careful, baby,* and you meant my tongue, the stud—it hurt you—and I thought of the handcuffs in my bag, stolen from the Halloween man, the last one, the white one—he was cursing me even now. I could have cuffed you to your wheel, left you to explain. I imagined myself in your coat, carrying your gun.

But I loved you.

I mean, I didn't want to go.

The rain slowed. Fog blew across the road. You drove. I wore your gloves, felt the fur of the animal around every finger. I stared at the lights till my eyes were holes.

You were tired. You were sorry. It was too late to throw me out. You said we'd stop at a motel. You said we'd sleep. You said, *What happened back there—don't worry.* You meant it wasn't going to go any further. You meant you thought it was your fault.

I disgusted you now. I saw that. Your tongue hurt. My sour breath was in your mouth. *Never,* you thought. *Not with her.* Dirty Nadine. Nothing like my pretty sister. Pale half sister. Daughter of the father before my father. Not like Clare, lovely despite her filth, delicate Clare, thin as your daughter—you could hold her down. You could take her to any room. You could wash her. You could break her with one blow. You would never guess how dangerous she is. You can't see the shadows on her lungs, her hard veins, her brittle bones. You can't see the bloom of blood. Later I'll tell you about the handprints on all the doors of the disappeared. Later I'll explain the lines of her open palm.

Is she alive? Try to find her. Ask her yourself.

Never is the car door slamming. *Never* is the key in the lock, the Traveler's Rest Motel, the smell of disinfectant, the light we don't turn on. *Never* is the mattress so old you feel the coils against your back when you fall. My tongue's in your mouth. Your cock's hard against my thigh. *Never.*

Clare has a game. We strobe. She grabs my hand, sticks the wire in the socket. She dares me to hang on.

I'm a thief. It's true.

I turn you into a thief. It's necessary. You'll think of that forever, the sheet you had to steal to get out of the motel. You'll remember your bare legs in the truck, the cold vinyl through thin cloth, the white half-moon hanging in the morning sky, facedown.

Days now and hundreds of miles since I left you. You wear your orange vest, carry your oiled gun. You follow tracks in snow. I follow Clare to the road. She wants me to find her, to feel what she feels, to do everything she's done.

When you see the doe at last, you think of me. You're alone with me—there's no one you can tell about the girl on the road, her sore tongue in your mouth. *Never*, you said, *no* and *no*, but you twitched under her, blinded by the flickering in your skull. No one will understand. You thought her hands would turn you inside out, but you held on. There's no one you can tell about the wallet she opened, the cash and pictures, the pants she stole.

Careful, baby.

I've got your life now—your little girl smiling in my hand, dressed in her white fairy costume, waving her sparkling fairy wand; I hold your sad wife in her striped bathing suit. If I could feel, her chubby knees would break my heart. I've got you in my pocket—your driver's license, my proof. I'm in your pants. I belt them tight. I keep your coins in my boots for good luck. I wear your hat, earflaps down. I bought a silver knife with your forty-three dollars. I carved your name in a cross on my thigh.

Yesterday I found a dump of jack-o'-lanterns in the ditch, the smashed faces of all the men I used to know. They grinned to show me the stones in their broken mouths. They've taken themselves apart. I'm looking for their unstuffed clothes, hoping they didn't empty their pockets before their skulls flamed out.

It's dark. Clare pulls me toward the gully. She wants me to run down between the black trees and twisting vines. She wants me to feel my way—she wants me to crawl.

Morning again, I saw a deer, only the head and legs, bits of hide, a smear of blood, five crows taking flight, wings hissing as they rose. Someone's accident butchered here, the stunned meat taken home. Before you fell asleep, I said, *Anyone can kill.*

She's in your sights. Nobody understands your fear, how you feel my hands even now, reaching for your wrists, slipping under your clothes. So many ways to do it, brutal or graceful, silent as the blood in my sister's veins or full of shattered light and sound. Kick to the shoulder, blast of the gun—she staggers, wounded, not killed all at once. There's snow on the ground, gold leaves going brown. There's light in the last trembling leaves, but the sun is gone. You follow her trail, dark puddles spreading in snow, black into white, her blood.

You remember a farmer straddling his own sheep. *Will it be like this?* The knife, one slit, precise. *Pain is just a feeling like any other feeling.* She never struggled. He reached inside, grabbed something, squeezed hard. *I can't tell you what it was.*

She won't drop in time, won't give up. When you put your hands in front of you, you almost feel her there: hair, flesh, breath, blood. She wants only what you want: to survive one minute more.

What would you do if you found her now, if her ragged breathing stopped? Too far to drag her back to the truck; you'd have to open her in the sudden dark, pull her steaming entrails into the snow.

I wait for the next ride. Clare wants me to follow in her tracks, to find her before she falls, to touch her, to wash her blood clean in this snow, to put it back in her veins, to make her whole.

You walk in a circle. You wonder if you're lost. The doe's following you now, but at a distance. She's trying to forgive you. If she could speak, she might tell you the way home. She might say, *You can climb inside me, wear my body like a coat.*

You can't explain this to anyone. *Never, no.* You need

me. I'm the only one alive who knows your fear, who understands how dangerous we are to each other in these woods, on this road.

II. XMAS, JAMAICA PLAIN

I'm your worst fear.

But not the worst thing that can happen.

I lived in your house half the night, I'm the broken window in your little boy's bedroom. I'm the flooded tiles in the bathroom where the water flowed and flowed.

I'm the tattoo in the hollow of Emile's pelvis, five butterflies spreading blue wings to rise out of his scar.

I'm dark hands slipping through all your pale woman underthings; dirty fingers fondling a strand of pearls, your throat, a white bird carved of stone. I'm the body you feel wearing your fox coat.

Clare said, *Take the jewelry; it's yours.*

My heart's in my hands: what I touch, I love; what I love, I own.

Snow that night and nobody seemed surprised, so I figured it must be winter. Later I remembered it was Christmas, or it had been, the day before. I was with Emile, who wanted to be Emilia. We'd started downtown, Boston. Now it was Jamaica Plain, three miles south. *Home for the holidays,* Emile said, some private joke. He'd been working the block around the Greyhound station all night, wearing nothing but a white scarf and black turtleneck, tight jeans. *Man wants to see before he buys,* Emile said. He meant the ones in long cars, cruising, looking for fragile boys with female faces.

Emile was sixteen, he thought.

Getting old.

He'd made sixty-four dollars, three tricks with cash, plus some pills—a bonus for good work, blues and greens, he didn't know what. Nobody'd offered to take him home, which is all he wanted: a warm bed, some sleep, eggs in the morning, the smell of butter, hunks of bread torn off the loaf.

Crashing, both of us, ragged from days of speed and crack, no substitute for the smooth high of pure cocaine but all we could afford. Now, enough cash between us at last. I had another twenty-five from the man who said he was in the circus once, who called himself the Jungle Creep—on top of me he made that sound. Before he un-locked the door, he said, *Are you a real girl?* I looked at his plates—New Jersey; that's why he didn't know the lines, didn't know that the boys as girls stay away from the Zone unless they want their faces crushed. He wanted me to prove it first. Some bad luck once, I guess. I said, *It's fucking freezing. I'm real. Open the frigging door or go.*

Now it was too late to score, too cold, nobody on the street but Emile and me, the wind, so we walked, we kept walking. I had a green parka, somebody else's wallet in the pocket—I couldn't remember who or where, the coat sto-len weeks ago and still mine, a miracle out here. We shared, trading it off. I loved Emile. I mean, it hurt my skin to see his cold.

Emile had a plan. It had to be Jamaica Plain, *home*—
enough hands as dark as mine, enough faces as brown as
Emile's—not like Brookline, where we'd have to turn our-
selves inside out. Jamaica Plain, where there were pretty
painted houses next to shacks, where the sound of bursting
glass wouldn't be that loud.

Listen, we needed to sleep, to eat, that's all. So thirsty
even my veins felt dry, flattened out. Hungry somewhere
in my head, but my stomach shrunken to a knot so small
I thought it might be gone. I remembered the man, maybe
last week, before the snow, leaning against the statue of
starved horses, twisted metal at the edge of the Common.
He had a knife, long enough for gutting fish. Dressed in
camouflage but not hiding. He stared at his thumb, licked
it clean, and cut deep to watch the bright blood bubble out.
He stuck it in his mouth to drink, hungry, and I swore I'd
never get that low. But nights later I dreamed him beside
me. Raw and dizzy, I woke, offering my whole hand, begging him to cut it off.

We walked around your block three times. We were
patient now. Numb. No car up your drive and your porch
light blazing, left to burn all night, we thought. Your house
glowed, yellow even in the dark, paint so shiny it looked
wet, and Emile said he lived somewhere like this once, when
he was still a boy all the time, hair cropped short, before lipstick and mascara, when his cheeks weren't blushed, before
his mother caught him and his father locked him out.

In this house Emile found your red dress, your slippery
stockings. He was happy, I swear.

So why did he end up on the floor?

I'm not going to tell you; I don't know.

First, the rock wrapped in Emile's scarf, glass splintering in the cold, and we climbed into the safe body of your house. Later we saw this was a child's room, your only one. We found the tiny cowboy boots in the closet, black like Emile's but small, so small. I tried the little bed. It was soft enough but too short. In every room your blue-eyed boy floated on the wall. Emile wanted to take him down. Emile said, *He scares me.* Emile said your little boy's too pretty, his blond curls too long. Emile said, *Some night the wrong person's going to take him home.*

Emile's not saying anything now, but if you touched his mouth you'd know. Like a blind person reading lips, you'd feel everything he needed to tell.

We stood in the cold light of the open refrigerator, drinking milk from the carton, eating pecan pie with our hands, squirting whipped cream into our mouths. You don't know how it hurt us to eat this way, our shriveled stomachs stretching; you don't know why we couldn't stop. We took the praline ice cream to your bed, one of those tiny containers, sweet and sickening, bits of candy frozen hard. We fell asleep and it melted, so we drank it, thick, with your brandy, watching bodies writhe on the TV, no sound: flames and ambulances all night; children leaping; a girl in mud under a car, eight men lifting; a skier crashing into a wall—we never knew who was saved and who was not. Talking heads spat the news again and again. There was no reason to listen—tomorrow exactly the same things would happen, and still everyone would forget.

There were other houses after yours, places I went alone, but there were none before and none like this. When I want to feel love I remember the dark thrill of it, the bright sound of glass, the sudden size and weight of my own heart in my own chest, how I knew it now, how it was real to me in my body, separate from lungs and liver and ribs, how it made the color of my blood surge against the backs of my eyes, how nothing mattered anymore because I believed in this, my own heart, its will to live.

No lights, no alarm. We waited outside. Fifteen seconds. Years collapsed. We were scared of you, who you might be inside, terrified lady with a gun, some fool with bad aim and dumb luck. The boost to the window, Emile lifting me, then I was there, in you, I swear, the smell that particular, that strong, almost a taste in your boy's room, his sweet milky breath under my tongue. Heat left low, but to us warm as a body, humid, hot.

My skin's cracked now, hands that cold, but I think of them plunged deep in your drawer, down in all your soft underbelly underclothes, slipping through all your jumbled silky womanthings.

I pulled them out and out.

I'm your worst fear. I touched everything in your house: all the presents just unwrapped—cashmere sweater, rocking horse, velvet pouch. I lay on your bed, smoking cigarettes, wrapped in your fur coat. How many foxes? I tried to count.

But it was Emile who wore the red dress, who left it crumpled on the floor.

Thin as he is, he couldn't zip the back—he's a boy, after all—he has those shoulders, those soon-to-be-a-man bones. He swore trying to squash his boy feet into the matching heels; then he sobbed. I had to tell him he had lovely feet, and he did, elegant, long—those golden toes. I found him a pair of stockings, one size fits all.

I wore your husband's pinstriped jacket. I pretended all the gifts were mine to offer. I pulled the pearls from their violet pouch.

We danced.

We slid across the polished wooden floor of your living room, spun in the white lights of the twinkling tree. And again, I tell you, I swear I felt the exact size and shape of things inside me, heart and kidney, my sweet left lung. All the angels hanging from the branches opened their glass mouths, stunned.

He was more woman than you, his thick hair wound tight and pinned. *Watch this*, he said. *Chignon.*

I'm not lying. He transformed himself in front of your mirror, gold eyeshadow, faint blush. He was beautiful. He could have fooled anyone. Your husband would have paid a hundred dollars to feel Emile's mouth kiss all the places you won't touch.

Later the red dress lay like a wet rag on the floor. Later the stockings snagged, the strand of pearls snapped and the beads rolled. Later Emile was all boy, naked on the bathroom floor.

I'm the one who got away, the one you don't know; I'm the long hairs you find under your pillow, nested in your drain, tangled in your brush. You think I might come back. You dream me dark always. I could be any dirty girl on the street, or the one on the bus, black lips, just-shaved head. You see her through mud-spattered glass, quick, blurred. You want me dead—it's come to this—killed, but not by your clean hands. You pray for accidents instead, me high and spacy, stepping off the curb, a car that comes too fast. You dream some twisted night road and me walking, some poor drunk weaving his way home. He won't even know what he's struck. In the morning he'll touch the headlight I smashed, the fender I splattered, dirt or blood. In the light he'll see my body rising, half remembered, snow that whirls to a shape then blows apart. Only you will know for sure, the morning news, another unidentified girl dead, hit and run, her killer never found.

I wonder if you'll rest then, or if every sound will be glass, every pair of hands mine, reaching for your sleeping son.

How can I explain?

We didn't come for him.

I'm your worst fear. Slivers of window embedded in carpet. Sharp and invisible. You can follow my muddy footprints through your house, but if you follow them backward they always lead here: to this room, to his bed.

If you could see my hands, not the ones you imagine but my real hands, they'd be reaching for Emile's body. If you looked at Emile's feet, if you touched them, you could feel us dancing.

This is all I want.

After we danced, we lay so close on your bed I dreamed

we were twins, joined forever this way, two arms, three legs, two heads.

But I woke in my body alone.

Outside, snow fell like pieces of broken light.

I already knew what had happened. But I didn't want to know.

I heard him in the bathroom.

I mean, I heard the water flow and flow.

I told myself he was washing you away, your perfume, your lavender oil scent. Becoming himself. Tomorrow we'd go.

I tried to watch the TV, the silent man in front of the map, the endless night news. But there it was, my heart again, throbbing in my fingertips.

I couldn't stand it—the snow outside; the sound of water; your little boy's head propped on the dresser, drifting on the wall; the man in the corner of the room, trapped in the flickering box: his silent mouth wouldn't stop.

I pounded on the bathroom door. I said, *Goddamn it, Emile, you're clean enough.* I said I had a bad feeling about this place. I said I felt you coming home.

But Emile, he didn't say a word. There was only water, that one sound, and I saw it seeping under the door, leaking into the white carpet. Still I told lies to myself. I said, *Shit, Emile—what's going on?* I pushed the door. I had to shove hard, squeeze inside, because Emile was there, you know, exactly where you found him, facedown on the floor. I turned him over, saw the lips smeared red, felt the water flow.

I breathed into him, beat his chest. It was too late, God, I know, his face pressed to the floor all this time, his face in the water, Emile dead even before he drowned, your bottle of Valium empty in the sink, the foil of your cold capsules punched through, two dozen gone—this is what did it: your brandy, your Valium, your safe little pills bought in a store. After all the shit we've done—smack popped under the skin, speed laced with strychnine, monkey dust—it comes to this. After all the nights on the streets, all the knives, all the pissed-off johns, all the fag-hating bullies prowling the Fenway with their bats, luring boys like Emile into the bushes with promises of sex. After all that, this is where it ends: on your clean wet floor.

Above the thunder of the water, Clare said, *He doesn't want to live.*

Clare stayed very calm. She said, *Turn off the water, go.*

I kept breathing into him. I watched the butterflies between his bones. No flutter of wings and Clare said, *Look at him. He's dead.* Clare said she should know.

She told me what to take and where it was: sapphire ring, ivory elephant, snakeskin belt. She told me what to leave, what was too heavy: the carved bird, white stone. She reminded me, *Take off that ridiculous coat.*

I knew Clare was right; I thought, Yes, everyone is dead: the silent heads in the TV, the boy on the floor, my father who can't be known. I thought even you might be dead— your husband asleep at the wheel, your little boy asleep in the back, only you awake to see the car split the guardrail and soar.

I saw a snow-filled ravine, your car rolling toward the river of thin ice.

I thought, You never had a chance.

But I felt you.

I believed in you. Your family. I heard you going room to room, saying, *Who's been sleeping in my bed?* It took all my will.

I wanted to love you. I wanted you to come home. I wanted you to find me kneeling on your floor. I wanted the wings on Emile's hips to lift him through the skylight. I wanted him to scatter: ash, snow. I wanted the floor dry, the window whole.

I swear, you gave me hope.

Clare knew I was going to do something stupid. Try to clean this up. Call the police to come for Emile. Not get out. She had to tell me everything. She said again, *Turn the water off.*

In the living room the tree still twinkled, the angels still hung. I remember how amazed I was they hadn't thrown themselves to the floor.

I remember running, the immaculate cold, the air in me, my lungs hard.

I remember thinking, I'm alive, a miracle anyone was. I wondered who had chosen me.

I remember trying to list all the decent things I'd ever done.

I remember walking till it was light, knowing if I slept, I'd freeze. I never wanted so much not to die.

I made promises, I suppose.

In the morning I walked across a bridge, saw the river frozen along the edges, scrambled down. I glided out on it; I walked on water. The snowflakes kept getting bigger and bigger, butterflies that fell apart when they hit the ground, but the sky was mostly clear and there was sun.

Later, the cold again, wind and clouds. Snow shrank to ice. Small, hard. I saw a car idling, a child in the back, the driver standing on a porch, knocking at a door. Clare said, *It's open.* She meant the car. She said, *Think how fast you can go.* She told me I could ditch the baby down the road.

I didn't do it.

Later I stole lots of things, slashed sofas, pissed on floors.

But that day, I passed one thing by; I let one thing go.

When I think about this, the child safe and warm, the mother not wailing, not beating her head on the wall to make herself stop, when I think about the snow that day, wings in the bright sky, I forgive myself for everything else.

III. HOME

November again. Harvard Square. I called Adele. Not the first time. One ring, two—never more than this. If my mother loved me, she'd pick it up that quick.

Don't be stupid, Clare said.

No answer, no surprise. Coins clanging down. *Jackpot*, Clare said.

I saw Emile across the street. He was a Latino boy with cropped hair, reaching for his mother's hand.

Then it was December third. I remember because afterward I looked at a paper in a box so I'd know exactly when.

One ring. My mother there, whispering in my ear.

Now you've done it, Clare said.

Past noon, Adele still fogged. I knew everything from the sound of her voice, too low, knew she must be on night shift again: nursing home or bar, bringing bedpans or beers—it didn't matter which. I saw the stumps of cigarettes in the ashtray beside her bed. I saw her red hair matted flat, creases in her cheek, the way she'd slept. I smelled her, the smoke in her clothes, the smoke on her breath. I remembered her kissing me one night before I knew any words—that smell: lipstick and gin. I heard Clare sobbing in the bunk above mine, her face shoved into her pillow, and then our mother was gone—we were alone in the dark, and if I'd had any words I would have said, *Not again.*

Who is it? Sharper now, my mother, right in my hand. A weird warm day, so the Haitian man was playing his guitar by the Out of Town News stand. He'd been dancing for hours, brittle legs, bobbing head. You never saw a grown man that thin. Sometimes he sang in French, and that's when I understood him best, when his voice passed through me, hands through water, when the words stopped making sense.

I wanted to hold out the phone, let my mother hear what I heard. I wanted to say, *Find me if you can.*

It's me, Nadine, I said.

I heard the match scrape, the hiss of flame burning air. I heard my mother suck in her breath.

Your daughter, I almost said.

Where are you?

I thought she was afraid I might be down the road, already on my way, needing money, her soft bed. I saw her there on the edge of the bunk, yellow spread wrapped around her shoulders, cigarette dangling from her lips. I saw the faded outlines of spilled coffee, dark stains on pale cloth, my mother's jittery hand.

Not that close, I said.

Muffled words. I thought she said, *I'm glad.* The Haitian man kept jumping, dreadlocks twisting, pants flapping—those legs, no flesh, another scarecrow man. Dollar bills fluttered in his guitar case, wings in wind. *Un coeur d'oiseaux brisés*, he sang, and I almost knew what he meant. A crowd had gathered to listen, two dozen, maybe more, all those people between us, but he was watching me; I was watching him.

I'm glad you called, my mother said again.

And I swear, I knew then.

Je ne pleure pas, the Haitian man said.

For a moment both his feet were off the ground at once. For a moment his mouth stayed open, stunned. He was a dark angel hanging in blue air. I saw his heart break against his ribs. For a moment there were no cars and no breath.

Then every sound that ever was rushed in. Horns blaring, exploding glass; ice cracking on the river; *On the ground, motherfucker*—all this again.

I said, *Clare's dead.*

Tell me where you are, Nadine.

Fuck you, Clare said.

The Haitian man fell to earth. I heard the bones of his legs snap. He wouldn't look at me now. He was bent over his case, stuffing bills in his pockets.

The voice came over the phone, the one that says you have thirty seconds left. I said, *I'm out of quarters*. I said, *Maybe I'll call you back.*

That night I found a lover.

I mean, I found a man who didn't pay, who let me sleep in his car instead. He told me his name and I forget. Fat man with a snake coiled in the hair of his chest. I kept thinking, All this flesh. When he was in me, I thought I could be him.

Clare said, *I tried to come home once, but the birds had eaten all the crumbs. There was no path.*

The next night, another lover, another man with gifts. Two vials of crack we smoked, then heroin to cut the high. *Got to chase the dragon*, he said. No needles. Clean white smack so pure we only had to breathe it in. *Safe this way*, he said. He held a wet cloth, told me, *Lean back*, made me snort the water too, *got to get the last bit*. When he moved on top of me, I didn't have a body: I was all head.

Then it was day and I was drifting, knowing that by dark I'd have to look again.

Emile appeared on Newbury Street, shop window, second floor: he was a beautiful mannequin in a red dress.

Listen, you think it's easy the way we live? Clare told me this: *I never had a day off. I had to keep walking. I could never stay in bed.*

So she was glad when they put her in a cell, glad to give them all she had: clothes, cash, fingerprints. She said, *I knew enough not to drink the water, but nobody told me not to breathe the air.*

No lover that night. I found a cardboard box instead. Cold before dawn, and I thought, *Just one corner, just the edge.* When the flames burst, I meant to smother them. I felt Earl, his cool metal grasp. *Get out,* he said. Ashes floated in the frozen air, the box gone that fast. Clare said, *Look at me: this is what they did.* Later my singed hair broke off in my hands.

In the morning, I called Adele again. *Tell me,* I said.

I thought she might know exactly where and when. I thought there might be a room, a white sheet, a bed, a place I could enter and leave, the before and after of my sister's death.

But there were only approximate details, a jail, stones, barbed wire somewhere.

No body. She meant she never saw Clare dead.

Clare said she tried to get home in time, but the witch caught her and put her in the candy house instead.

Busted. Prostitution and possession.

Let me answer the charges.

This is Clare's story.

Let me tell you what my sister owned.

In her pocket, one vial of crack, almost gone. In her veins, strangers' blood. She possessed ninety-six pounds. I want to be exact. The ninety-six pounds included the weight of skin, coat, bowels, lungs; the weight of dirt under

her nails; the weight of semen, three men last night and five
the night before.

The ninety-six pounds included the vial, a rabbit's foot
rubbed so often it was nearly hairless, worn to bone.

Around her wrist she wore her own hair, what was
left of it, what she'd saved and braided, a bracelet now. In
her left ear, one gold hoop and one rhinestone stud, and
they didn't weigh much but were included in the ninety-
six pounds.

She possessed the virus.

But did not think of it as hers alone.

She passed it on and on.

Stripped and showered, she possessed ninety-one
pounds, her body only, which brings me to the second
charge.

Listen, I heard of a man who gave a kidney to his brother.
They hadn't spoken for eleven years. A perfect match in
spite of this. All that blood flowed between them, but the
brother died, still ranting, still full of piss and spit.

Don't talk to me about mercy.

The one who lived, the one left unforgiven, the one
carved nearly in half, believed in justice of another kind: *If
we possess our bodies only, we must offer up this gift.*

You can talk forever about risk.

New York City, Clare. Holding pen. They crammed her
in a room, two hundred bodies close, no windows here.
They told her to stand and stand, no ventilation, only
a fan beating the poison air. And this is where she came
to possess the mutant germ, the final gift. It required no

consensual act, no exchange of blood or semen, no mother's milk, no generous brother willing to open his flesh.

Listen, who's coughing there?

All you have to do is breathe it in.

It loved her, this germ. It loved her lungs, first and best, the damp dark, the soft spaces there. But in the end, it wanted all of her and had no fear.

December still, Clare eight months dead. Adele knew only half of this.

You can always come home, she said.

I went looking for my lover, the fat one with the car, anybody with a snake on his chest.

I found three men in the Zone, all with cash—no snakes and none that fat. Tomorrow I'd look again. I wanted one with white skin and black hair, a belly where my bones could sink so I wouldn't feel so thin. I wanted the snake in my hands, the snake around my neck; I wanted his unbelievable weight to keep me pinned.

Ten days in a cell, Clare released. Two hundred and fifty-three hours without a fix—she thought she might go straight, but it didn't happen like that.

She found a friend instead. *You're sad, baby*, he said. She dropped her pants. Not for sex, not with him, only to find a vein not scarred too hard. When your blood blooms in the syringe, you know you've hit.

Listen, nobody asks to be like this.

If the dope's too pure, you're dead.

This is Clare's story. This is her voice speaking through me. This is my body. This is how we stay alive out here.

Listen. *It's hope that kills you in the end.*

On Brattle Street I saw this: tall man with thick legs, tiny child clutching his pants. Too beautiful, I thought, blue veins, fragile skull, her pulse flickering at the temple where I could touch it if I dared. The man needed a quarter for the meter. He asked me for change, held out three dimes. *A good trade,* I said. He stepped back toward the car, left the girl between us. I crouched to be her size, spoke soft words, nonsense, and she stared. When I moved, she moved with me. The man wasn't watching. I wanted to shout to him, *Hold on to this hand.* I wanted to tell him, *There's a boneyard in the woods, a hunter's pile of refuse, jaw of a beaver, vertebrae of a deer.* I wanted to tell him how easily we disappear.

That night I found Emile sleeping in a doorway. Shrunken little man with a white beard. No blanket, no coat. He opened one eye. *Cover me,* he said.

I held out my hands, empty palms, to show him all I had. *With your body,* he said.

He held up his own hands, fingerless. *I froze once,* he said.

In the tunnel I found the Haitian man. Every time a train came, people tossed coins in his case and left him there. Still he sang, for me alone, left his ragged words flapping in my ribs.

Listen, the lungs float in water.

Listen, the lungs crackle in your hands.

Out of the body, the lungs simply collapse.

For my people, he said.

His skin was darker than mine, dark as my father's

perhaps. His clothes grew bigger every day: he was singing himself sick. By February he'd be gone. By February I'd add the Haitian manchild to my list of the disappeared.

But that night I threw coins to him.

That night I believed in the miracles of wine and bread, how what we eat becomes our flesh.

It was almost Christmas. I put quarters in the phone to hear the words. *Come home if you want*, Adele said.

Clare made me remember the inside of the trailer. She made me count the beds. *Close the curtains—it's a box*, she said.

Clare made me see Adele at the table the morning she told me she was going to marry Mick. *It's my last chance*, my mother said. I wanted the plates to fly out of the cupboard. I wanted to shatter every glass.

I smoked a cigarette instead.

I was thirteen.

It was ten a.m.

I drank a beer.

I felt sorry for Adele, I swear. She was thirty-four, an old woman with red hair. She said, *Look at me*, and I did, at her too-pale freckled skin going slack.

I thought, How many men can pass through one woman? I thought, How many children can one woman have? I tried to count: Clare's father and Clare, my father and me, two men between, two children never born whose tiny fingers still dug somewhere. She didn't need to make the words, *I feel them*; didn't need to touch her body, *here*. I knew everything. It was her hand reaching for the cigarettes. It was the way she had to keep striking the match to get it lit. It was the color of her nails—pink, chipped.

If she'd been anyone but my mother I would have forgiven her for what she said.

I can't do it again. She meant she had another one on the way. She meant she couldn't make it end. So Mick was coming here, to live, bringing his already ten-year-old son, child of his dead first wife; the boy needed a mother, God knows, and I saw exactly how it would be with all of them, Mick and the boy and the baby—I could hear the wailing already, the unborn child weeping through my mother's flesh.

Clare made me remember all this. Clare made me hang up before my mother said the words *come home* again.

Storm that night, snow blown to two-foot drifts; rain froze them hard. *Forever*, Clare said.

She didn't know which needle, didn't know whose blood made her like this. She didn't know whose dangerous breath blew through her in the end. She told me she had a dream. We were alone in the trailer. Our little hands cast shadows on the wall: rabbit, bird, devil's head. She said, *Someone's hand passed over my lungs like that.*

I wanted to go home. I didn't care what she said. I saw the trailer in the distance, the colored lights blinking on and off, the miles of snow between me and them. I saw the shape of my mother move beyond curtain and glass.

It's too late to knock, Clare said.

She made me remember our first theft, Adele's car, all the windows down, made me see her at fifteen, myself at ten. We weren't running away: we were feeling the wind. We drove north, out of the dusty August day into the surprising twilight. I remember the blue of that sky, dark and brilliant, dense, like liquid, cool on our skin. And then ahead of us, glowing in a field, we saw a carnival tent, lit from inside.

Freaks, we thought, and we wanted to see, imagined we'd find the midget sisters, thirty-three inches high; the two-headed pig; the three-hundred-pound calf.

We wanted to see Don Juan the Dwarf, that silk robe, that black mustache. We wanted to buy his kisses for dimes. Wanted him to touch our faces with his stubby hands.

We wanted the tattooed woman to open her shirt. Pink-eyed albino lady. We wanted her to show us the birds of paradise on her old white chest.

We wanted to go into the final room, the draped booth at the far corner of the tent. Wanted to pay our extra dollar to see the babies in their jars: the one with half a brain and the twins joined hip to chest. We wanted to see our own faces reflected in that glass, to know our own bodies, revealed like this.

We wanted freaks, the strange thrill of them.

But this is what we found instead: ordinary cripples, a man in a violet robe promising Jesus would heal them.

We found children in wheelchairs. We saw their trembling limbs.

We saw a bald girl in a yellow dress.

Two boys with withered bodies and huge heads.

We saw all the mothers on their knees. We thought their cries would lift this tent.

Busted driving home. Adele knew who had the car but turned us in. *That's why I left*, Clare said.

I'm waiting for you on the road.

You could be anyone: a woman with a blond child, or the man in the blue truck come back. You could be the one who wants me dead. We meet at last.

I'm not trying to go home. I'm heading north instead.

Clare's tired. Clare's not talking now. If you're dangerous, I don't think she'll tell me.

I see swirling snow, pink light between bare trees, your car in the distance, moving fast. I speak out loud to hear myself. *Clare's gone*, I say. But when you spot me, when you swerve and stop, she surprises me. She says, *Go, little sister, get in.*

She whispers, *Yes, this is the one.*

I don't know what she means.

If you ask me where I want to go, I'll tell you this: *Take me out of the snow. Take me to a tent in a field. Make it summer. Make the sky too blue. Make the wind blow. Let me stand here with all the crippled children. Give me twisted bones and metal braces. Give me crutches so I can walk. Let my mother fall down weeping, begging the man in a violet robe to make me whole.*

First, Body

TWO NURSES WITH SCISSORS could make a man naked in eleven seconds. Sid Elliott had been working Emergency eight months and it amazed him every time. Slicing through denim and leather, they peeled men open faster than Sid's father flayed rabbits.

Roxanne said it would take her longer than eleven seconds to make him naked. "But not that much longer." It was Sunday. They'd met in the park on Tuesday and she hadn't left Sid's place since Friday night. She was skinny, very dark skinned. She had fifteen teeth of her own and two bridges to fill the spaces. "Rotted out on smack and sugar. But I don't do that shit anymore." It was one of the first things she told him. He looked at her arms. She had scars, hard places where the skin was raised. He traced her veins with his fingertips, feeling for bruises. She was never pretty. She said this too. "So don't go thinking you missed out on something."

He took her home that night, to the loft in the warehouse overlooking the canal, one room with a high ceiling, a mattress on the floor beneath the window, a toilet behind a screen, one huge chair, one sink, a hot plate with two burners, and a miniature refrigerator for the beer he couldn't drink anymore.

"It's perfect," she said.

Now they'd known each other six days. She said, "What do you see in me?"

"Two arms, two ears. Someone who doesn't leave the room when I eat chicken."

"Nowhere to go," she said.

"You know what I mean."

He told her about the last boy on the table in Emergency. He'd fallen thirty feet. When he woke, numb from the waist, he said, *Are those my legs?* She lay down beside him, and he felt the stringy ligaments of her thighs, the rippled bone of her sternum; he touched her whole body the way he'd touched her veins that night in the park, by the water.

He sat at his mother's kitchen table. "What is it you do?" she said.

"I clean up."

"Like a janitor?"

Up to our booties in blood all night, Dr. Enos said. "Something like that."

She didn't want to know, not exactly, not any more than she'd wanted to know what his father was going to do with the rabbits.

She nodded. "Well, it's respectable work."

She meant she could tell her friends Sid had a hospital job.

He waited.

"Your father would be proud."

He remembered a man slipping rabbits out of their fur coats. His father had been laid off a month before he thought of this.

Tonight his mother had made meat loaf, which was safe—so long as he remembered to take small bites and chew slowly. Even so, she couldn't help watching, and he kept covering his mouth with his napkin. Finally he couldn't chew at all and had to wash each bite down with milk. When she asked, "Are you happy there?" he wanted to tell her about the men with holes in their skulls, wanted to bring them, trembling, into this room. Some had been wounded three or four times. They had beards, broken teeth, scraped heads. The nurses made jokes about burning their clothes.

But the wounds weren't bullet holes. Before the scanners, every drunk who hit the pavement got his head drilled. "A precautionary measure," Dr. Enos explained. "In case of hemorrhage."

"Did the patient have a choice?"

"Unconscious men don't make choices."

Sid wanted to tell his mother that. *Unconscious men don't make choices.* He wanted her to understand the rules of Emergency: first, body, then brain—stop the blood, get the heart beating. No fine-tuning. Don't worry about a man's head till his guts are back in his belly.

Dr. Enos made bets with the nurses on Saturday nights. By stars and fair weather they guessed how many motor-cyclists would run out of luck cruising from Seattle to

Marysville without their helmets, how many times the choppers would land on the roof of the hospital, how many men would be stripped and pumped but not saved.

Enos collected the pot week after week. "If you've bet on five and only have three by midnight, do you wish for accidents?" Dr. Roseland asked. Roseland never played. She was beyond it, a grown woman. She had two children and was pregnant with the third.

"Do you?" Enos said.

"Do I what?"

Enos stared at Roseland's swollen belly. "Wish for accidents," he said.

Skulls crushed, hearts beating, the ones lifted from the roads arrived all night. Enos moved stiffly, like a man just out of the saddle. He had watery eyes—bloodshot, blue. Sid thought he was into the pharmaceuticals. But when he had a body on the table, Enos was absolutely focused.

Sid wanted to describe the ones who flew from their motorcycles and fell to earth, who offered themselves this way. *Like Jesus.* His mother wouldn't let him say that. *With such grace.* He wished he could make her see how beautiful it was, how ordinary, the men who didn't live, whose parts were packed in plastic picnic coolers and rushed back to the choppers on the roof, whose organs and eyes were delivered to Portland or Spokane. He was stunned by it, the miracle of hearts in ice, corneas in milk. These exchanges became the sacrament, transubstantiated in the bodies of startled men and weary children. Sometimes the innocent died and the faithless lived. Sometimes the blind began to see. Enos said, "We save bodies, not souls."

Sid tasted every part of Roxanne's body: sweet, fleshy lobe of the ear, sinewy neck, sour pit of the arm, scarred hollow of the elbow. He sucked each finger, licked her salty palm. He could have spent weeks kissing her, hours with his tongue inside her. Sometimes he forgot to breathe and came up gasping. She said, "Aren't you afraid of me?"

And he said, "You think you can kill me?"

"Yes," she said. "Anybody can."

She had narrow hips, a flat chest. He weighed more than twice what she did. He was too big for himself, always— born too big, grown too fast. Too big to cry. Too big to spill his milk. At four he looked six; at six, ten. Clumsy, big-footed ten. Slow, stupid ten. *Like living with a bear,* his mother said, something broken every day, her precious blown-glass ballerina crumbling in his hand, though he held her so gently, lifting her to the window to let the light pass through her. He had thick wrists, enormous thumbs. Even his eyebrows were bushy. *My monster,* Roxanne said the second night. *Who made you this way?*

"How would you kill me?" he said. He put one heavy leg over her skinny legs, pinning her to the bed.

"You know, with my body."

"Yes, but how?"

"You know what I'm saying."

"I want you to explain."

She didn't. He held his hand over her belly, not quite

touching, the thinnest veil of air between them. "I can't think when you do that," she said.

"I haven't laid a finger on you."

"But you will," she said.

He'd been sober twenty-seven days when she found him. Now it was forty-two. Not by choice. He'd had a sudden intolerance for alcohol. Two shots and he was on the floor, puking his guts out. He suspected Enos had slipped him some Antabuse and had a vague memory: his coffee at the edge of the counter, Enos drifting past it. Did he linger? Did he know whose it was? But it kept happening. Sid tried whiskey instead of rum, vodka instead of whiskey. After the third experiment he talked to Roseland. "Count your blessings," she said. "Maybe you'll have a liver when you're sixty." She looked at him in her serious, sad way, felt his neck with her tiny hands, thumped his back and chest, shined her flashlight into his eyes. When he was sitting down, she was his height. He wanted to lay his broad hand on her bulging stomach.

No one was inclined to offer a cure. He started smoking pot instead, which was what he was doing that night in the park when Roxanne appeared. *Materialized,* he said afterward, *out of smoke and air.*

But she was no ghost. She laughed loudly. She even breathed loudly—through her mouth. They lay naked on the bed under the open window. The curtains fluttered and the air moved over them.

"Why do you like me?" she said.

"Because you snore."

"I don't."

"How would you know?"

"It's my body."

"It does what it wants when you're sleeping."

"You like women who snore?"

"I like to know where you are."

He thought of his sister's three daughters. They were slim and quick, moving through trees, through dusk, those tiny bodies—disappearing, reassembling—those children's bodies years ago. Yes, it was true. His sister was right. Better that he stayed away. Sometimes when he'd chased them in the woods, their bodies had frightened him—the narrowness of them, the way they hid behind trees, the way they stepped in the river, turned clear and shapeless, flowed away. When they climbed out downstream, they were whole and hard but cold as water. They sneaked up behind him to grab his knees and pull him to the ground. They touched him with their icy hands, laughing like water over stones. He never knew where they might be, or what.

He always knew exactly where Roxanne was: behind the screen, squatting on the toilet; standing at the sink, splashing water under her arms. Right now she was shaving her legs, singing nonsense words, *Sha-na-na-na-na*, like the backup singer she said she was once. "The Benders—you probably heard of them." He nodded but he hadn't. He tried to picture her twenty-four years younger, slim but not scrawny. Roxanne with big hair and white sequins.

Two other girls just like her, one in silver, one in black, all of them shimmering under the lights. "But it got too hard, dragging the kid around—so I gave it up." She'd been with Sid twenty-nine days and this was the first he'd heard of any kid. He asked her. "Oh yeah," she said. "Of course." She gave him a look like, *What d'you think—I was a virgin?* "But I got smart after the first one." She was onto the second leg, humming again. "Pretty kid. Kids of her own now. I got pictures." He asked to see them, and she said, "Not *with* me."

"Where?" he said.

She whirled, waving the razor. "You the police?"

She'd been sober five days. That's when the singing started. "If you can do it, so can I," she'd said.

He reminded her he'd had no choice.

"Neither do I," she said. "If I want to stay."

He didn't agree. He wasn't even sure it was a good idea. She told him she'd started drinking at nine: stole her father's bottle and sat in the closet, passed out and no one found her for two days. Sid knew it was wrong, but he was almost proud of her for that, forty years of drinking—he didn't know anyone else who'd started so young. She had conviction, a vision of her life, like Roseland, who said she'd wanted to be a doctor since fifth grade.

Sid was out of Emergency. Not a demotion. A lateral transfer. That's what Mrs. Mendelson in Personnel said. Her eyes and half her face were shrunken behind her glasses.

"How can it be lateral if I'm in the basement?"

"I'm not speaking literally, Sid."

He knew he was being punished for trying to stop the girl from banging her head on the wall.

Inappropriate interference with a patient. There was a language for everything. *Sterilized equipment contaminated.*

Dropped—he'd dropped the tray to help the girl.

"I had to," he told Roxanne.

"Shush, it's okay—you did the right thing."

There was no reward for doing the right thing. When he got the girl to the floor, she bit his arm.

Unnecessary risk. "She won't submit to a test," Enos said after Sid's arm was washed and bandaged. Sid knew she wasn't going to submit to anything—why should she? She was upstairs in four-point restraint, doped but still raving; she was a strong girl with a shaved head, six pierced holes in one ear, a single chain looped through them all. Sid wanted Enos to define *unnecessary.*

Now he was out of harm's way. Down in Postmortem. The dead don't bite. *Unconscious men don't make choices.* Everyone pretended it was for his own sake.

Sid moved the woman from the gurney to the steel table. He was not supposed to think of her as a woman, he knew this. She was a body, female. He was not supposed to touch her thin blue hair or wrinkled eyelids—for his own sake. He was not supposed to look at her scars and imagine his mother's body—three deep puckers in one breast, a raised seam across the belly—was not supposed to see the ghost there, imprint of a son too big, taken this way, and later another scar, something else stolen while she slept. He was not to ask what they had hoped to find, opening her again.

Roxanne smoked more and more to keep from drinking. She didn't stash her cartons of cigarettes in the freezer anymore. No need. She did two packs a day, soon it would be three. Sid thought of her body, inside: her starved, black lungs shriveled in her chest, her old, swollen liver.

He knew exactly when she started again, their sixty-third day together, the thirty-ninth and final day of her sobriety.

He drew a line down her body, throat to belly, with his tongue. She didn't want to make love. She wanted to lie here, beneath the window, absolutely still. She was hot. He moved his hands along the wet, dark line he'd left on her ashy skin, as if to open her.

"Forget it," she said. The fan beat at the air, the blade of a chopper, hovering. He smelled of formaldehyde, but she didn't complain about that. It covered other smells: the garbage in the corner, her own body.

They hadn't made love for nineteen days. He had to go to his mother's tonight but was afraid to leave Roxanne naked on the bed, lighting each cigarette from the butt of the last one. He touched her hip, the sharp bone. He wanted her to know it didn't matter to him if they made love or not. If she drank or not. He didn't mind cigarette burns on the sheets, bills missing from his wallet. As long as she stayed.

The pictures of his three nieces in his mother's living room undid him. He didn't know them now, but he remembered their thin fingers, their scabbed knees, the way Lena kissed him one night—as a woman, not a child, as if she saw already how their lives would be—a solemn kiss, on the mouth, but not a lover's kiss. Twelve years old, and she must have heard her mother say, *Look, Sid, maybe it would be better if you didn't come around—just for a while—know what I mean?* When he saw her again she was fifteen and fat, seven months pregnant. Christina said, *Say hello to your uncle Sid,* and the girl stared at him, unforgiving, as if he were to blame for this too.

These were the things that broke his heart: his nieces on the piano and the piano forever out of tune; dinner served promptly at six, despite the heat; the smell of leather in the closet, a pile of rabbit skin and soft fur; the crisp white sheets of his old bed and the image of his mother bending, pulling the corners tight, tucking them down safe, a clean bed for her brave boy who was coming home.

Those sheets made him remember everything, the night sweats, the yellow stain of him on his mother's clean sheets. He washed them but she knew, and nothing was the way they expected it to be, the tossing in the too-small bed, the rust-colored blotches in his underwear, tiny slivers of shrapnel working their way to the surface, wounding him again. *How is it a man gets shot in the ass?* It was a question they never asked, and he couldn't have told them without answering other questions, questions about what had happened to the men who stepped inside the hut, who didn't have time to turn and hit the ground, who blew sky-high and fell down in pieces.

He touched his mother too often and in the wrong way. He leaned too close, tapping her arm to be sure she was listening. He tore chicken from the bone with his teeth, left his face greasy. Everything meant something it hadn't meant before.

She couldn't stand it, his big hands on her. He realized now how rarely she'd touched him. He remembered her cool palm on his forehead, pushing the hair off his face. Did he have a temperature? He couldn't remember. He felt an old slap across his mouth for a word he'd spat out once and forgotten. He remembered his mother licking her thumb and rubbing his cheek, wiping a dark smudge.

He thought of the body he couldn't touch, then or now— her velvety, loose skin over loose flesh, soft crepe folding into loose wrinkles.

His father was the one to tell him. They were outside after dinner, more than twenty years ago, but Sid could see them still, his father and himself standing at the edge of the yard by the empty hutches. Next door, Ollie Kern spoke softly to his roses in the dark. Sid could see it killed his father to do it. He cleared his throat three times before he said, "You need to find your own place to live, son." Sid nodded. He wanted to tell his father it was okay, he understood, he was ready. He wanted to say he forgave him—not just for this, but for everything, for not driving him across the border one day, to Vancouver, for not suggesting he stay there a few days, alone, for not saying, "It's okay, son, if you don't want to go."

Sid wanted to say no one should come between a husband

and a wife, not even a child, but he only nodded, like a man, and his father patted his back, like a man. He said, "I guess I should turn on the sprinkler." And Sid said, "I'll do it, Dad."

They must have talked after that, many times. But in Sid's mind this was always the last time. He remembered forever crawling under the prickly juniper bushes to turn on the spigot as the last thing he did for his father. Remembered forever how they stood, silent in the dark, listening to water hitting leaves and grass.

He was in the living room now with his mother, after all these years, drinking instant coffee made from a little packet—it was all she had. It was still so hot. She said it. *It's still so hot.* It was almost dark, but they hadn't turned on the lights because of the heat, so it was easy for Sid to imagine the shadow of his father's shape in the chair, easy to believe that now might have been the time his father said at last, *Tell me, son, how it was, the truth, tell me.* It was like this. Think of the meanest boy you knew in sixth grade, the one who caught cats to cut off their tails. It's like that. But not all the time. Keep remembering your eleven-year-old self, your unbearable boy energy, how you sat in the classroom hour after hour, day after day, looking out the window at light, at rain. Remember the quivering leaves, how you felt them moving in your own body when you were a boy—it's like that, the waiting, the terrible boredom, the longing for something to happen, *anything*, so you hate the boy with the cat but you're thrilled too, and then you hate yourself, and then you hate the cat for its ridiculous howling and you're glad when it runs into the street crazy with pain—you're glad when the car hits it, smashes it flat. Then the bell rings, recess is over, and you're in the room again—you're taking your pencils out of your little wooden desk. The girl in front of you has long, shiny braids you know you'll never touch, not now, not after what you've seen, and then you imagine the braids in your hands, limp as cats' tails, and Mrs. Richards is saying the words *stifle, release, mourn,* and you're supposed to spell them, print them on the blank page, pass the paper forward, and later you're supposed to think the red marks—her sharp corrections, her grade—matter.

He could be more specific. If his father wanted to know. At night, you dig a hole in red clay and sleep in the ground. Then there's rain. Sheets and rivers and days of rain. The country turns to mud and smells of shit. A tiny cut on your toe festers and swells, opens wider and wider, oozes and stinks, an ulcer, a hole. You think about your foot all the time, more than you think about your mother, your father, minute after minute, the pain there, you care about your foot more than your life—you could lose it, your right big toe, leave it here, in this mud, your foot, your leg, and you wonder, how many pieces of yourself can you leave behind and still be called yourself? Mother, father, sister—heart, hand, leg. One mosquito's trapped under your net. You've used repellent—you're sticky with it, poisoned by it—but she finds the places you've missed: behind your ear, between your fingers. There's a sweet place up your sleeve, under your arm. And you think, *This is the wound that will kill me.* She's threading a parasite into your veins. These are the enemies: mud, rain, rot, mosquito. She's graceful, not malicious. She has no wish to harm, no intention. She wants to live, that's all. If she finds you, she'll have you. She buzzes at your head, but when she slips inside there's no sound.

It's still so hot. He wants to bang the keys of the out-of-tune piano. He wants a racket here, in his mother's house. He longs for all the dark noise of Roxanne, his plates with their tiny roses smashing to the floor two nights ago, his blue glasses flying out of the drainer. She wanted a drink, and he said she could have one, and she told him to fuck himself, and then the dishes exploded. He thinks of her walking through the broken glass, barefoot but not cutting her feet, brilliant Roxanne. *Roxanne Roxanne.* He has to say her name here, now, bring her into this room where the silent television flickers like a small fire in the corner. He wants to walk her up the stairs to that boy's room, wants her to run her fingers through the silky fur of rabbit pelts in the closet, wants to explain how fast his father was with the knife but too old, too slow, to collect tolls for the ferry. He wants to show her the tight corners of the white sheets, wants her to touch him, here, in this room, to bring him back together, who he was then, who he is now.

So he is saying it, her name. He is telling his mother, *I've been seeing someone,* and his mother is saying, *That's nice, Sid—you should bring her to dinner,* and he understands she means sometime, in some future she can't yet imagine, but he says, *Next week?*

She sips at her too-hot coffee, burns her pursed lips, says, *Fine, that would be fine.*

Roxanne will never agree to it. He knows this. He sees the glow of her cigarette moving in the dark, hand to mouth. He knows he won't ask because he can't bear the bark of her laughter. He doesn't turn on the light, doesn't speak. He sees what's happening, what will happen—this room in winter, the gray light leaking across the floor, the windows closed, the rain streaming down the glass.

He lies down beside her. She stubs out her cigarette, doesn't light another, says nothing but moves closer, so the hair of her arm brushes the hair of his.

He knows she hasn't eaten tonight, hasn't moved all day, living on cigarettes and air, a glass of orange juice he brought her hours ago. Roxanne. But she must have stood at the windows once while he was gone, he sees that now: the blinds are down; the darkness is complete, final, the heat close. There's only sound: a ship's horn on the canal; a man in the distance who wails and stops, wails and stops, turning himself into a siren. She rolls toward him, touches his lips with her tongue, presses her frail, naked body against him. He feels the bones of her back with his fingers, each disk of the spine. He knows he can't say anything—now or forever—such tender kisses, but he's afraid she'll stop, that she'll break him here, on this bed, so he holds back, in case she says she's tired or hungry, too hot, though he's shaking already, weeks of wanting her pulled into this moment. He touches her as if for the first time, each finger

forming a question: *Here and here, and this way, can I?* He's
trembling against his own skin, inside. If she says no, he'll
shatter, break through himself, explode. She's unbutton-
ing his shirt, unzipping his pants, peeling him open. She's
tugging his trousers down toward his feet but not off—
they shackle him. And he knows if they make love this way,
without talking, it will be the last time. He wants to grab
her wrists and speak, but he can't—the silence is everything, hope and the lack of it. He wants the dark to come
inside him, to be him, and there are no words even now, no
sounds of pleasure, no soft murmurs, no names, no gods,
only their skin—hot, blurred—their damp skin and the
place where his becomes hers no longer clear, only her hair
in his mouth, her eyes, her nose, her mouth in his mouth,
her nipple, her fingers, her tongue in his mouth, brittle
Roxanne going soft now, skinny Roxanne huge in the heat
of them, swollen around him, her body big enough for all
of him and he's down in her, all the way down in the dark
and she has no edges, no outline, no place where her dark
becomes the other dark, the thinning, separate air, and he
doesn't know his own arms, his own legs, and still he keeps
moving into her, deeper and deeper, feeling too late what
she is, what she's become, softer and softer under him, the
ground, the black mud, the swamp swallowing him—he's
there, in that place, trying to pull himself out of it, but his
boots are full of mud—he's thigh-deep, falling facedown
in the swamp, and then he feels fingernails digging into his
back, a bony hand clutching his balls. He tries to grab her
wrist but she's let go—she's slipped away from him, and he

knows he never had a chance—this swamp takes everyone. He's gasping, mouth full of mud, and then there's a word, a name, a plea: *Stop, Sid, please,* and then there's a body beneath him, and then there's his body: heavy, slick with sweat, and then there's a man sitting on the edge of a mattress, his head in his hands, and then there's the air, surprising and cool, the fan beating and beating.

He opens the shades and rolls a joint, sits in the big chair, smoking. She's fallen asleep—to escape him, he thinks, and he doesn't blame her. If his father moved out of these shadows, Sid would say, Look at her. It was like this, exactly like this. After the rain, after the toe heals, after you don't die of malaria. The sniper's bullet whizzes past your ear, and you're almost relieved. You think this is an enemy you'll know. Bouncing Bettys and Toe Poppers jump out of the ground all day. Two wounded, two dead. The choppers come and take them all. You expect it to happen and it does, just after dark: one shot, and then all of you are shooting—you tear the trees apart. In the morning, you find them, two dead boys and a girl in the river. Her blood flowers around her in the muddy water. Her hands float. Her long black hair streams out around her head and moves like the river. She's the one who strung the wire, the one who made the booby trap with your grenade and a tin can. She tried to trip you up, yesterday and the day before. She's the sniper who chose you above all others. Her shot buzzed so close you thought she had you. She looks at the M-16 slung over your shoulder. She looks at your hands. She murmurs in her language, which you will never understand. Then she speaks in your language. She says, Your bullet's in my liver. She tells you. Your bullet ripped my bowel. She says, Look for yourself if you don't believe me. You try to pull her from the water. You slip in the mud. The water here knows her. The mud filling your boots is her mud. Slight as she is, she could throw you down and hold you under.

How would you kill me?

You know, with my body.

But you get her to the bank. You pull her from the river. Then the medic's there and he tells you she's dead, a waste of time, *unnecessary risk,* and you tell him she wasn't dead when you got there, she wasn't, and you look at her lying on the bank, and she's not your enemy now, she's not anyone's enemy—she's just a dead girl in the grass, and you leave her there, by the river.

Sid thinks of the doctors at the hospital, their skills, how they use them, their endless exchanges—merciful, futile, extravagant—hearts and lungs, kidneys and marrow. What would they have given her, what would they have taken?

If his mother had looked out the window soon enough, if Sid had been there to carry him to the car, his father could have been saved by a valve; but the man was alone, absolutely, and the blood fluttering in his heart couldn't flow in the right direction. So he lay there in his own backyard, the hose in his hand, the water running and running in the half dark.

·   ·   ·

Sid no longer knows when Roxanne will be lying on his bed and when she won't. She's got her own life, she tells him, and suddenly she does: friends who call at midnight, business she won't describe. One night she doesn't come home at all, but the next morning she's there, downstairs, hunched in the entryway, one eye swollen shut. *Mugged,* she says. *Son of a bitch.* And he knows what's happened. Even her cigarettes stolen. She forages for butts, checking the ashtray, the garbage. There aren't many. She's smoked them down to the filters almost every time, but she finds enough to get by while he runs to the store for a carton, for juice and bread, a jar of raspberry jam. He wants her to eat, but she won't. She doesn't give a shit about that. She doesn't give a shit about him. One line leads to the next. He nods, he knows this. She says she loves whiskey more than she loves him—the park, the tracks, the ground more than a mattress on the floor. She says the bottle's always there and sometimes he's not and who the fuck does he think he is, Jesus? And he says no, he never saved anyone. And then she's crying, beating his chest with her fists, falling limp against him, sobbing so hard he thinks her skinny body will break and he holds her until she stops and he carries her to the bed. He brings her orange juice, the jar of jam, ice in a rag for her swollen eye. She eats jam by the spoonful but no bread. He combs her tangled hair. He lays her down and she wants to make love but they don't, he can't, and he doesn't go to work that day but he does the next and then she's gone.

·   ·   ·

Days become weeks become winter, the one he imagined, the rain on the window. She's here but not here. She's left the smell of her hair on the pillow, her underpants twisted in the sheet at the foot of the bed, the butts of her cigarettes in the ashtray. He sees her everywhere. She's the boy in the hooded sweatshirt huddled on the stoop, whispering *I got what you need,* trying to sell crack or his own thin body. She's the bloated woman asleep on a bench in the park, the newspaper over her face coming apart in the rain. She's the bearded man at Pike's Market who pulls fishbones from the trash to eat the raw flesh. She's the dark man cuffed and shoved into the cruiser. She turns to stare out the back window, blaming him. She's the girl on Broadway with blond hair shaved to stubble. She's fifteen. She wears fishnets under ripped jeans, black boots, a leather jacket with studded spikes along the shoulders. She smacks gum, smokes, says *Fuck you* when he looks too long. He wants to stop, wants to warn her of the risks, wants to say, *Just go home.* But she can't, he knows; at least it's strangers on the street, not someone you know. *And anyway, what about you?* she'd say. She'd drop her cigarette, grind it out. She'd whisper, *I saw Roxanne—she's not doing too good, she's sick—so don't be giving me any shit about risk.*

She's the scarred man on the table with his twice-cleaved chest and gouged belly. When they open him, they'll find things missing. She's the woman without a name, another body from the river. He knows her. She rises, floating in the dirty water.

.   .   .

Dr. Juste says, "Shove her up there on the slab any way you can."

This one's fat. That's the first thing Sid notices. Later there will be other things: the downy hair on her cheeks, the long black hairs sprouting from her blotched legs, the unbelievable white expanse of her breasts. And she's dead, of course, like the others.

But she's not exactly like them, not dead so long, not so cold or stiff. He'd thought he could no longer be surprised, but she surprises him, Gloria Luby, the fattest dead person he has ever seen.

She weighs three hundred and twenty-six pounds. That gives her eighty-three on Sid and the gravity of death.

Dr. Juste turns at the door. He's lean and hard, not too tall, bald; he has a white beard, the impatience of a thin man. He says, "You'll have to roll this one." He says, "She won't mind."

Now they're alone, Gloria and Sid. She was a person a few hours ago, until the intern blasted her eyes with light and the pupils stayed frozen. Sid can't grasp it, the transformation. If she was a person in the room upstairs, she's a person still. He imagines her alive in her bed, a mountain of a woman in white, her frizz of red hair matted and wild, no one to comb it. Blind, unblinking as a queen, she sat while the interns clustered around her and the head resident told them about her body and its defeats, the ravages of alcohol and the side effects of untreated diabetes: her engorged cirrhotic liver, the extreme edema of her abdomen, fluid accumulating from her liver disease, which accounted for her pain—were they listening to her moan?—which put pressure on her lungs till she could barely breathe—did they see her writhing under the sheets? It was the gastrointestinal bleeding that couldn't be stopped, even after the fluid was drained from the belly.

She pissed people off, getting fatter every day, filling with fluids and gases, seventeen days in all. If she'd lived two more, they would have taken her legs, which Dr. Juste says would have been a waste because it wouldn't have saved her but might have prolonged this. Sid wanted to ask what he meant, exactly, when he said *this*.

She's valuable now, at last: she's given herself up, her body in exchange for care. In an hour, Dr. Juste will begin his demonstration and Gloria Luby will be exposed, her massive mistakes revealed.

Sid thinks they owe her something, a lift instead of a shove, some trace of respect. He won't prod. He isn't going to call another orderly for help, isn't going to subject Gloria Luby to one more joke. *How many men does it take to change a lightbulb for a fat lady?*

Later, he may think it isn't so important. Later, he may realize no one was watching, not even Gloria Luby. But just now this is his only duty: clear, specific. It presented itself.

None, she has to turn herself on. He knew what Juste would say when the interns gathered: *Shall we cut or blast?*

A first-timer might be sick behind his mask when they opened her abdomen and the pools of toxins began to drain into the grooves of the metal table, when the whole room filled with the smell of Gloria Luby's failures.

But everyone would keep laughing, making cracks about women big enough for a man to live inside. He knew how scared they'd be, really, looking at her, the vastness of her opened body, because she *was* big enough for a man to crawl inside, like a cow, like a cave. Hollowed out, she could hide him forever. Some of them might think of this later, might dream themselves into the soft swamp of her body, might feel themselves waking in the warm, sweet, rotten smell of it, in the dark, in the slick, glistening fat with the loose bowels tangled around them. They might hear the jokes and wish to speak. Why didn't anyone notice? There's a man inside this woman, and he's alive. But he can't speak—she can't speak—the face is peeled back, the skull empty, and now the cap of bone is being plastered back in place, and now the skin is being stitched shut. The autopsy is over—she's closed, she's done—and he's still in there, with her, in another country, with the smell of shit and blood that's never going to go away, and he's not himself at all, he's her, he's Gloria Luby—bloated, full of gas, fat and white and dead forever.

It could happen to anyone. Anytime. Sid thinks, The body you hate might be your own; your worst fear might close around you, might be stitched tight by quick, clever hands. You might find yourself on this table. You might find yourself sprawled on a road or submerged in a swamp; you might find yourself in a bed upstairs, your red hair blazing, your useless legs swelling. Shadows come and go and speak, describing the deterioration of your retinas, the inefficiency of your kidneys, the necessity of amputation due to decreasing circulation in the lower extremities. *Extremities.* Your legs. They mean your legs. You might find yourself facedown in your own sweet backyard, the hose still in your hand.

He doesn't think about God or ask himself what he believes—he knows: he believes in her, in Gloria Luby, in the three-hundred-and-twenty-six-pound fact of her body. He is the last person alive who will touch her with tenderness.

The others will have rubber gloves, and masks, and knives.

So he is going to lift her, gently, her whole body, not her shoulders, then her torso, then her terrible bruised thighs. She's not in pieces, not yet—she's a woman, and he is going to lift her as a woman. He is going to move her from the gurney to the table with the strength of his love.

He knows how to use his whole body, to lift from the thighs, to use the power of the back without depending on it. He crouches. It's a short lift, but he's made it harder for himself, standing between the gurney and the table. If he pressed them together, they'd almost touch—a man alone could roll her.

He squats. He works his arms under her, surprised by the coolness of her flesh, surprised, already, by her unbelievable weight.

For half a second, his faith is unwavering, and he is turning with her in his arms; they're almost there, and then something shifts—her immense left breast slaps against his chest, and something else follows; her right arm slips from his grasp—and he knows, close as they are, they'll never make it: an inch, a centimeter, a whole lifetime, lost. He feels the right knee give and twist, his own knee; he feels something deep inside tear, muscle wrenching, his knee springing out from under him, from under them. And still he holds her, trying to take the weight on the left leg, but there's no way. They hit the gurney going down, send it spinning across the room. The pain in his knee is an explosion, a booby trap, a wire across a path and hot metal ripping cartilage from bone, blasting his kneecap out his pants leg.

When they hit the floor, his leg twists behind him, and he's howling. All three hundred and twenty-six pounds of Gloria Luby pin him to the cold concrete.

She amazes him. She's rolled in his arms so his face is pressed into her soft belly. The knee is wrecked. He knows that already, doesn't need to wait for a doctor to tell him. *Destroyed.* He keeps wailing, though there's no point, no one in that room but the woman on top of him, insisting she will not hear, not ever. There's no one in the hallway, no one in the basement. There are three closed doors between Sidney Elliott and all the living.

He has to crawl out from under her, has to prod and shove at her thick flesh, has to claw at her belly to get a breath. Inch by inch he moves, dragging himself, his shattered leg, across the smooth floor. He leaves her there, just as she is, facedown, the lumpy mound of her rump rising in the air.

·   ·   ·

Dr. Enos is trying not to smile while Sid explains, again, how it happened. Everyone smiles, thinking of it, Sid Elliott on the floor underneath Gloria Luby. They're sorry about his leg, truly. It's not going to be okay. There'll be a wheelchair, and then a walker. In the end, he'll get by with a cane. If he's lucky. It's a shame, Dr. Roseland tells him, to lose a leg that way, and Sid wonders if she thinks there are good ways to lose a leg. He remembers the boy on the table. He remembers all the boys. *Are those my legs?*

He's drifting in and out. He hears Roxanne laughing in the hallway. Then he sees her at the window, her mouth tight and grim as she sucks smoke.

She wants to know if it's worth it, the risk, the exchange: Gloria Luby's dignity for his leg. The *idea* of her dignity. She laughs, but it's bitter. She tells him he's a failure; she tells him how they found Gloria Luby. It took six orderlies to get her on the slab. They grunted, mocking her, cursing him.

He sleeps and wakes. Roxanne's gone. Even her smoke is gone. He asks the nurse, a thin, dark-skinned man, *Where is she?* And the nurse says, *Where's who, baby? Nobody been here but you and me.*

His father stands in the corner, shaking his head. He can't believe Sid's come back from the jungle, nothing worse than shrapnel in his ass, only to get it from a three-hundred-pound dead woman in a hospital in Seattle. *Three hundred and twenty-six*, Sid says. *What? Three hundred and twenty-six pounds.* His father looks as if he wants to weep, and Sid's sorry—not for himself, he'd do it again. He's sorry for his father, who's disappointed, and not just in him. He's been standing in the closet in Sid's old room all these years, sobbing in the musty dark, pressing his face into the soft rabbit fur. He's been in the other room, in the summer heat, listening to Sid plead with Roxanne, *Just let me lick you.* He's been in the kitchen, watching Sid's mother fry pork chops, chop onions, mash potatoes. He's tried to tell her something and failed. He's stood there, silent in the doorway, while she and Sid sat at the table chewing and chewing. Now, at last, when he speaks to his son, he has nothing to tell him, no wisdom to impart, only a phrase to mutter to himself, *What a waste, what a waste,* and Sid knows that when he says it he's not thinking of the leg. He wants to forgive his father for something, but the old man's turned down his hearing aid. He looks befuddled. He says, *What is it, Sid?*

The nurse shows him the button to press when the pain comes back. *Straight into the vein, babe. No need to suffer. Just give yourself a little pop. Some people think they got to be strong, lie there sweating till I remind them. Not me, honey— you give me one of those, I'd be fine all the time.* He grins. He has a wide mouth, bright teeth; he says, *You need me tonight, honey, you just buzz.*

Gloria Luby lies down beside him. She tells him, *I was exactly what they expected me to be. My brain was light, my liver heavy; the walls of my heart were thick. But there were other things they never found.* She rolls toward him, presses herself against him. Her soft body has warmth but no weight. She envelopes him. She says, *I'll tell you now, if you want to know.*

The blond girl with the spikes on her jacket leans in the doorway. Outside, the rain. Behind her, the yellow light of the hall. She's wearing her black combat boots, those ripped fishnets, a sheer black dress, a black slip. She says, *Roxanne's dead. So don't give me any of that shit about risk.* He turns to the wall. He doesn't have to listen to this. *All right then*, she says. *Maybe she's not dead. But I saw her—she don't look too good.*

She comes into the room, slumps in the chair by the bed. She says, *I heard all about you and that fat lady.*

She's waiting. She thinks he'll have something to say. She lights a cigarette, says, *Wanna drag?* And he does, so they smoke, passing the cigarette back and forth. She says, *Roxanne thinks you're an idiot, but who knows.* She grinds the cigarette out on the floor, then stuffs the filter back in the pack, between the plastic and the paper. She says, *Don't tell anybody I was here.*

The nurse brings Sid a wet cloth, washes his face, says, *You been talking yourself silly, babe.*

You know what I did?

The nurse touches Sid's arm, strokes him from elbow to wrist. *You're famous here, Mr. Elliott—everybody knows what you did.*

Roxanne sits on the windowsill. She says, *Looks like you found yourself another sweetheart.*

Sid's forehead beads with sweat. The pain centers in his teeth, not his knee; it throbs through his head. He's forgotten the button on his IV, forgotten the buzzer that calls the nurse. Roxanne drifts toward the bed like smoke. She says, *Does it hurt, Sid?* He doesn't know if she's trying to be mean or trying to be kind. She says, *This is only the beginning.* But she presses the button, releases the Demerol into the tube. She stoops as if to kiss him but doesn't kiss. She whispers, *I'm gone now.*

Sidney Elliott stands in a white room at the end of a long hallway. He's alone with a woman. He looks at her. He thinks, Nobody loved you enough or in the right way.

In some part of his mind, he knows exactly what will happen if he lifts her, if he takes her home, but it's years too late to stop.

He tries to be tender.

He prays to be strong.

Father, Lover, Deadman, Dreamer

I WAS A NATURAL LIAR, LIKE MY MOTHER. One night she told my daddy she was going to the movies with her girlfriend Marlene. Drive-in, double feature, up in Kalispell. Daddy said, *How late will you be?* And my mother said she didn't know.

Hours later, we tried to find her. I remember my father hobbling from car to car while I sat in the truck. The faces on the screen were as big as God's. Their voices crackled in every box. I was certain my mother was here, stunned and obedient. Huge bodies floated over the hill. They shimmered, lit from inside. This was how the dead returned, I thought, full of grace and hope.

It was midnight. I was nine years old. By morning I understood my mother was five hundred miles gone.

I remember the clumsy child I was. Bruises on my arms, scabbed knees. Boys chased me down the gully after school. I remember falling in the mud. They stole things I couldn't get back, small things whose absences I couldn't explain to my father now that we lived alone: a plastic barrette shaped like a butterfly, one shoelace, a pair of white underpants embroidered with the word *Wednesday*. I was Wednesday's child. I wore my Tuesday pants twice each week, the second day turned inside out.

Careless girl, the nuns said, immature, a dreamer. They told my father they had to smack my hands with a ruler just to wake me up.

I was afraid of the lake, the dark water, the way rocks blurred and wavered, the way they grew long necks and fins and swam below me.

I was afraid of the woods where a hunter had killed his only son. An accident, he said: the boy moved so softly in his deer-colored coat. When the man saw what he'd shot, he propped the gun between his feet and fired once more. He bled and bled. Poured into the dry ground. Unlucky man, he lived to tell.

I was afraid of my father's body, the way he was both fat and thin at the same time, like the old cows that came down to the water at dusk. Bony haunches, sagging bellies—they were pitiful things. Daddy yelled at them, waving his stick, snapping the air behind their scrawny butts. They looked at him with their terrible cow eyes. Night after night they drank all they wanted, shat where they stood. Night after night the stick became a cane, and my father climbed the path, breathing hard. He'd been a crippled child, a boy with a metal brace whose mother had had to teach him to walk a second time when he was six, a boy whose big sister lived to be ten. She drowned in air, chest paralyzed, no iron lung to save her. I thought it was this nightly failure, the cows' blank eyes, that made my mother go.

My daddy worked for a man twelve years younger than he was, a doctor with an orchard on the lake. We lived in the caretaker's cottage, a four-room cabin behind the big house. Lying in my little bed, the one Daddy'd built just for me, I heard leaves fluttering, hundreds of cherry trees; I heard water lapping stones on the shore. Kneeling at my window, I saw the moon's reflection, a silvery path rippling across the water. I smelled the pine of the boards beneath me, and pines swaying along the road. Then, that foot-dragging sound in the hall.

I remember the creak of the hinge, my father's shape and the light behind him as he stood at my door. This was another night, years before the movie, another time my mother lied and was gone. He said, *Get dressed, Ada, we have to go.* He meant we had to look for her. He meant he couldn't leave me here alone. I wore my mother's sweater over my nightgown, the long sleeves rolled up.

This time we drove south, down through the reservation, stopping at every bar. We drove past the Church of the Good Shepherd, which stayed lit all night, past huddled trailers and tar-paper shacks, past the squat house where two dogs stood at the edge of the flat tin roof and howled, past the herd of white plaster deer that seemed to flee toward the woods.

We found my mother just across the border, beyond the reservation, in a town called Paradise, the Little Big Man Bar. Out back, the owner had seven junked cars. He called it his Indian hotel. For a buck, you could spend the night, sleep it off.

My mother was inside that bar, dancing with a dark-skinned man. Pretty Noelle, so pale she seemed to glow. She spun, head thrown back, eyes closed. She was dizzy, I was sure. The man pulled her close, whispered to make her laugh. I swear I heard that sound float, my mother's laughter weaving through the throb of guitar and drum, whirling around my head like smoke. I swear I felt that man, his hand on my own back, the shape of each finger, the sweat underneath my nightgown, underneath his palm.

Then it was my father's hand, clamping down.

I am a woman now. I have lovers. I am my mother's daughter. I dance all night. Strangers with black hair hold me close.

I remember driving home, the three of us squeezed together in the truck. I was the silence between them. I felt my father's pain in my own body, as if my left leg were withered, my bones old. Maybe I was dreaming. I saw my mother in a yellow dress. She looked very small. A door opened, far away, and she stumbled through it to a field of junked cars.

The windows in the truck were down. I was half in the dream, half out. I couldn't open my eyes, but I knew where we were by smell and sound: wood fires burning, the barking of those dogs.

I remember my prayers the morning after, boys lighting candles at the altar, my mother's white gloves.

Green curtain, priest, black box—days later I was afraid of the voice behind the screen, soft at first and then impatient, what the voice seemed to know already, what it urged me to tell. I was afraid of stained-glass windows, saints and martyrs, the way sunlight fractured them, the rocks they made me want to throw.

Sometimes my father held me on his lap until I fell asleep. He stroked my hair and whispered, *So soft.* He touched my scraped shin. *What happened, Ada, did you fall down?* I nodded and closed my eyes. I thought about the boys, the gully, the things they stole. I learned that the first lie is silence. And I never told.

Then I was a girl, twelve years old, too big for my father's lap. I dove from the cliffs into the lake. I told myself the shapes waffling near the bottom were only stones.

I played a game in the woods with my friend Jean. We shot each other with sticks and fell down in the snow. We lay side by side, not breathing. My chest felt brittle as glass. If I touched my ribs, I thought I'd splinter in the cold. The first one to move was the guilty father. The first one to speak had to beg forgiveness of the dead son.

I worked for the doctor's wife now. My mother's words hissed against those walls. I knew the shame she felt, how she hated that house, seeing it so close, getting down on her knees to wax its floors, how she thought it was wrong for an old man like my father to shovel a young man's snow.

But Daddy was glad the snow belonged to someone else. That doctor had nothing my father wanted to own. He said, *The cherry trees, they break your heart.* He meant something always went wrong: thunderstorms in July; cold wind from Canada; drought. I remember hail falling like a rain of stones, ripe fruit torn from trees. I remember brilliant sunlight after the storm, glowing ice and purple cherries splattered on the ground. My father knelt in the orchard, trying to gather the fruit that was still whole.

Then I was sixteen, almost a woman. I went to public school. I knew everything now. I refused to go to mass with my father. I said I believed in Jesus but not in God. I said if the father had seen what he'd done to his child, he would have turned the gun on himself. I thought of the nuns, my small hands, the sting of wood across my palms. I remembered their habits, rustling cloth, those sounds, murmurs above me, that false pity, *poor child*, how they judged me for what my mother had done.

I knew now why my mother had to go. How she must have despised the clump and drag of my father's steps in the hall, the weight of him at the table, the slope of his shoulders, the sorrow of his smell too close. He couldn't dance. Never drank. Old man, she said, and he was. Smoking was his only vice, Lucky Strikes, two packs a day, minus the ones I stole.

He tried not to look at me too hard. I was like her. He saw Noelle when I crossed my legs or lit my cigarette from a flame on the stove.

He gave me what I wanted—the keys to his truck, money for gas and movies, money for mascara, a down vest, a cotton blouse so light it felt like gauze. He thought if I had these things I wouldn't be tempted to steal. He thought I wouldn't envy the doctor's wife for her ruby earrings or her tiny cups rimmed with gold. Still, I took things from her, small things she didn't need: a letter opener with a silver blade and a handle carved of bone; a silk camisole; oily beads of soap that dissolved in my bathwater and smelled of lilac. I lay in the tub, dizzy with myself. The dangerous knife lay hidden, wrapped in underwear at the bottom of my drawer. Next to my skin, the ivory silk of the camisole was soft and forbidden, everything in me my father couldn't control.

The same boys who'd chased me down the gully took me and Jean to the drive-in movies in their Mustangs and Darts. Those altar boys and thieves who'd stolen my butterfly barrette pleaded with me now: *Just once, Ada—I promise I won't tell.*

I heard Jean in the backseat, going too far.

Afterward, I held her tight and rocked. Her skin smelled of sweet wine. I said, *You'll be okay. I promise, you will.*

I am a woman now, remembering. I live in a trailer, smaller than my father's cottage. I am his daughter after all: there's nothing I want to own. I drive an old Ford. I keep a pint of whiskey in the glovebox, two nips of tequila in my purse. I don't think I know as much as I used to know. I sit in the car with my lights off and watch my father, the slow shape of him swimming through the murky light of his little house. He's no longer fat and thin. It scares me, the way he is thin alone. He's had two heart attacks. His gall-bladder and one testicle are gone. In January, the doctors in Spokane opened his chest to take pieces of his lungs. Still he smokes. He's seventy-six. He says, *Why stop now?*

I smoke too, watching him. I drink. I tell myself I'm too drunk to knock at the door, too drunk to drive home.

In the grass behind my father's cottage, a green truck sits without tires, sinking into the ground. If I close my eyes and touch its fender, I can feel everything: each shard, the headlight shattering, the stained-glass windows bursting at last, the white feet of all the saints splintering, slicing through a man's clothes.

Twenty-one years since that night, but if I lie down beside that truck, I can feel every stone of a black road.

Fourth of July, 1971. This is how the night began, with my small lies, with tepid bathwater and the smell of lilac— with ivory silk under ivory gauze—with the letter opener slipped in my purse. I was thinking of the gully long before, believing I was big enough to protect myself.

Jean and I knew other boys now. Boys who crashed parties in the borderlands at the edge of every town.

I asked my father for the truck. I promised: *Jean's house, then up the lake to Bigfork to see the fireworks and nowhere else.* I said, *Yes, straight home.* I twisted my hair around my finger, remembering my mother in a yellow dress, lying to my father and me, standing just like this, all her weight on one foot, leaning against the frame of this door.

We drove south instead of north. A week before, two boys in a parking lot had offered rum and let us sit in the backseat of their car. They said, *Come to the reservation if you want to see real fireworks.*

We scrambled down a gulch to a pond. Dusk already and there were maybe forty kids at the shore.

We were white girls, the only ones.

Jean had three six-packs, two to drink and one to share. I had a pint of vodka and a quart of orange juice, a jar to shake them up. But the Indian kids were drinking pink gasoline—Hawaiian Punch and ethanol—chasing it down with bottles of Thunderbird. They had boxes full of fire-crackers, homemade rockets and shooting stars. They had crazyhorses that streaked across the sky. Crazy, they said, because they fooled you every time: you never knew where they were going to go.

The sky sparked. Stars fell into the pond and sizzled out. We looked for the boys, the ones who'd invited us, but there were too many dressed the same, in blue jeans and plaid shirts, too many cowboy hats pulled down.

One boy hung on to a torch until his whole body glowed. I saw white teeth, slash of red shirt, denim jacket open down the front. I thought, *He wants to burn.* But he whooped, tossed the flare in time. It spiraled toward the pond, shooting flames back into the boxes up the shore. Firecrackers popped like guns; red comets soared; crazy-horses zigzagged along the beach, across the water, into the crowd.

The boy was gone.

In the blasts of light, I saw fragments of bodies, scorched earth, people running up the hill, people falling, arms and legs in the flickering grass, one hand raised, three heads rolling, and then the strangest noise: giggles rippling, a cho-rus of girls.

They called to the boy, their voices like their laughter, a thin, fluttery sound. *Niles.* They sang his name across the water.

Then I was lying in the grass with that boy. Cold stars swirled in the hole of the sky. In the weird silence, bod-ies mended; bodies became shape and shadow; pieces were found. Flame became pink gasoline guzzled down. Gunfire turned to curse and moan.

This boy was the only one I wanted, the brave one, the crazy one, the one who blazed out. He rose up from the water, red shirt soaked, jacket torn off. I said, *You were something,* and he sat down. Now I was wet too, my clothes and hair dripping, as if he'd taken me into the sky, as if we'd both fallen into the pond.

I whispered his name, *Niles,* hummed it like the girls, but soft. He said, *Call me Yellow Dog.*

My purse was gone, the letter opener and my keys lost. The boy kept drinking that pink gasoline and I wondered how he'd die, if he'd go blind on ethanol or catch fire and drown. I'd heard stories my whole life. The Indians were always killing themselves: leaping off bridges, inhaling ammonia, stepping in front of trucks. Barefoot girls with bruised faces wandered into the snow and lay down till the snow melted around them, till it froze hard.

But tonight this boy was strong.

Tonight this boy could not be killed by gas or flame or gun.

He had a stone in his pocket, small and smooth, like a bird's egg and almost blue. He let me touch it. He said it got heavy sometimes. He said, *That's when I watch my back— that's how I know.* I kissed him. I put my tongue deep in his mouth. I said, *How much does it weigh now?* And he said, *Baby, it's dragging me down.*

My clothes dried stiff with mud. I remember grabbing his coarse braid, how it seemed alive, how I wanted it for myself. I thought I'd snip it off when he passed out. His hands were down my cutoff jeans. He knew my thoughts exactly. He whispered, *I'll slit your throat.* I let his long hair go. His body on me was heavy now. I thought he must be afraid. I thought it must be the stone. He held me down in the dirt, pressed hard: he wanted to stop my breath; he wanted to squeeze the blood from my heart. I clutched his wrists. I said, *Enough.*

I imagined my father pacing the house, that sound in the hall. I heard my own lies spit back at me, felt them twist around bare skin, a burning rope.

I remember ramming my knee into the boy's crotch, his yelp and curse, me rolling free. I called to Jean, heard her blurred answer rise up from distant ground.

I remember crawling, scraping my knees, feeling for my purse in the grass. Then he was on me, tugging at my un-zipped jeans, wrenching my arm. He said, *I could break every bone.* But he didn't. He stood up, this Niles, this Yellow Dog. He said, *Go home.*

He was the one to find my purse. He took the letter opener, licked the silver blade, slid it under his belt. He dropped my keys beside me. He said, *I could have thrown these in the water.* He said, *I didn't. You know why? Because I want your white ass gone.*

When I looked up, the stars above him spun.

I yelled Jean's name again. I said, *Are you okay?* And she said, *Fuck you—go.*

I staggered up the hill. I saw my father at the kitchen table, his head in his hands. I heard every word of his prayers as if I were some terrible god. I felt that tightness in my chest, his body. I felt my left leg giving out.

I saw what he saw, my mother's yellow dress, me standing in the door. I smelled his cigarettes. He said, *The cherry trees, they break your heart.*

I drove up that road through the reservation, my mother's laughter floating through the open windows of the truck. She made me dizzy, all that dancing—I felt myself pulled forward, twirled, pushed back, hard.

The lights of the steeple still burned. I was Noelle, the same kind of woman, a girl who couldn't stand up by herself. I wanted to weep for my father. I wanted not to be drunk when I got home, not to smell of boy's sweat, sulfur and crushed lilacs, mud. I wanted to stop feeling hair between my fingers, to stop feeling hands slipping under my clothes.

The dogs on the roof growled. All the white plaster deer surged toward the road. Wind on my face blew cold.

Past the Church of the Good Shepherd, a hundred pairs of eyes watched from the woods, all the living deer hidden between trees along this road. I practiced lies to tell when I got home. I thought, My mother and I, we're blood and bone. I saw how every lie would be undone. I watched a dark man wrap his arms around my pale mother and spin her into a funnel of smoke.

Then he was there, that very man, rising up in a swirl of dust at the side of the road—a vision, a ghost, weaving in front of me. Then he was real, a body in dark clothes.

There was no time for a drunken girl to stop.

No time to lift my heavy foot from the gas.

I saw his body fly, then fall.

I saw the thickness of it, as if for a moment the whole night gathered in one place to become that man, my mother's lover. A door opened at the back of a bar in Paradise. His body filled that space, so black even the stars went out.

I am a woman now, remembering. I am a woman drinking whiskey in a cold car, watching the lights in my father's house. I am a woman who wants to open his door in time, to find her father there and tell.

Twenty-one years since I met Vincent Blew on that road, twenty-one years, and I swear, even now, when I touch my bare skin, when I smell lilacs, I can feel him, how warm he was, how his skin became my shadow, how I wear it still.

He was just another drunken Indian trying to find his way home. After he met me, he hid his body in the tall grass all night and the next day. Almost dusk before he was found. There was time for a smashed headlight to be reassembled. Time for a dented fender to be pounded out and dabbed with fresh green paint. Time for a girl to sober up. Time for lies to be retold. Here, behind my father's cottage, I can feel the body of the truck, that fender, the edges of the paint, how it chipped and peeled, how the cracks filled with rust.

I waited for two men in boots and mirrored glasses to come for me, to take me to a room, close the door, to ask me questions in voices too low for my father to hear, to urge and probe, to promise no one would hurt me if I simply told the truth.

Imagine: *No hurt.*

But no one asked.

And no one told.

I wanted them to come. I thought their questions would feel like love, that relentless desire to know.

I waited for them.

I'm waiting now.

I know the man on the road that night was not my mother's lover. He was Vincent Blew. He was mine alone.

He lies down beside me in my narrow bed. I think it is the bed my father built. The smell of pine breaks my heart. He touches me in my sleep, traces the cage of my ribs. He says, *You remind me of somebody.* He wets one finger and carves a line down the center of my body, throat to crotch. He says, *This is the line only I can cross.* He lays his head in the hollow of my pelvis. He says, *Yes, I remember you, every bone.*

He was behind me now, already lost.

I didn't decide anything. I just drove. My hands were wet. Blood poured from my nose. I'd struck the steering wheel. I was hurt, but too numb to know. Then I was sobbing in my father's arms. He was saying, *Ada, stop.*

Finally I choked it out.

I said, *I hit something on the road.*

And he said, *A deer?*

This lie came so easily.

All I had to do was nod.

He wrapped me in a wool blanket. Still I shivered, quick spasms, a coldness I'd never known, like falling through the ice of a pond and lying on the bottom, watching the water close above you, slowly freezing hard. He washed the blood from my face with a warm cloth. His tenderness killed me, the way he was so careful, the way he looked at the bruises and the blood but not at me. Every gesture promised I'd never have to tell. He said, *You'll have black eyes, but I don't think your nose is broken.* These words—he meant to comfort me—precious nose—as if my own face, the way it looked, could matter now.

He said he had to check the truck. He took his flashlight, hobbled out. I couldn't stand it, the waiting—even those minutes. I thought, My whole future, the rest of my life, like this, impossibly long.

I moved to the window to watch. I tried to light a cigarette, but the match kept hissing out. I saw the beam moving over fender and grille, my father's hand touching the truck. I imagined what he felt—a man's hair and bones. I believed he'd come back inside and sit beside me, both of us so still. If he touched me, I'd break and tell.

But when he came inside, he didn't sit, didn't ask what, only where. I could have lied again, named a place between these orchards and Bigfork, that safe road, but I believed my father was offering me a chance, this last one. I thought the truth might save us even now. I described the place exactly, the curve, the line of trees, the funnel of dust. But I did not say one thing, did not tell him, *Look for a man in the grass.*

He said, *You sleep now.* He said, *Don't answer the phone.*

I had this crazy hope. I'd heard stories of men who slammed into trees, men so drunk their bodies went limp as their cars were crushed. Some walked away. Some sailed off bridges but bobbed to the surface faceup. I remembered the man's grace when we collided, the strange elegance of his limbs as he flew.

I believed in my father, those hands holding blossoms in spring, those fingers touching the fender, my face—those hands wringing the rag, my blood, into the sink. I believed in small miracles, Niles flying into the pond hours ago, Yellow Dog wading out.

I imagined my crippled father helping the dazed man stumble to the truck, driving him to the hospital for X-rays or just taking him home. I thought my father had gone back alone so that he could lift the burden of my crime from me and carry it himself, to teach me suffering and sacrifice, the mercy of his God.

Even if the police came, they'd blame the Indian himself. He'd reel, still drunk, while my father, my good father, stood sober as a nun.

For almost an hour I told myself these lies. Confession would be a private thing, to my father, no one else. He would decide my penance. I would lie down on any floor. I would ask the Holy Mother to show me how I might atone. I would forgive the priest his ignorance when wine turned to blood in my mouth.

I thought of the cherries my father found after the hail, the bowl of them he brought back to the cottage—I thought of this small miracle, that any had been left whole. We ate them without speaking, as if they were the only food. I saw my father on his knees again, the highway. He

gathered all the pieces. Glass and stone became the body of
a man. My father's fingers pressed the neck and found the
pulse. I knew I couldn't live through fifteen minutes if what
I believed was not so.

Two hours gone. I saw the bowl slipping from my
hands, my faith shattered, cherries rolling across the floor.
I saw the man more clearly than I had on the road, the impossible angles of his body, how he must have broken when
he fell.

I heard my father say, *Thou shalt not kill.*

But this was not my crime. The Indian himself told me
he accepted accidents, my drunkenness as well as his own.
Then he whispered, *But I don't understand why you left me
here alone.*

I knew I should have gone with my father, to show him
the way. I imagined him limping up and down that stretch
of highway, waving his flashlight, calling out. On this road,
wind had shape and leaves spoke. A bobcat's eyes flashed.
A coyote crossed the road. I felt how tired my father must
be, old pain throbbing deep in bone.

I tried not to count all the minutes till dawn. I tried to
live in this minute alone. I wanted to speak to the man, to
tell him he had to live like me, like this, one minute to the
next. I knew the night was too long to imagine while his
blood was spilling out. I promised, *He'll come.* I said, *Just
stay with your body that long. There's a hospital down the road
where they have bags of blood to hang above your bed, blood to
flow through tubes and needles into your veins—enough blood
to fill your body again and again.*

I went to the bathroom, turned on the heater. I needed this, the smallest room, the closed door. I crushed the beads of lilac soap till I was sick with the smell. I heard the last crickets and the first birds, and I thought, *No, not yet.* I heard the man say, *I'm still breathing but not for long.* He told me, *Once I sold three pints of blood in two days.* He said, *I could use some of that back now.*

Then there were edges of light at the window and the phone was ringing. Jean's mother, I thought. I saw my friend naked, passed out in the dirt or drowned in the pond. This too, my fault.

The phone again. The police at last.

I must have closed my eyes, relieved, imagining questions and handcuffs, a fast car, a safe cell. Soon, so soon, I wouldn't be alone.

I must have dreamed.

The phone kept ringing.

This time I picked it up.

It was the Indian boy. He said, *I'll slit your throat.*

Past noon before my father got home. I understood exactly what he'd done as soon as I saw the truck: the fender was undented, the headlight magically whole. I knew he must have gone all the way to Missoula, to a garage where men with greasy fingers asked no questions, where a man's cash could buy a girl's freedom.

I couldn't believe this was his choice. Couldn't believe that this small thing, the mockery of metal and glass, my crime erased, was the only miracle he could trust.

He said, *Did you sleep?* I shook my head. He said, *Well, you should.*

I thought, How can he speak to me this way if he knows what I've done? Then I thought, We, not I—it's both of us now.

The phone once more. I picked it up before he could say *Stop.* The police, I hoped. They'll save me since my father won't. But it was Jean. *Thanks a lot,* she said. *I'm grounded for a month.*

Then she hung up.

Vincent Blew was long dead when he was found. The headline said, UNIDENTIFIED MAN VICTIM OF HIT AND RUN. One paragraph. Enough words to reveal how insignificant his life was. Enough words to lay the proper blame: "elevated blood alcohol level indicates native man was highly intoxicated."

I thought, Yes, we will each answer for our own deaths.

Then there were these words, meant to comfort the killer, I suppose: "Injuries suggest he died on impact."

I knew what people would think, reading this. Just one Indian killing another on a reservation road. Let the tribal police figure it out.

Still, the newspaper gave me a kind of hope. I found it folded on the kitchen table, beside my father's empty mug. I thought, He believed my lie about the deer until today. He is that good. He fixed the truck so the doctor wouldn't see. He was ashamed of my drunkenness, that's all.

I was calm.

When he comes home, we'll sit at this table. He'll ask nothing. Father of infinite patience. He'll wait for me to tell it all. When I stop speaking, we'll drive to town. He'll stay beside me. But he won't hang on.

I was so grateful I had to lean against the wall to keep from falling down.

I thought, He loves me this much, to listen, to go with me, to give me up.

All these years I'd been wrong about the hunter. Now I saw the father's grief, how he suffered with his wounds, how his passion surpassed the dead son's. I saw the boy's deception, that deer-colored coat. I understood it was the child's silent stupidity that made the father turn the gun on himself.

I meant to say this as well.

But my father stayed in the orchard all day. At four, I put on dark glasses and went to the doctor's house. I polished gold faucets and the copper bottoms of pots; I got down on my hands and knees to scrub each tile of the bathroom floor. The doctor's wife stood in the doorway, watching me from behind.

She said, *That's nice, Ada.*

She said, *Don't forget the tub.*

When I came back to the cottage, I saw the paper stuffed in the trash, the mug washed. My father asked what I wanted for dinner, and I told him I was going to town. He said I could use the truck, and I said, *I know.*

I meant I knew there was nothing he'd refuse.

He saw me held tight in the dead Indian's arms. He was afraid of me, the truth I could tell.

Sometimes when I dream, the night I met Vincent Blew

is just a movie I'm watching. Every body is huge. Yellow Dog's brilliant face fills the screen. He grins. He hangs on to that torch too long. I try to close my eyes, but the lids won't come down. His body bursts, shards of light; his body tears the sky apart. Then everything's on fire: pond, grass, hair—boy's breath, red shirt.

But later he's alive. He's an angel rising above me. He's Vincent Blew hovering over the road. The truck passes through him, no resistance, no jolt—no girl with black eyes, no body in the grass, no bloody nose. There's a whisper instead, a ragged voice full of static coming up from the ground. It's Vincent murmuring just to me: *You're drunk, little girl. Close your eyes. I'll steer. I'll get us home.*

And these nights, when he takes the wheel, when he saves us, these nights are the worst of all.

Three days before the man was known. His cousin claimed him. She said she danced with him the night he died. In Ronan, at the Wild Horse Bar. Then he was Vincent Blew, and she was Simone Falling Bear. It amazed me to think of it, the dead man dancing, the dead man in another woman's arms.

She said he died just a mile from her house. I knew then that her cousin Vincent was her lover too, that her house was a tar-paper shack at the end of a dirt road, that her refrigerator was a box of ice, her heater a woodstove. She'd have a bag of potatoes in a pail under the sink, a stack of cans with no labels on the shelf.

I saw that even in his stupor Vincent Blew remembered the way home.

She said he'd been an altar boy, that he knew the words

of the Latin mass by heart. She said he'd saved two men at Ia Drang and maybe more. She had his Medal of Honor as proof. She said he wanted to open a school on the reservation where the children would learn to speak in their own tongue.

But that was before the war, before he started to drink so much.

He had these dreams. He had a Purple Heart. *Look at his chest. They had to staple his bones shut.*

I don't know what lies the reporter told to make Simone Falling Bear talk. Perhaps he said, *We want people to understand your loss.*

That reporter found Vincent's wife in Yakima, living with another man. He asked her about Vietnam, and she said she never saw any medals. She said Vincent's school was just some crazy talk, and that boy was drinking beer from his mama's bottle when he was three years old. When the reporter asked if Vincent Blew was ever a Catholic, she laughed. She said, *Everybody was.*

In a dream I climb a hill to find Vincent's mother. She lives in a cave, behind rocks. I have to move a stone to get her out. She points to three sticks stuck in the dirt. She says, *This is my daughter; these are my sons.*

September, and Vincent Blew was two months dead. I was supposed to go to school, ride the bus, drink milk. But I couldn't be with those children. Couldn't raise my hand or sit in the cafeteria and eat my lunch. I went to the lake instead, swam in the cold water till my chest hurt and my arms went numb. Fallen trees lay just below the surface;

rocks lay deeper still. I knew what they were. I wasn't afraid. Only my own shadow moved.

I came home at the usual time to make dinner for my father. Fried chicken, green beans. I remember snapping each one. He didn't ask, *How was school?* I thought he knew, again, and didn't want to know, didn't want to risk the question, any question—my weeping, the truth sputtered out at last, those words so close: *Daddy, I can't.*

The next day I lay on the beach for hours. I burned. My clothes hurt my skin. I thought, He'll see this.

But again we ate our dinner in silence, only the clink of silverware, the strain of swallowing, his muttered *Thank you* when I cleared his plate. He sat on the porch while I washed the dishes, didn't come back inside till he heard the safe click, my bedroom door closed.

I saw how it was between us now. He hated each sound: the match striking, my breath sucked back, the weight of me on the floor. He knew exactly where I was—every moment—by the creak of loose boards. I learned how words stung, even the most harmless ones: *Rice tonight, or potatoes?* He had to look away to answer. *Rice, please.*

His childhood wounds, his sister's death—those sorrows couldn't touch his faith. My mother, with all her lies, couldn't break him. Only his daughter could do that. I was the occasion of sin. I was the road and the truck he was driving. He couldn't turn back.

The third day, he said, *They called from school.*

I nodded. *I'll go,* I said.

He nodded too, and that was the end of it.

But I didn't go. I hitched to Kalispell, went to six restaurants, finally found a job at a truck stop west of town.

That night I told my father I needed the truck to get to work, eleven to seven, graveyard.

I knew he wouldn't speak enough words to argue.

I married the first trucker who asked. I was eighteen. It didn't last. He had a wife in Ellensburg already, five kids. After that I rented a room in Kalispell, a safe place with high, tiny windows. Even the most careless girl couldn't fall.

Then it was March, the year I was twenty, and my father had his first heart attack. I quit my job and tried to go home. I thought he'd let me take care of him, that I could bear the silence between us.

Three weeks I slept in my father's house, my old room, the little bed.

One morning I slept too long. Light filled the window, flooded across the floor. It terrified me, how bright it was.

I felt my father gone.

In his room, I saw the bed neatly made, covers pulled tight, corners tucked.

I found him outside the doctor's house. He had his gun in one hand, the hose in the other. He'd flushed three rats from under the porch and shot them all.

He meant he could take care of himself.

He meant he wanted me to go.

I got a day job, south of Ronan this time, the Morning After Café. Seventeen years I've stayed. I live in a trailer not so many miles from the dirt road that leads to Simone Falling Bear's shack.

Sometimes I see her in the bars—Buffalo Bill's, Wild Horse, Lucy's Chance. She recognizes me, a regular, like herself. She tips her beer, masking her face in a flash of green glass.

When she stares, I think, She sees me for who I really am. But then I realize she's staring at the air, a place between us, and I think, Yes, if we both stare at the same place at the same time, we'll see him there. But she looks at the bottle again, her loose change on the bar, her own two hands.

Tonight I didn't see Simone. Tonight I danced. Once I was a pretty girl. Like Noelle, shining in her pale skin. It's not vain to say I was like that. I'm thirty-seven now, already old. Some women go to loose flesh, some to hard bone. I'm all edges from years living on whiskey and smoke.

But I can still fool men in these dim bars. I can fix myself up, curl my hair, paint my mouth. I have a beautiful blue dress, a bra with wires in the cups. I dance all night. I spin like Noelle; I shine, all sweat and blush and will.

Hours later, in my trailer, it doesn't matter, it's too late. The stranger I'm with doesn't care how I look: he only wants me to keep moving in the dark.

Drifters, liars—men who don't ask questions, men with tattoos and scars, men just busted out, men on parole; men with guns in their pockets, secrets of their own; men who can't love me, who don't pretend, who never want to stay too long: these men leave spaces, nights between that Vincent fills. He opens me. I'm the ground. Dirt and stone. He digs at me with both hands. He wants to lie down.

Or it's the other way around. It's winter. It's cold. I'm alone in the woods with my father's gun. I'll freeze. I'll starve. I look for rabbits, pray for deer. I try to cut a hole in the frozen earth, but it's too hard.

It's a bear I have to kill, a body I have to open if I want to stay warm. I have to live in him forever, hidden in his fur, down deep in the smell of bear stomach and bear heart. We lumber through the woods like this. I've lost my human voice. Nobody but the bear understands me now.

Last week my lover was a white man with black stripes tattooed across his back. His left arm was withered. *Useless*, he told me. *Shrapnel, Dak To.*

He was a small man, thin, but heavier than you'd expect.

He had a smooth stone in his pocket, three dollars in his hatband, the queen of spades in his boot. He said, *She brings me luck.*

He showed me the jagged purple scar above one kidney, told the story of a knife that couldn't kill.

The week before, my lover was bald and pale, his fingers thick. He spoke Latin in his sleep; he touched my mouth.

It's always like this. It's always Vincent coming to me through them.

This bald one said he loaded wounded men into helicopters, medevacs in Song Be and Dalat. Sometimes he rode with them. One time all of them were dead.

He was inside me when he told me that.

He robbed a convenience store in Seattle, a liquor store in Spokane. He did time in Walla Walla. I heard his switchblade spring and click. Felt it at my throat before I saw it flash.

He said, *They say I killed a man.*

He said, *But I saved more than that.*

He had two daughters, a wife somewhere. They didn't want him back.

The cool knife still pressed my neck. He said, *I'm innocent.*

I have nothing to lose. Nothing precious for a lover to steal—no ruby earrings, no silver candlesticks.

In my refrigerator he'll find Tabasco sauce and mayonnaise, six eggs, a dozen beers.

In my freezer, vodka, a bottle so cold it burns your hands.

In my cupboard, salted peanuts, crackers shaped like little fish, a jar of sugar, an empty tin.

In my closet, the blue dress that fooled him.

If my lover is lucky, maybe I'll still have yesterday's tips.

When he kisses me on the steps, I'll know that's my thirty-four dollars bulging in his pocket. I'll know I won't see him again.

He never takes the keys to my car. It's old, too easily trapped.

But tonight I have no lover. Tonight I danced in Paradise with a black-haired man. I clutched his coarse braid. All these years and I still wanted it. He pulled me close so I could feel the knife in his pocket. He said, *Remember, I have this.*

I don't know if he said the words out loud or if they were in my head.

When I closed my eyes I thought he could be that boy, the one who blew himself into the sky, whose body fell down in pieces thin and white as ash and bread, the one who rose up whole and dripping, who slipped his tongue in my mouth, his hands down my pants.

He could have been that boy grown to a man.

But when I opened my eyes I thought, No, that boy is dead.

Later we were laughing, licking salt, shooting tequila. We kissed, our mouths sour with lime. He said we could go out back. He said if I had a dollar he'd pay the man. I gave him five, and he said we could stay the week for that. I kissed him one more time, light and quick. I said I had to use the ladies' room.

Lady? he said, and laughed.

I decided then. He was that boy, just like him. I said, *Sit tight, baby, I'll be right back.* He put his hand on my hip. *Don't make me wait,* he said.

I stepped outside, took my car, drove fast.

Don't get me wrong.

I'm not too good for Niles Yellow Dog or any man. I'm not too clean to spend the night at that hotel. It wouldn't be the first time I passed out on a backseat somewhere, hot and drunk under someone's shadow, wrapped tight in a man's brown skin.

But tonight I couldn't do it. Tonight I came here, to my father's house, instead. Tonight I watch him.

He's stopped moving now. He's in the chair. There's one light on, above his head. I can't help myself: I drink the whiskey I keep stashed. It stings my lips and throat, burns inside my chest. But even this can't last.

I don't believe in forgiveness for some crimes. I don't believe confessions to God can save the soul or raise the dead. Some bodies are never whole again.

I cannot open the veins of my father's heart.

I cannot heal his lungs or mend his bones.

Tonight I believe only this: we should have gone back. We should have crawled through the grass until we found that man.

If Vincent Blew had one more breath, I should have lain down beside him—so he wouldn't be cold, so he wouldn't be scared.

If Vincent Blew was dead, we should have dug the hard ground with our bare hands. I should have become the dirt if he asked. Then my father could have walked away, free of my burden, carrying only his own heart and the memory of our bones, a small bag of sticks light enough to lift with one hand.

Necessary Angels

DORA'S DISAPPEARED AGAIN. I see her lying in the field, in the abandoned refrigerator. She's not sleeping and she's not dead: she's between these places. And though I'm afraid for her even now, from this distance of years I can tell you Dora Stone is going to live.

The first time it happened, she was five years old, thirty-six pounds. While Mother dozed in the shade of her striped umbrella, Dora wandered up the beach, into the cool waves. She felt sand shifting under her feet, her small body sinking in the tug of an undertow. One man up the shore was close enough to save her. One fat white man burned red seemed to stare. But he didn't come. Was he blind behind his glasses, or was he curious, wanting to see what the child might do?

She wasn't that deep really. She wasn't going to drown. She was her own voice whispering in her own ear, *Just walk out*. Mother found her, safe and dry, so Lily's fury, stripped of fear, was pure, and the slaps were quick and hard, familiar— Dora knew how to let them fall: no crying, no ducking. The sting went away soon enough, and Mommy was sorry in the dark; Mommy came to Dora's room and lay down beside her in the blue bed. Mommy cried and held Dora, stroked her precious body, touched arm and neck and thigh as if to be sure the child was all there. She said, *What would Mommy do if she lost you?*

These are the bodies Lily's lost already: the husband with another wife and two sons; the mother shrinking in the bed, wrinkling into the sheets till she was gone; the half-man down the hall, her father, lost; her own unknown self. She's not fat but blurred, lost in her body: drooping breasts and buttocks, spread white belly—lily-white Lily Stone, not a flower now though her skin is still petal soft and that pale, that easily bruised. Don't touch Mommy too hard, don't hug her too close, but she can touch you where and how she wants, can slap your head on the beach or swat your butt, can come to your room and lie beside you in your little bed, her breath wine sweet, her body a weight and heat that fills your room till you blur too, into her, *precious baby*, the place that is yourself and not yourself has disappeared, but you don't look at her here, and she's come to this room so many times you're not scared—why would you be scared of your own mother, who only wants to lie this close? Yes, it's hot, but you're used to that, so you let her sleep and do not tell her of waves or undertow, do not speak of sand, though you feel them in your body now, in your body that remembers everything, the pull and lick, the ground beneath you slipping. You do not speak of the burning man. He's yours. You keep these places to go alone: the water, the blind man's eyes, the stranger's hands.

·   ·   ·

The next time, Dora's six, tied in the closet, forgotten by twelve-year-old Max, her cousin and best friend, who has used his favorite knot, the Lazarus loop, so called because a person has roughly the same chance of escaping it as she has of rising from the dead.

It will happen again. Dora's bike is in the reeds by the canal. But eight-year-old Dora is gone. Or she's eleven, drunk on beer with Max, who is no longer allowed in their grandfather's house. They dance in the back of the truck, radio blaring, doors flung open, yellow light spilling into the swamp. The man in the song says he's a razor he's a rifle he's the water and Max says, *You're dangerous, girl.* Hours later, in the still dark, Dora wakes groggy and mystified on her own front lawn.

In the morning she'll learn of the stolen truck, Max's escape from the Alpena School for Boys, a string of gas stations robbed from Michigan to Florida and one attendant shot in the hand, *So if you know, little girl, you better tell us where.* Armed and dangerous, sweet tender Max, shaved almost bald—Max, whose dirty fingers snarled your long hair when he pulled you close. You should have known.

She's seven, she's twelve, she's fourteen, she's gone.

I see a dark-skinned boy on a bike riding toward the refrigerator in the field. He doesn't know what's in it, but he spots the silver bicycle sparkling in the grass. He can't believe what he finds. He's only a child, but he knows she's dangerous to him. He doesn't check for breath or pulse, doesn't lean close to see she's just a girl. He's smart enough not to touch. He flies across the field, pumping harder than he thought he could while the sun blazes and spits in the bleached white sky.

I'm Dora. I'm the girl in the refrigerator. I'm the girl in the closet. I'm the girl who's left her bike in the reeds by the canal. I can't be found.

I know you're afraid of where I'm going when I tell you this. I'm afraid. But I can't stop. Forgetting is the first lie, a little death. I won't abandon myself piece by piece. I know what happens to wicked runaway girls. You find us in rivers of grass, or floating in ponds. You find us under our own beds or stuffed in the hedges of our own yards. You find our shoes in trash heaps. When we surface at last, you give numbers to our bones. But this isn't one of those stories. See, these are my hands. This is my voice talking. As long as you hear me, I'm alive.

One night my father forgot to come home. Max forgot the boy with the bullet in his palm, forgot a woman pushed from her truck to the road. Max says, *I never did nothin' wrong.* My grandfather sits in the wheelchair upstairs, touching his right hand with his left, trying to remember when his body had two sides and the words that might explain. Mother says, *Just a bad dream, baby.*

They leave me to remember it all.

These are the rules:

> Don't sit in the sun.
> Don't ride your bike on the road.
> Don't walk by the canal.

Everything here is dangerous: heat, wind, days of rain—
this water wants to rise, wants to take back this ground;
waves want to splinter boats and wash dark bodies to the
shore. Grass cuts your hand if you grab it; leaves tipped
with poison pierce your clothes. The alligator in the sun
looks harmless as rubber, a truck's blown tire, only the eyes
moving, but one flick of the tail and you'll be in the water,
legs broken, back numb.

But Dora always disobeyed; Dora always walked home
along the canal. Even the ducks were fierce. She swatted at
them with a stick. One bit her cheek—see, beneath the eye,
this white scar.

Grandpa said, *Go get my gun*. He hated the ducks. Their
noise. Their shit on his lawn. Dora promised to stay on the
road, but he said, *Actions have consequences*. She knows she
is the consequence of certain actions for which her mother
is to blame. She knows she can't stop him now. This has
nothing to do with her, the wound on the cheek, the eye
that could have been lost. This is the voice of the gun, the
stutter in the brain, the trembling hand, a hurt so old it's
hard and small as the bullet in the heart of the gun.

She knows where it is, exactly, where it stands in the
closet, propped against the wall—the clean, oiled, loaded
rifle. She knows already how it feels in her small hands—
exactly how long, how smooth. She knows its surprising
weight.

Her grandfather once dreamed cities into being—the
straight grids of streets, the safe repetition of houses—
raised them out of wet ground. Now he speaks with a

stutter; his walk is a stutter too. He's had one stroke already, will have six more before he dies, so Dora's mother says, *He couldn't have killed the ducks*, but Dora remembers the heavy bodies of birds falling from the sky.

And she remembers the girl. The moon was new, a carved blade slung low at twilight, reflected in water. She wanted to dive through it, into the rippling shadows of palms, wanted to swim away from her grandfather, whose hand was hot, whose whole body smelled of the swamp. But she was more afraid of the canal: reeds to wrap ankle and wrist, mud to suck you down.

This is why her grandfather dragged her here. This is what she saw. A pale girl in dark water. Floating. Facedown.

Her grandfather squeezes her hand so tight her face goes numb.

This is her proof: her own feet cut by the shells embedded in the road. Fine scars now.

A dream, Mother says. *Yes, a girl did drown, but your grandfather was in a wheelchair by then, so how could he take you to the canal?*

Dora can't ask him. He doesn't know.

She's the only one who remembers how the water looked that night, smooth and slow, its surface tight as skin and just as fragile. How the girl's body seemed not to have fallen. She rose. She broke the skin. She was the white scar on the black surface of memory. Whether she existed or not, she was the place you entered if you wanted to remember it all.

This part Dora doesn't remember—she can't, she wasn't there. So she doesn't know how the boy who found her in the refrigerator told nobody all day, how he hid instead under his own porch, hoping that what he'd seen wasn't real, that he'd wake and forget. His mother stood at the door calling his name. The earth was dark, the sky still blue. The third time, her voice broke him, and the child crawled out.

He talks his way backward till he sees more at dusk than he saw in the scorched field. He knows now she's only a girl, very white but burned red, almost blistering, her eyelids—Did he come that close? Yes, now he remembers—and her thighs streaked with dirt—no, not dirt, something dry, rust-colored, flaking off her skin.

His mother is afraid for him in a new way, not afraid as she was when she stood alone and her son was only her voice, an image in her mind, the shape of her lips in the dark—now he's here, with her, in her arms, dirty, whole, but she's afraid because she wonders what they'll think when he tells them, *It's been hours.* She hears herself pleading, *He's only eight years old.* She wants to hide under the porch with him and wait till dawn—she's a mother, after all—but she sees the girl, those sore eyes. She believes in grace and knows this child, like hers, might be alive.

Dora doesn't remember how the boy led dogs and men back to the field in the now complete dark, doesn't remember how they questioned him, how they tried to make him conjure somebody else in that field, tried to make him believe that man's face was dark and familiar and this was the reason for his silence.

And she doesn't remember the hands under her, the hands on her chest pumping, the mouth on her mouth breathing, doesn't remember her body lifted to the stretcher, the white ambulance, the mask over nose and mouth, the needle jabbed in the vein and taped to the hand, doesn't remember the long white hall or the cool metal of the scissors cutting her out of her clothes, doesn't remember all the hands on her, where they touched and how.

Remembers only this: waking in the white room and her mother there asleep in the chair beside her, her mother opening her eyes at the same moment Dora opened hers, and in this way she thought her mother must know what had happened but won't say now or ever what it was, will only refer to it in the future as the time Dora rode her bike too long in the sun, the time Dora passed out and nearly died in the heat—and hadn't she been warned?

She doesn't feel anything inside. Feels only her burned skin. She would tell her mother something if she knew where to start.

Imagine this: another boy, not the one who will find her. None of that has happened yet. This one's no boy really and no stranger. *Lewis Freyer.* Like *prayer,* Dora thinks—when she remembers her hands on him it's that quiet.

Estrelle, who is his mother, used to come twice a week to clean the house, and Lewis came too sometimes until Estrelle caught them: filthy, together. Now she comes every day to take care of Dora's grandfather. She has a mother of her own at home, an old woman in a chair but not a wheelchair—they don't have money for that—and anyway, Lewis is strong enough to lift her anywhere she needs to go. She was six feet tall, a prison guard, and now she's only four feet long, got one wooden leg and one stump, and if there's any sense in that Estrelle doesn't know. Dora's never seen her, has only heard Estrelle talk. For years Estrelle has walked to and from this house, across fields and roads, a mile and a half each way, but Estrelle's not a young woman, you know, and lately her feet have been bothering her, swollen and a bit numb, and this is how her mother's troubles started, so now Lewis brings her in the morning, returns for her in the afternoon.

He's sullen. No matter how hot it is, he stays in the gold Impala. He won't come out for iced tea or lemonade, won't sit in the shade, won't answer Dora when she says, *You're melting, Lewis.*

He sits like a deaf man, refuses to wipe his face though the sweat trickles into ears and eyes, though the salt burns. Yes, he's melting, but he can sit still as plaster and stare through the skinny white girl.

Dora says, *You go too long without blinking, your eyes gonna dry up and fall out of your skull.*

Still nothing—as if he's forgotten how they crawled through culverts under roads, snagged their clothes on barbed wire, fell down in the field alone.

He's a grown man, eighteen years old, so he can't remember the weight of her small body on his, her dirty hand over his mouth. Remembers only this: Estrelle in the yard, Estrelle descending—*I'm gonna beat your black skin blue*—remembers that the seven-year-old girl who's now fourteen was the reason for this and other shame.

Silent as he is, Dora persists. It's hot. She's bored. Nobody but Estrelle has come to the house all summer. Nobody but the skittish boy with festering skin who brings groceries and cases of wine to the back door. Nobody but the Haitian gardener with his whirring blades who carves the hedges, trims the lawn, every day. She could ride down the road, swim a hundred laps in a tiny pool while two other girls her age, her friends, lie greased and golden in the blistering sun. But she'd rather wait here, with him.

On the twelfth day, he speaks.

He says, "What the fuck do you want?"

After all her pestering, she doesn't know. "Nothing," she says, and for three days doesn't go near the car. Then he's the one to tempt her. She's on the porch, and he gets out of the Impala, so she sees him, really, for the first time—a man, thin but hard, all long muscle, dark in the bright sun.

This Lewis, who grins, who says, "I am thirsty," who takes the lemonade in his big hand and drinks it all in one pull, this Lewis who gives her the empty glass, leaves her mute. It's his hands that silence her, the way they flutter like wings opening so she sees the pale undersides marked with fine dark lines. This Lewis who squints, who almost scowls, makes her feel ashamed of her small body. She hears Lily say, *Don't talk to strangers. Don't stand in the sun.* She hears Grandpa: *Go get the gun.* The heavy-bodied birds drop from the sky, and Max whispers, *You're dangerous, girl.* It must be true, because even though she never said a word, Max, her sweetheart, her first love, was caught again.

Lewis says, "You meet me up the road I'll take you for

a ride someday." She says she can't, and he laughs but it's mean. He says, "I thought you liked me."

She thinks of Max in jail, Max blaming her all these years, dangerous eleven-year-old Dora getting him drunk.

She says, "It's not what you think."

Lewis is sliding his long body into the gold Impala; he's closing the door slowly, a deliberate softness, he's whispering his words so she has to lean close; he's saying, *Tell me what I think.*

"Tomorrow," she says. And though she's afraid of what she'll do to him, she can't stop what they've begun.

They make love in her grandfather's car parked in the dark garage. They make love in the gold Impala at the end of a deserted road. They can't be seen together. They know this but never speak of it. They find a refrigerator in a field, a white box, a home, and they lie down but it's much too small. They remember childhood paths through woods and swamp, under barbed wire, over walls. Lewis knows how to come at night into the huge dark house, which door she's left unlocked; he knows how to be a shadow among shadows moving through the long halls, how to breathe as the house breathes, how to find Dora in the blue room in the soft bed, how to slip his hand over her mouth so she won't cry out, how to move like water through her and out of her, how to flow down the dark stairs into the dark yard before gathering himself into the hard shape of a man. *Go get the gun.* There's nobody here to say it now, nobody but the old man with half a face, the old man who can't get out of bed alone, who lies like a bug on his back till morning when Estrelle comes. There's nobody here but the mother fallen across the couch, snoring in wine-thick sleep. Nobody here but little Dora in the damp bed.

Tonight he lifted his grandmother, carried her from the chair where she sits all day to the couch where she sleeps. Even without her legs she's a big woman, heavy. She never leaves this house, but she sees far beyond these walls. She feels the heat of the boy's skin where he touches. She knows. She says, *You watch yourself, Lewis.* She says, *Your mama's had all the sorrow she can bear.*

He would never tell Dora, would never name his mother's grief, would never describe the three rooms where he lives with her and her mother and two sisters, the kitchen table where he and his sisters and brother were born, would never try to explain what it means to be the youngest child of seven and the only man in the house.

But somehow she knows. She imagines the old woman in his arms, knows that despite her losses she weighs more than Dora ever will, that this weight is a thing he carries every time he climbs the stairs of her house.

He does not find her pretty in any way. She has a flat butt, barely swollen breasts. The thick blue veins roping her thin arms seem unnatural on a girl so small. Her blond hair is clipped short, dyed black, but comes in yellow at the roots. In any light she looks too naked, not just stripped but skinned.

He's had girls before. Women, he calls them. They knew what to do. They had red mouths, quick hands. They were never this naked. They were wet and open, their bodies full and safe and soft. They had rubbers in their purses. He could meet them anywhere, anytime. No one had to lie.

He and Dora never talk. They know everything and nothing; they're bound: his mother combs her grandfather's hair, clips his nails, wipes his bum. She's more than wife or daughter ever was. What the old man feels for Estrelle is his secret but will never be as fragile or forgettable as love.

The blue car.

The stifling heat of the garage.

He says, "Does it scare you?"

She knows he means his body, how long it is, how dark, and she thinks of her mother climbing out of the tub, all that flesh rushing toward her, loose breasts flapping, dimpled thighs whispering where they rub—she thinks of her grandfather grabbing with his one good hand, the thumbprint of bruise he leaves—she thinks of the cheek she's supposed to kiss, the rough white-whiskered skin—she imagines these familiar bodies, how they make her forget what's her and not her, how she's terrified of the place they blur.

Where Lewis touches, he defines—dark hand on white rib. So she's not afraid. But he is—afraid of these frail ribs. He can rest his long fingers in the spaces between them—she's that thin, and her skin too, so fine he feels he might put his hand through her. He would not say he loves her or even likes her. If he could explain it at all, he might say it is this fear that makes him tender, this fear that brings him to the house again and again—he sees her brittle ribs as the rigging of a tiny boat rocking on black water; it is this sound, waves lapping wood, that calls him. Small and breakable as the girl is, the body he enters is a way out.

Tonight Dora's grandfather could not be comforted. He rolled around and around the room, using his cane to move the chair with his strong left hand. He dumped the drawers, looking for something that can't be found. He refused to understand who Lily was, and finally she left him, locked him in the room so he wouldn't propel himself down the hall, so he wouldn't fly down the stairs. He banged the wheels of his chair against the door. He rattled the knob. When his yell broke to a whimper, it was Estrelle's name he called.

Dora tells Lewis none of this. She wants to be her body only, her body in the car, in the rain, out here on the black road. But her body is a map. Her body is a history. His fingers find every scar and bruise. *What happened here, and here?* He doesn't ask, but where he touches she remembers. She cries, and he holds her. He expects no explanation. He isn't scared of sorrow. It doesn't surprise him. When he's calmed her, he touches her again.

She imagines her grandfather upstairs in the house far from this road. He's rolled his chair close to the window. He's trying to see through the rain, trying to remember his right shoulder, how the raised rifle kicked as he fired. He's trying to count the ducks falling from the sky, but there are too many, they always come too fast, and then he sees, he understands this one thing: it's only the rain.

She imagines Lewis's grandmother—one stump, one wooden leg; Lewis is touching her legs—and she sees her own future, her body coming apart, how she'll lose it piece by piece. She doesn't know how he does this to her, why he won't stop. They make love so many times, so long, her fingers and feet and lips go numb.

They will be caught. It's necessary. They know this as they know each other: without words. They are waiting in their silence to see how it will happen.

The gold Impala, empty.

A dirt road.

Tonight they saw the pretty little horses, the setting sun.

Four ponies, lean and glowing in gold light. One deep ginger with hair like velvet. One the bleached white of bone. Two bays nuzzling. They heard the hum of insect wings, saw the ginger pony brace his legs to piss hard.

Later they stood on a bridge, watching gulls swoop high, then dive toward water, saw them vanish at the surface as if a blue hole opened between air and river.

Tonight when they lay down in the woods where palm and pine grow together, they touched each other's bones: hips, cheeks, spine. Tonight, for the first time, they closed their eyes and almost slept, the man enfolding the child, one bird fallen—her body the white belly, his the dark wings—and it is in this way they wake to the sound of glass shattering on the road.

It's only boys, three of them, nine or ten years old.

They beat the car with sticks and rocks. Lewis knows that if he closes his eyes the bare-chested boys with sticks will become men with guns. He lies naked, watching children destroy the car. His hand clamps Dora's mouth, and she wonders, Does he think I'm fool enough to yell? It's not that simple, his fear. What he wants is for the body beneath his body to be gone. But her body insists. Still as it is, it is too many sharp bones. It will not soften, will not be hidden, will not sink into this ground. The boys jab their little knives into tires; the air escaping hisses off the road. His body hot on top of hers has a smell of something smoldering, about to burn, and then the match is struck, the first one, and the vinyl seats are split open with the sharp knives and the stuffing spills out—the first match is thrown and the second match is struck and the smell in the night is melting plastic. Together, two boys stand on the hood to drop a rock onto the windshield, and the glass is a shattered web caved in that does not break apart. Black smoke billows from open doors. The man in the woods has pressed the air from the girl's lungs, and the boys, who are thrilled with their miraculous destruction, are mounting their bikes and pedaling home.

He is off her and she gulps air. He hates the boys, their bare white skin, their whoops and their strange silence in the end, but they're gone, so it's only the girl beside him now, silent but for her gasping, and he hates that sound, and he hates her bright reflecting skin—he can't see his own hand at the end of his own arm.

He wants her dressed, and she knows; she's quick. He wants to leave her or be able to love her despite everything. But he can't escape the smell of fear, strong as piss, rising from his skin. He can't escape the rage, a shaking too deep to stop, blood quivering in the veins. He wants to weep, thinking of his mother in the morning, walking to this girl's house.

There's nothing to do but let the car burn. The sky's gone green with clouds. If the storm comes soon enough, if the rain's hard, these flames might flicker out.

They walk together partway and then alone. They do not touch or speak. They do not look over their shoulders. They do not look up and hope.

When he disappears, he disappears completely, moving across the field, silent and invisible as the black canal. She thinks he is gone forever. She leaves no door unlocked. But that night he comes again.

He's green sky and wind. He swirls up from the south.

He's the wind uprooting palms, pavement that seems to melt and flow, the drone of pumps. He's three stones hitting the glass of her window, sharper than rain. He's all sound.

She's afraid of him but more afraid for him, his new recklessness, and what would happen if her mother woke and made one call? What would anyone see here but a dark-skinned man at a white girl's door? So she's opening the window, letting the rain pour in—she's speaking his name into the wind and he hears her—she's moving down the stairs to open the door so carefully locked.

He's inside, he's there, filling the doorway, dripping, dark, his clothes drenched, his skin wet, his hair full of rain. Water flows from him, puddles on the floor; muddy rivulets stream across the tile, and Dora thinks of Estrelle on her hands and knees tomorrow, Estrelle not asking, not her business what the white people do in their own house, just her business to make it right when they stop.

She's wearing a long T-shirt, her underpants. Nothing else. She's cold. But it's not cold. Her shaking is a spasm now, in her chest and knees. She leans against the door so she won't fall. She says, *Why are you here?* He moves close and she smells his breath and body, the burn of adrenaline, the acid rising in his throat. He grabs her wrist, pulls up his wet shirt to press her palm to his stomach. *Can you feel it?* he says. He means the quivering, the blood jumping under the skin—he believes she'll know. But she doesn't know.

He says, *I have to lie down.*

She thinks he wants to hurt her still. His body's hard against her—belly, hip, hand—hard. His fingers twist her hair and pull. She remembers the weight of him in the woods. He squeezes her bare arm, says again, *I have to lie down.* He says, *I want this to stop.*

He's following her up the stairs. He's leaving his muddy tracks through her house but he doesn't care—it's the last time, he's not coming back. So what if the doors are chained and bolted after this, what if there are big-headed dogs in the yard after this, what if the girl is slapped and questioned till she spits out a lie or the ridiculous, unbelievable truth, what does he care?

In the blue room, on the blue bed, he strokes her body
through the shirt; he strokes her bare thighs. She wants
him to hate her. She wants him to do this and be gone—
she wants to lie on the bed alone while the wind tears the
palms out of the ground, while the rain blown sideways
batters the house—she wants nothing left of him but the
damp place where he lay in his wet clothes. She wants him
not to kiss, not to touch her face, not to put his fingers in
her mouth; she wants him not naked, only unzipped—
quick, hard—she wants to hate him and be hurt and be
done. She wants him not to speak ever again. She wants
not to feel the short blades, not to hear the hiss of air, not
to smell the vinyl melting on his skin.

But he is naked. He's pulled the T-shirt over her head.
He's pulled the panties down to her ankles. She's small in
this room, in this bed, a child in this house, herself and
not herself—she's letting him touch her, everywhere—he's
inside her, everywhere, and it's wrong, she knows, to want
him and be this scared. She thinks of the grandfather down
the hall, wide-eyed and helpless in his bed. She imagines
he knows everything and wants to come but can't come.
She imagines him weeping, longing to put his big hands
on the smooth gun. And the man in this bed is kissing her
eyelids. His long fingers are in her mouth. She's terrified,
and he knows and he holds her head in both hands and
he moves so slowly, and his lips are almost touching hers
when he whispers, *Baby, no,* and she sees she's herself again,
not blurred with the boys on the road; she's his lover, and
that's what breaks her and breaks him, because they see the

muddy tracks through this house, because they can follow those footsteps back along a muddy road to a place where a gold car exploded hours ago and is burning still—it's a fire the rain can't put out.

He wants to go. He's pulling on his wet clothes. She knows how it ends here. He won't risk this again, for her. The boys in their bright skin will dance around this bed forever. The gold flames will rise forever from the road.

He's his own footprints wiped from the stairs. He's the rose-splattered bedspread washed and dried. He's the faint outline only she can find.

But it's not over.

It's just begun.

Hard as he tries to go, there's no way out of her. Not long now till she'll know. First the swelling. Then the sickness and no blood. *Actions have consequences.* Your grandfather can't say it now, but it doesn't matter: you know who can't help you, who can't be called. And the consequence of no action is to understand what you'll do alone.

It's easy to steal what you need. You don't ask yourself what's right. You think of boys with sticks and Max in jail, how dangerous you are, rocks thrown at your window, a wet man who flows through you: first rain, then fire. You imagine your life forever in this house.

There's cash in Lily's purse, wads of it, uncounted—for Estrelle and the gardener, for any shy boy who might bring wine to the back door. You know how much to take each week for four weeks. You know how soon and where to go.

Seven miles. It's not that far. You ride your bike. You don't think what you'll do after. *After* is another country, a place you can't know.

The woman at the desk counts your money, says, *Age?*, squints when you say *Eighteen* but writes it down. She says, *How will you get home?* And Dora says her boyfriend will come; he's got a car and all she has to do is call, and the woman Dora won't remember says, *That's fine, but we can't let you go till somebody comes,* and Dora nods, of course, somebody will come.

There's the finger to be pricked and one drop of blood. There's a movie and a clever girl who shows you the pink model of your uterus, who explains what she calls *the procedure.* There's the yellow pill to calm you and seven colored birds hanging from the ceiling, twisting on their strings over the table. There's the clever girl in green scrubs now, offering two fingers for you to grip. She says, *You can't hurt me.* And the doctor comes in his white mask. He's a face you won't know and don't want to know, and he says, *You're a little one*; he's already between your legs, so you're not sure what he means, but you can squeeze too hard, and the girl says, *Let go.* The sound is water in a vacuum. The paper birds spin. The curved blade is quick, and the doctor says, *That's all.*

In a room with tiny windows too high there are eleven beds; you are number eight. You eat cookies, drink juice— obedient Dora, you hold out your arm, let one more woman in green take the pressure of your blood, ninety over sixty, a lie, what could they know about your blood?

A third woman tells you to rest now, just for an hour, don't move—here's a pad, your underwear, call me if there's too much blood.

How much is too much?

How many times do the little boys jab their knives into soft tires?

How many matches make a car explode? She's too weak to do what she needs to do. She drifts and wakes. A woman's whispering, *We've got a bleeder.* Dora hopes it's not her. She feels the stabbing from inside, the doctor again, the bright boys. It could be her. She checks her underwear, sees the black clots, the thin red streaks—not too much—there's so much more blood in a body than this—and the woman who is the bleeder is screaming now, feeling the blood beneath her, slippery, the blood, and the three women in green hold her down.

Dora sees and takes her one chance, gathers her clothes in a ball, slips from the bed and out the door.

In the bathroom she wads the paper gown in the trash with the soaked pad. She stuffs paper towels in her underpants. She doesn't look. What good would it do to know? Her shoes are in the other room where the woman has stopped wailing.

The window here is wide enough, and Dora Stone is gone.

I see her on the road, riding. I know it's true but still don't quite believe she's doing this. She's dizzy. She can't sit down. The air rises in waves off the pavement. It's not the heat but the light she can't bear. She weaves and cars honk,

but nobody stops and the sound of horns is a distant sound
to her, a sound from her life, before. She can't see anything
except her own hands on the bike, gleaming metal, and the
road moving under her. She means to go home, but it's too
far, and she goes to the field instead, lies in the refrigerator instead, and this is where the things she can't remember begin:

> the boy on the bike
> the mother on the porch
> the dogs in the dark
> their smell, her smell
> and then the men
> the needle, the mask, the scissors gliding along
> > her skin.

This is where you wake in a white room. This is where
the mother, your mother, opens her eyes at exactly the same
moment you open yours.

You do not think of God or mercy. You think of water,
cows and trailers swirling across flooded lawns; you think
of wind, the furious swaying heads of palms in the moments before they fall; you think of your grandfather's cities, the ones he built and can't remember now, the cities
where streets flow with mud and hail, rivers of forgetful-
ness, and the roofless identical houses split open, walls and
rafters splinter on the ground; you think of boats, their
crammed cargo, arms and legs dangling over rails, torsos
twisting, all those dark bodies straining toward this shore.

Now it's the blue room at night, and Estrelle stands in the
corner, and Dora thinks she should have gone home hours

ago, and why does she stand there, and Estrelle says, *Don't you ever tell.*

She thinks he comes again. She thinks he's a scatter of stones, but it's only rain. She thinks he must know what's happened to her body, how she's forever changed. But only Estrelle comes, only Estrelle speaks. *Boys like mine still rising out of the swamps because of ignorant girls like you.*

He who's touched her everywhere, who touches her now, who's asked with his silent hands what happened here and here—green bruise, white scar—he who's seen her body in every light, touched her body in every dark place, whose fingers brush her lips like moth wings, he never comes.

He's lying in his bed and she can't believe he doesn't feel the hard table beneath them, doesn't see the paper birds, doesn't ride and ride and then lie down forever in the white box, doesn't lie down to burn in the field with her.

It's September. Dora Stone is still fourteen, starting ninth grade. She trims the dark ends of her hair, lets it grow back blond. She visits friends. She swims in tiny turquoise pools. She drinks rum and orange juice like the other girls. A glass shatters on concrete. She laughs at her own stupid hands, her own foot bleeding.

Dora's sixteen, and Estrelle's in the kitchen crying, saying her poor mama's dead at last and Lewis going to be married next week, moving north with his pretty wife, baby coming a little bit soon but not too soon, and Lewis gonna get that training, be an EMT like he always wanted. *Did he?* Dora doesn't know. Think of it, her boy, saving lives every night, and yes she's worried and yes she'll miss him but mostly she's proud. Estrelle's in the blue room in the middle of the night. She's got her hand over Dora's mouth. Grandfather's had the seventh stroke. The wind blows the curtains over the bed; the woman's gone.

There's a man on the television. Mugged having a heart attack. Detroit. *Lewis, is this where you are?* Revived by an off-duty EMT. *Did you save him? Did you rip his shirt, put your hands on his chest, your mouth on his mouth?*

Dora's twenty. She lives alone, has left her mother forty miles north in the big house, alone. She has a job.

Collecting urine.

Taking blood.

Everybody in this city is terrified: the men with big veins, the women with no hair, the little girls pissing in jars. Nobody wants to find out. She knows what to do. She knows how scared they are, that later, when they know for sure, they'll be hurt all the time. So she's careful with the needle and the rubber hose. She doesn't want to hurt them now.

She's had lovers, a string of them, a parade—the serial lovers, she calls them, one after another. She's dangerous still—this body, this skin, this blood—*don't touch me if you don't want to know.* But they do touch. They come and go. They pass through her and under her. They pin her down.

Sometimes she thinks he'll come the way the others come. They're muddied reflections in black water—they're imprints in white sand—they're mouths opening in the rain—her lovers—they're a line of men in white masks and white gowns—they're the wrinkled sheets—they're naked boys. They want her to lie down.

He thinks he was the one in danger. You could argue with him now. You could show him your rubber gloves, the vials of blood, the spit in the sink, the warm yellow fluid trembling in glistening jars. You could tell him how careful you are at work, how careless at home. You could tell him how it felt on the hard table, on the long ride, in the refrigerator, in the dark room, how it was through the days of silence that followed and now through the years of fear when you think this will happen again and again—to your body alone— this will keep happening until one day, one day you really will be gone. You could tell him how terrifying it is to live in your bright skin. You could make him touch the place it still burns. You could touch him. You could open his veins. You could drink his blood. You could tell him the one thing that matters now: *Listen, it won't be that long—unknown and unforgiven as I am, I want to live in my body somehow.* You could ask him who he saved tonight. You could make him tell you what he sees when he closes his eyes and the heart beneath his hands starts to beat again.

New Stories
(2002–2010)

Heavenly Creatures:

for wandering children and their delinquent mother

I. FATHERS

DIDI KINKAID AND HER THREE CHILDREN by three fathers lived in a narrow pink-and-green trailer at the end of a rutted road in Paradise Hollow. One wintry November night, fifteen days after my father died, eleven days after he was buried, Didi's only son climbed the hill to our house, leaped from our bare maple to a windowsill on the second floor, shattered the glass above my mother's bed, and burst, bleeding, onto her pillows.

The house was dark, all his—Mother and I had gone to town that night to eat dinner by the hot-bellied stove in my brother's kitchen.

Evan Kinkaid helped himself to twenty-two pounds of frozen venison, a bottle of scotch, six jars of sweet peaches. The boy carried away my down comforter, a green sleeping bag, our little black-and-white television. He found Mother's cashmere scarf, rolled tight and tucked safe in a shoebox full of cedar chips, never worn because it was too precious. Now it was gone, wrapping Evan's throat, a lovely gift, something soft and dear for him to wear home and offer Didi. The starved boy crushed chocolate cookies in a bowl of milk and sugar. He stopped to eat, then slipped his hands in Daddy's gloves: deerskin dyed black, lined with the silky fur of a white rabbit.

In exchange, he left his blood, his dirt, his smell of bonfire smoke everywhere.

On the playground the next day, I saw the little wolf in sheep's clothing: Evan Kinkaid dressed in red wool and green flannel, my father's vest and shirt—both ridiculously loose, two sizes too big for a skinny child from the Hollow.

Why should the hungry repent? Evan Kinkaid wanted me to betray him. I stared, defiant as he was. *Mine*, I thought, *one holy secret*. Mother didn't deserve to know the truth, she who had sent me to school that day, against my will, against what I believed to be my father's deepest wishes. He would have wanted me home, with her, waiting till dawn to fold the clothes Evan tossed and trampled in their bedroom. Daddy would have wanted me to crawl under their bed, to find every stray sock, to lay my little hands on each one of his tattered undershirts as if cloth, like skin, might still be healed. Neither he nor I wanted to lie in the dark, listening to Mother scour and scurry.

By the mercy of morning light, Daddy hoped I would discover his last words, a note to himself still crumpled in the pocket of his wrinkled trousers: *Don't forget! Honey Walnut*. A loaf of sweet bread for me or a color of stain for a birdhouse?

The dead speak in riddles and leave us to imagine.

Face-to-face with the righteous thief, I made a vow to keep my silence. I was ten years old that winter day, arrogant enough to feel pity for this failure of a boy, Evan Kinkaid, stooped and pale, a fourteen-year-old sixth grader who had flunked three times, Evan Kinkaid, who would never go to high school.

Less than a year later, Didi Kinkaid's pink trailer burned so hot even the refrigerator melted. By then, Didi lived in the Women's Correctional Facility in Billings, and Evan at the Pine Hills School for Boys in Miles City. Meribeth, seventeen, the oldest Kinkaid, a good girl, a girl who might grow up to be useful, lived in Glasgow with foster parents and eight false siblings. Fierce little Holly, just eleven—the dangerous child who once stole my lunch and slammed me to the wall of the girls' bathroom when I accused her—had become the only daughter of a hopeful Pentecostal minister and his barren wife in Polebridge.

So nobody was home the night the Kinkaids' trailer sparked, nobody real, though on any given night there might have been six or ten or twenty-nine tossed-out, worthless, wild kids crashing at Didi's, wishing she would return, their darling delinquent mother, dreaming she would appear in time to cook them breakfast, hoping to hear the roar and grind of her battered baby-blue Apache.

What a truck! Dusty, rusty, too dented to repair—you could squeeze thirty stray kids in the back and whoop all the way to Kalispell—you could pad the bed with leaves or rags or borrowed blankets, sleep out under the stars, warm and safe even in December.

Oh, Didi—slim in the hips, tiny at the waist—she might have been one of them, the best one, if you didn't spin her around too fast, if you didn't look too closely. The lost children built shelters of sticks and tarps in the woods behind her trailer. She let them drink beer in her yard. She gave them marshmallows and hot dogs to roast over the bonfire where she burned her garbage.

No wonder they loved her.

Any day now, Didi might honk her horn and rev the engine hard to wake them. *Sweet Mother of God!* Didi, home at last with four loaves of soft white bread and a five-pound tub of creamy peanut butter.

In half-sleep, the throwaway children kept their faith, but when they woke, they remembered: Mother in chains, Didi in prison. Of her seventeen known accomplices, three were willing to testify against her. *Three of them!* Sheree, Vince, Travis. *Traitors, snitches.* Three who still believed in real homes: mothers, fathers, feather pillows, fleece blankets.

Every night, these three lay alone between clean sheets, trying to be good, trying to be quiet, taking shallow breaths, hoping their clean and perfect mothers might slip into their rooms, kneel by their beds, and with tender mouths kiss them, kiss them, kiss them.

But only Didi came, in dreams, to mock and then forgive them.

Didi Kinkaid was made for trouble, slender but round, lovely to touch, lovely to hold, and mostly she liked it. To Didi Kinkaid, any roadside motel seemed luxurious.

What she liked best was the bath after, when the man,

whoever he might be that night, was drowned in sleep on the bed and she was alone, almost floating, warm in the warm water, one with the water—not like the trailer where there was only a cramped closet with a spitting shower, three kids and twelve minutes of scalding water to share among them.

Any night of the week Didi might be lucky or unlucky enough to glimpse the father of one of her children—one good ole boy pumping quarters in the jukebox to conjure Elvis, one sweet, sorry sight for sore eyes slumped on a bar stool—and a feeling long lost might rise up: pity, fear, hope, desire.

There was Billy Hayes, Meribeth's father, and she'd loved him best, and she might have married him. But Billy was too young for Didi even when she was young—just sixteen when she was twenty—a skinny golden boy with a fuzz of beard and long flowing hair. Billy got sad when he drank and started looking like Jesus. She didn't have a chance with Billy Hayes, a boy still in high school, a child living with his parents. Didi knew from the start a woman from the Hollow could never keep him.

Now, the taxidermist Billy Hayes was old enough, and the years between them made no difference; his hair was thin and short; he had four kids and a wife named Mary. Mary Patrillo's patient parents had taught Billy Hayes to stuff the bodies of the dead and make the mouths of bob-cats and badgers look ferocious, but the place he'd opened in Didi Kinkaid stayed empty forever.

When she told him she was pregnant, he never seemed

to imagine any choice for them but having the baby—*I'll help you*, he said. And so it was: Meribeth came to be; and though Didi thought she'd loved Billy as much as she could love anybody, the child was her first true love, her first true blessing.

Billy helped her steal a crib and a high chair, booties and bibs, disposable diapers. *Shopping*, he called it. One night, their last night, he came to the trailer with a blue rubber duck and seven white rubber ducklings, toys to float in the tub Didi didn't have, so they put Meribeth in the kitchen sink with her eight ducks, and Billy, Sweet Billy Boy, hummed lullabies while he washed her.

Evan's dad was a different story, a mean sonuvabitch if ever there was one—Rick McQueen, Mister Critter Control, who was kind enough in the beginning, who rescued her at two-thirty one morning when she came home to discover pack rats had invaded the trailer. It didn't occur to her that a man willing to drown rats and feed cyanide to coyotes might harbor similar attitudes toward his own child. Evan swore to this day that he remembered his first beating. *Before I was born, when I was inside you.*

He banged his head and bruised his eye. Even now, when he's tired or mad or hungry, that place around the socket still hurts him. He traces the bone. *You have hard hips*, he says, and this much is true, so what about the rest of it?

Didi remembers how Evan kicked and punched, twisting inside her womb for days after the pummeling. She thought he'd choke, furious and desperate enough to strangle himself with his own umbilical cord. Maybe Evan truly remembers the beating, and maybe he's only heard Didi's story. Truth or tale—what does it matter in the end if a boy believes he felt his father's fists hammering?

You saved me, Didi says, and this is fact. The baby fought the man. If she'd had any inclination to forget, if she'd been tempted by Rick McQueen's tears, scared by his threats, or lulled by his promises, the baby unknown and unnamed reminded her night and day: *You let him stay, I'll kill him.*

Holly's father could have been any one of three people—it was a long winter, too cold, so it was hard to keep track of who was when, what might be possible. There was Didi's cousin, Harlan Dekker, and a fat man by the river whose name she's blissfully forgotten, and a third man too thin, like a freak, like the Emaciated Marvel in a cage at the carnival. *Half my life behind bars*, he said, *a guard, not a prisoner.* Now he lived on the road, *free*, he said, in his rust-riddled Mustang.

The man who could suck his belly back to his spine didn't have the cash for even one night at a motel, so Didi, in her kindness, in her mercy, brought him back to the trailer, and they made love right there with three-year-old Evan and five-year-old Meribeth wide awake, no doubt, and listening. He had a pretty name, *Aidan Cordeaux.* The last part meant fuse, and the first was the fire, so maybe the flickering man did spark inside her.

Strange as it was, she often hoped the starved prison guard was Holly's father, that the night she'd conceived her youngest child, Evan and Meribeth had been there with her. *Little angels!* She felt them hovering all night, close and conscious, her darlings lying together in the narrow bunk above the bed where she and the Living Skeleton made love, where she touched the man's sharp ribs and knotted vertebrae, where she prayed, *yes, prayed,* for God to give him flesh, to restore him.

She heard her two children breathing slowly afterward, asleep at last, and the man was asleep too, up in smoke, and so she was alone, yes, but safe unto herself, blessed by her children, and the sound of their quiet breath was so sweet and familiar that she felt them as breath in her own body, as wings of sparrows softly fluttering. *God,* she thought, *his messengers.*

She was drunk enough to pretend, drunk enough to imagine. Later, the cries of feral cats in the woods sounded half-human, and she had to laugh at herself. What a hoot to think God might send angels to Didi Kinkaid in her trailer. *Just my own damn kids, but Christ, it was comforting.*

Her cousin Harlan was probably Holly's dad. It made the most sense: Holly and Harlan with that bright blond hair, those weird white eyelashes. Harlan's wife lived in Winnipeg all that winter, following her senile mother out in the snow, lifting her crippled father onto the toilet. Harlan and Didi met four times at the Kozy Kabins: twice to make love, once to watch television, once to be sorry.

More than anything, Didi wanted to believe Holly's father wasn't the fat man in his truck who passed out on top of her. She'd escaped inch by inch, hoping his cold sweat wouldn't freeze them together. She walked back to the Deerlick Saloon, to her own car, a yellow Dodge Dart that year, lemon yellow, a tin heap destined for the junkyard. She thought she should tell somebody he was out there alone at the edge of the river. She pictured him rolling off the seat to the floor, pants pulled down to his ankles, ripe body wedged underneath the dashboard. He could die tonight, numb despite all that flesh, and Didi Kinkaid would be his killer.

But the bar had been closed for hours, and her fingers were so stiff she could barely turn the key in the lock of her car door, arms so sore she could barely grip the wheel. Didi didn't feel sorry for anybody but herself by then, so she didn't stop at the all-night gas station, and she didn't call the police when she got home—she didn't even tell Rita LaCroix, her neighbor, the babysitter—she just dropped into bed, shivering, and the truth was she was so damn cold she forgot the man, his flesh and sweat, his terrible whinny of high laughter.

In the morning, she smelled his skin on her skin and she used every drop of hot water in the shower, all twelve minutes, and she drank bright green mouthwash straight from the bottle and she listened to the news on the radio. There was no report of a dead man gone blue as ice by the river. She figured he'd been spared and so had she, but when she thought of it now, she hoped to God she hadn't been cruel or stupid enough to abandon the one who was Holly's true father.

When Didi Kinkaid's child splintered the window above my mother's bed and entered our lives, her story became my story—her only son burst in my heart, her bad boy broke me open. My father was dead. Eleven months later, the second night of November, the night Didi's pink-and-green trailer burned and melted, I knew my mother was dying.

Didi had been in prison since August. When I imagined her children—the desperate ones she'd borne and the wild ones she'd rescued, when I imagined all the sooty-faced, tossed-up runaways left to wander—I understood there are three hundred ways for a family to be shattered.

Soon, so soon, I too would be an orphan.

II. FIRE

The fire was revenge, intimate and tribal. We came to witness, we people of the hills and hollows, lured up Didi's road by smoke and sirens. Through the flames, I saw the glowing faces of Didi's closest neighbors: Nellie Rydell and Doris Kelso, Lorna Coake and Ruby Whipple. I thought that one of them must have sparked this blaze—with her own two hands and the holy heat of her desire.

Who poured the stream of gasoline, who struck the match, who lit the torch of wood and paper? *Tell me now. I keep all secrets.* Was it one of you alone, or did all four conspire?

For the small crime of arson, no respectable woman ever stood trial. The trailer was a temptation and an eyesore, a refuge for feral cats, a sanctuary for wayward children. Now Didi's home could be hauled away, a heap of melted rubble. *An accident,* Ruby said. *A blessing,* Lorna whispered.

Who can know for sure? Maybe the small boy called Rooster lit a pile of sticks to warm the fingers of his twelve-year-old girlfriend, Simone, so that it wouldn't hurt where she touched him. Maybe cross-eyed Georgia squirted loops of lighter fluid into the blaze just to see what would happen, and all the children danced in the dark, hot at last, giddy as the fire spread, too joyful now to try to smother it.

But I will always believe those four women in their righteous rage burned Didi out forever.

Didi Kinkaid trespassed against us: She harbored fugitives; she tempted boys; she tempted husbands. She slept with strangers and her own cousin—and despite all this generous love, Didi Kinkaid still failed to marry the father of even one of her children.

Compared with these transgressions, the crimes named by County Prosecutor Marvin Beloit—the violations for which Didi Kinkaid was shackled, chained, and dumped in prison—seemed almost trivial: receiving and selling stolen goods, felony offenses, theft of property far exceeding $1,000. To be precise: forty-one bicycles snatched by children and fenced by Didi over a thirteen-month period.

Forty-one, including the three treasures in her last load: a black-and-yellow 1947 Schwinn Hornet Deluxe with its original headlight, worth an astonishing $3,700; the 1959 Radiant Red Phantom, a three-speed wonder with lavish chrome, almost a motorcycle—and radiant, yes—worth $59.95 new, and now, lovingly restored by Merle Tremble's huge but delicate hands, worth $3,250; finally, the lovely 1951 Starlet painted in its original Summer Cloud White with Holiday Rose trim and pink streamers, worth only $1,900, but polished inch by inch for the daughter Merle never had. To him, priceless.

In court, Merle Tremble confessed: The jeweled reflector for the Phantom cost him $107. *A perfect prism of light, worth every penny.* He found a seat for the Hornet, smooth leather with a patina like an antique baseball glove, worn shiny by one particular boy's bones and muscles. *No man can buy such joy with money.*

For six years, Merle Tremble had haunted thrift stores and junkyards, digging through steaming heaps of trash to recover donor bikes with any precious piece that might be salvageable. Under oath, Merle Tremble swore to God he loved his bikes like children.

No wonder Didi laughed out loud, a snort that filled the courtroom. A man who believes he loves twisted chrome as much as he might love a human child deserves to lose everything he has, deserves fire and flood and swarms of locusts. But Didi's lack of remorse, her justifiable scorn, didn't help her.

For crimes named and trespasses unspoken, Didi Kinkaid received ten years, the maximum sentence.

Ten years. More than any man gets for beating his wife or stabbing his brother. More years than a man with drunken rage as his excuse might serve for barroom brawl and murder.

Didi's transgressions wounded our spirits. She fed the children no mother could tame. She loved them for a night or for an hour, just as she loved the men who shared all her beds in all those motel rooms, and this terrifying, transient love, this passion without faith that tomorrow will be the same or ever come, this endless offering of the body and the soul and the self was dangerous, dangerous, dangerous.

If she was good, then we were guilty. Exile wasn't enough. We had to burn her.

When Didi heard about the fire, she knew. *Busybody do-gooders*, she said, *always coming to my door with their greasy casseroles and stale muffins, acting all high and holy when all they really wanted was to get a peek inside, see if I had some tattooed cowboy sprawled on my bed, find out how many kids were crashing at my place and if my own three were running naked. Kindhearted ladies benevolent as that did the same damn thing to my mother. Ran her out of Riverton in the end. Killed her with their mercy.*

The bikes were just an excuse. *It could have been anything*, she said, *but in the end, I made it easy.*

III. BICYCLE BANDITS

Didi never asked the stray children for anything. Rooster and Simone brought the first bike to her doorstep, a silver mountain bike with gloriously fat tires, tires nubbed and tough enough to ride through snow and slush and mud and rivers, a bike sturdy enough to carry two riders down ditches and up the rocky road to Didi's trailer. A small gift, for all the times she'd fed them. Rooster said, *I've got a number and a name, a guy willing to travel for a truckload.*

Stealing bikes was a good job, one the children could

keep, without bosses or customers, time clocks or hairnets. They loved mountain bikes best—so many gears to grind, so many colors: black as a black hole black, metallic blue, fool's gold, one green so bright it looked radioactive. Rooster had to ride that bike alone: his Kootenai girlfriend was afraid to touch it.

There was a dump in the ravine behind Didi's trailer, *The Child Dump,* she called it, because sometimes it seemed the children just kept crawling out of it. They glued themselves together from broken sleds and headless dolls and bits of fur and scraps of plastic. Their bones were splintered wood. Their hearts were chicken hearts. Their little hands were rubber.

She expected them to stop one day—she thought there might be nine or ten or even forty—but they just kept rising out of the pit. In court, the day three testified against her, County Prosecutor Marvin Beloit said he had reason to believe more than three hundred homeless children roamed the woods surrounding Kalispell.

They slept in abandoned cars and culverts. Busted the locks of sheds. Shattered the windows of cabins. Desperate in a blizzard last winter, two cousins with sharp knives stabbed Leo Henry's cow in the throat, split her gut with a hatchet and pulled her entrails out so that they could sleep curled up safe in the cave of her body.

Three hundred homeless children.

Sleep was good, was God, their only comfort.

Nobody in court wanted to believe Marvin Beloit. *Not in our little town.* Didi pitied him—her brother, her prosecutor—a man alone, besieged by visions. She knew the truth, but couldn't help him.

Ferris, Cate, Luke, Scarla—Hansel, Heidi, Micah, LaFlora—Dawn, Daisy, Duncan, Mirinda. These children offered themselves to Didi in humility and gratitude. Joyfully and by design, they became thieves. They'd found their purpose.

Sometimes when a child stole a bike, he stole a whole family, and they lived in his mind, a vision of the life he couldn't have: they pestered, they poked him. Nuke was sorry after he took the candy-striped tandem with a baby seat and a rack to carry tent and camp stove. That night he dreamed he was the smiling infant who had no words, who knew only the bliss of pure sensation. Wind in his face carried the scent of his mother: sweet milk and clean cotton, white powder patted soft on his own bare bottom. Daddy pedaled hard in front, and the sun seemed so close and hot the baby believed he could touch it.

But Nuke woke on the hard dirt to the spit of his real name, *Peter Petrosky,* his mother's curse: *not in my house, you little fucker.* Then he was an only child caught smoking weed laced with crack in his mother's house, in his father's shower. Doctor Petrosky was a genius, an artist with a scalpel who could scoop a pacemaker from a dead man and set it humming inside the chest of a black Labrador. Peter didn't wait to receive his clever father's pity or redemption. Sick with sound and light, the boy lay under his bed for an hour then climbed out the window. Now he was Nuke the nuke, a walking holocaust, sending up mushroom clouds with every footstep.

Wendy, Wanda, Bix, Griffin.

Tianna found a smoked chrome BMX with a gusseted frame and scrambler tires. She could fly on this bike, airborne off every mogul. Indestructible. *Tianna!* Thirteen years old and four fingers gone to frostbite last winter. *No more piano lessons,* she said, *no flute, no cello.* Tianna imagined sitting at the polished mahogany piano in her parents' cedar house, high on a hill, overlooking the valley. Oh! How strange and lovely the music would sound, true at last, with so many of the notes missing.

She might lie down, *just for a moment,* and fall asleep on her mother's creamy white leather sofa. Sleeping outside was torture. Tianna sucked and bit her stumps. The fingers she'd lost itched in the heat and stung in the cold. *They're still there,* she said, *but I can't see them.*

Naomi, Rose, Garth, Devon.

Angel Donner bashed into his own basement and stole his own bike, a black and orange Diablo Dynamo that any kid could see was just a pitiful imitation of a Stingray, worth less than fifty dollars new and now worth nothing. He remembered it under the Christmas tree, his father's grin, his mother's joy, his pit of disappointment.

Laurel, Grace, Logan, Nikos.

There was the one who called herself Trace because she'd vanished without one. *Idaho, Craters of the Moon, family vacation.* Cleo Kruse climbed out the bathroom window while Daddy and his new wife and Cleo's two baby stepsisters lay sweetly sleeping. *Knew I was gone before it was light, but didn't start looking till sunset. I read about me in the paper. Daddy thought it was just my way—doing all I could to cause him trouble.*

Trace was the little thief who jimmied the lock of the garage where Merle Tremble had laced each spoke of his Hornet Deluxe, his Starlet, his Phantom. Cleo disappeared at eight, and now the girl gone without a trace was barely eleven. *Too big for your britches*, Daddy always said, but anybody could see she was puny. She wore loose T-shirts and baggy jeans, chopped her hair short, turned her baseball cap backwards. *I'm a boy*, she said, *halfway. That's the real problem.* She could never mind her p's and q's, never cross her legs in church, never sit still like a lady. Cleo Kruse was a six-year-old bully, suspended from first grade—two months for pinning and pounding a third-grade boy who called her *Little It*, who pulled her from the monkey bars, flipped up her skirt and said, *If you're a real girl, show me.*

Boy or girl, what did it matter now? Out here in the woods, down in The Child Dump, everybody was half-human. If you stole groceries to eat in Depot Park, you could convince yourself you might go home someday, scrub yourself clean, eat at your mother's table. But if one day in August you got so hungry you ate crackling bugs rolled in leaves, you had to believe you'd turned part lizard and grown the nub of a tail. Cleo had eaten bugs in leaves so many times she decided she liked them.

Jodie, Van, Kane, Kristian—Faith, Finn, Trevor, Nova. They broke Didi's heart with their gifts and their hunger.

Sufi wanted to twirl like a dervish, spin herself into a blur, turn so fast the back became the front, the air the breath, the girl nothing. She wanted to stop eating forever, to grow crisp and thin, to see through herself like paper.

She didn't believe in theft. If nothing belonged to anybody, how could anything be stolen? Objects passed, one hand to another, and this was good, what God wanted, so she was glad to ride the Starlet out of Merle Tremble's garage, grateful to be God's vessel, perfectly at peace as she watched Cleo buzz ahead on the Hornet, and Nuke disappear on the Phantom.

Caspar, Skeeter, Dillon, Crystal—Renée, Rhonda, Bird, JoJo—Margot, Madeleine, Quinn, Ezekiel. Swaddled in her narrow prison bed, Didi counts the lost children as she tries to fall asleep—so many came to her door, and now she wants to remember. *Cody, Kira, Joyce, Jewell.* If ninety-nine were found and one missing, she wouldn't sleep: she'd search the woods all night, calling. Nate carved his own name into his own white belly, a jagged purple wound that kept opening. *If my head's smashed flat, my mother will still know me.* Ray taught the others to make beds of boughs. Cedar is soft enough, and young fir with blistered bark smells of balsam, but spruce will stab your hands and back: a bed of spruce is a bed of nails.

Didi tries to rock herself to sleep, but the rocking brings the children close, and she sees their lives, so quick and sharp, one dark cradle to another.

Dustin, Sam, Chloë, Lulu—Betsy, Bliss, Malcolm, Neville. Oh, Didi, you sing their names. Mercy, Po, Hope, Isaac. Let them all join hands. Here is your ring of thieves. Let them dance like fire around us.

IV. THE LOVER

When Didi Kinkaid was good, she was very, very good. She fed the poor. She sheltered the homeless. She lived as Jesus asks us to live: turned only by love, purely selfless.

But when Didi Kinkaid was bad, she abandoned her own three children, deserted Evan and Holly and Meribeth for nine days one January while she lived with Daniel Lute in his log cabin, perched high on a snow-blown ridge above Lake Koocanusa. Later, she swore she didn't understand how far it was, how deep the snow, how difficult it might be to find a road in the grip of winter.

She slept fourteen, sixteen, twenty hours. She woke not knowing if it was morning or evening, November or April. Daniel Lute's cabin whistled in the wind at the edge of outer darkness.

He fed her glistening orange eggs, the fruit of the salmon, its smoked pink flesh, his Russian vodka. Ten words could fill a day, a hundred might describe a lifetime.

They made love under a bearskin, *a Kodiak from Kodiak,* and the bed rocked like a boat, like a cradle, and the cradle was a box, sealed tight, sinking to the bottom of the lake far below them.

Daniel was a bear himself, tall but oddly hunched, black hair and black beard tipped silver, a man trapped in his own skin, condemned to live in constant hunger until a virgin loved him. Didi couldn't break that spell, and for this she was truly sorry.

On the seventh day, Daniel dressed in winter camouflage

and left her alone while he stalked the white fox and the white weasel.

In utter silence, all the skinned Kodiaks walked the earth, bare and pink, like giant humans. Didi woke drenched in sweat, the skin of Daniel's bear stuck to her.

His fire flickered out. She'd never been so cold. She thought she'd die here, the stranger's captive bride, her face becalmed by hypothermia. But her children came to drag her home. Their muttering voices surged, soft at first, then angry. She tasted Holly's black-licorice breath and smelled Evan's wet wool socks. Meribeth said, *It's time, Mom. Get up.*

The children sat on the bed. Didi felt their weight, but never saw them. Tiny fingers pinched her legs like claws. Two little hands gripped her wrists and tugged. Six tight fists pressed hard: chest, rib cage, pelvis, throat.

The basin by the bed was full. It took all her strength and all her will to rise from this bed of death and go outside to piss in the snow. Her clamoring children had grown furiously still, unwilling to touch, unwilling to help. She ate smoked herrings from a tiny tin. They tasted terrible; they filled her up. She pulled Daniel Lute's wool pants over her own denim jeans and cinched them tight with his leather belt. Though the bearskin was heavy, she took it too, just in case she couldn't make it off the mountain, just in case she needed to lie down and sleep inside the animal.

She returned with gifts to appease her children: $309 in cash, two pounds of smoked salmon, a silver flask with a Celtic cross, still miraculously full of Daniel's brandy.

She came with a preposterous tale, the truth of sinking

thigh-deep in the snow as she climbed down the ridge, the luck of finding the road around the lake before dark, the blessing of hitching a ride with an old woman driving herself to the hospital in Libby. Adela Odegard had crackers in the car, five hand-rolled cigarettes, half a thermos of coffee. *The gifts of God for the people of God: Body, Blood, Holy Ghost.* Didi ate and drank and smoked in humble gratitude.

Adela Odegard looked shriveled up dark as an old potato, a woman so yellow, so thin, Didi thought she might be dead already, but her wild, white hair glowed and made her weirdly beautiful.

In Libby, Adela delivered Didi to her nephew, Milo Kovash, and Didi slept on his couch that night. In the morning, Milo gave her ten dollars and dropped her at the truck stop diner. He knew a waitress there named Madrigal, and the waitress had a friend named Fawn who had a little brother named Gabriel, *Gabe Lofgren*, sixteen years old and glad to skip school to drive Didi Kinkaid down to Kalispell.

A story like that could turn the hard of heart into believers, or the most trusting souls into cynics.

V. HOME

Didi's children chose to believe. *Mercy*, she thought, *who deserves it?* She smelled of creosote and pine, smoked herring, her own cold sweat gone rancid. She had Daniel's pants and belt as proof—so yes, some of what she remembered must have happened.

After her shower, Didi wore the bearskin around her naked self, his head above her head, and her children stroked her fur: their own mother, so soft everywhere. The Kodiak had a face like a dog's. He might be your best friend. *From a distance.*

Didi told her children that the cabin above the lake was dark as the inside of a bear's belly. *Swallowed alive*, she said, *but I had a silver fishing knife; I stole it from the trapper.* She showed them the jagged blade. *I cut myself out when the bear got sleepy.*

Now the Kodiak's skin was her skin, the gift of the father she never had, Daniel Lute: she could wear him like a coat, pin him to the wall, use him as her blanket.

Didi and her children drank Daniel's brandy, and the ones who wanted to forget almost did forget how they'd lived without her.

Two nights before Didi returned, little mother Meribeth, not yet thirteen, had made soup with ketchup and boiled water, crushed saltines and a shot of Tabasco. Every morning of the week, she got her ten-year-old brother and six-year-old sister to the bus on time—so nobody would know, so nobody would come to take them.

Though Evan might pull Holly from her swing, though Holly might bite him, though Meribeth might scold them both—*You little shits*, might cuss them down, *I'm so damn tired*—they belonged to one another in ways that children who live in real houses never belong to their brothers and sisters.

Only Holly stayed hard now, refusing to eat Daniel's

fish, loving the pang of her hunger, the fishing knife stuck
sharp in her belly. Brandy burned her throat and stomach,
and she loved that too, the way it hurt at first, then soothed
her. *Mother in a bottle, the slap before the kiss, the incredible
peace that comes after.*

What do I know of Didi's grief? Who am I to judge her?

The day I became a twenty-two-year-old widow, the
day my husband, who was a fireman, died by fire—not in
a trailer or a house, not as a hero saving a child, but as a
father driving home, as a husband who dozed, as a man
too weary to turn the wheel—that day when my husband's
silver truck skidded and rolled to the bottom of the gully—
when three men came to my door to tell me there was no
body for me to identify—only a man's teeth, only dental
records—that impossibly blue October day, I began to understand why a woman might refuse to dress and forget to
wash, how a mother might fail to rise, fail to love, fail to
wake and feed her children.

*Didi, I know what it means to melt away, to repent for-
ever in dust and ashes.* My daughters lived because my brother
found us. My children ate because my brother in his bitter mercy stole them.

*Lilla, Faye, Isabelle—most darling ones, most beloved—
though I lay in my own bed, I deserted them in spirit.*

In the days after the trailer burned, in the months after
Didi Kinkaid went to prison, people said she got what she
deserved. *But Didi, what about your children?*

One Friday night, as Didi lay rocking in the cradle of
Daniel Lute's bed, Meribeth and Holly dressed up in her

best clothes—a slinky green dress, a sparkly black sweater.
The little girls teetered on their mother's spiked heels. Evan
let Meribeth paint his nails pink and glossy. Holly rouged
his cheeks and smeared his mouth red while he was sleeping. In the morning, the boy glimpsed the reflection of his
own flushed face and soft lips, and before it occurred to
him to be ashamed, he thought, *Look at me! I'm pretty.*

*Didi, no matter what we deserved, our children deserved
to stay together.*

VI. MOTHER

After her nights under the bearskin, Didi made a promise
to always get herself home before dawn, to never again let
her children wake alone in daylight.

She vowed to love her work. That's where the trouble
started. She'd spent the whole dark day hunched over her
sewing machine, drinking and weeping like her own pitiful
mother. *Oh, Daphne!* Seven years gone, ashes scattered to
the wind from a high peak in Wyoming, and still, after all
this time, she could blow through a crack under the door
and make her daughter miserable.

They were ashamed together, mending clothes for the
dead who can't complain and don't judge you. Didi saw
Daphne's crippled hands, each joint twisted by arthritis.
Mother needed her whiskey sours, her Winston Lights, her
amber bottle of crushed pills—though the killers of pain
made it hard to sew, and the smoke made her bad eyes blurry.

Seeing her mother like this made Didi wish for the father

she didn't have. Murmuring beekeeper, Jehovah's Witness, busted-up rodeo rider with a broken clavicle—who was he?

Be kind, Daphne said. *Any man you meet might be your daddy.*

Didi's real father was probably the hypnotist at Lola Fiori's eighteenth birthday party, the Amazing Quintero, who chose Daphne because, he said, *Pretty girls with red hair are the most susceptible.*

Under his spell, Daphne was an owl perched on a stool, a wolf on all fours, a skunk, a snake, a jackrabbit, a burro. She hooted and howled. Quintero made her ridiculous.

Alone, in Quintero's room, the hypnotist blindfolded her with a silky cloth, its violet so deep she felt it bleeding into her.

Didi imagined her mother on her hands and knees again, not hypnotized, the scarf tied around her head like a halter. If this was the night, if Quintero was the father, if her mother hooted and howled and bucked and brayed the night Didi was conceived, the whole world was horrible.

As Didi sewed, as Didi drank whiskey and water, as her own fingers ached, as her own seams grew crooked, she thought, *There you are, Mama. I'm just like you.*

At dusk, she delivered the pressed clothes to Devlin Slade's Funeral Home: a gray suit for a handsome young man and a white christening dress for a newborn baby.

She meant to drive straight home. Rain had turned to sleet, and all the dead were with her. She was almost to the Hollow, almost safe with her children in the trailer, and the sleet softly became snow, and she thought God must love her even now, despite her fear, despite her sorrow. In the beams of her headlights, He showed her the secret of snow: each flake illuminated.

Each one of them, each one of us, is precious.

Mesmerized by snow, Didi didn't see the deer until the animal leaped, with astonishing grace, as if to die on purpose. The doe bounced onto the hood and crumpled on the slick pavement, but she didn't die, and Didi stopped and got out of the truck and walked back down the road to witness the creature's suffering. The animal lay on her side, panting hard, legs still running. Frenzied, she tried to stand on fractured bones. They'd done this to each other.

A man appeared, walking out of the snow, a ghost at first, then human. He'd seen it all, before it happened. The stranger had a gun in his glove box to put Didi and the deer out of their misery. The blast of the bullet through the doe's skull made Didi's bones vibrate. She felt snowflakes melting on her cheeks and was amazed again: this mercy in the midst of sorrow.

The man dragged the limp animal toward the woods, then knelt to wipe his hands in the snow. She would have gone anywhere with him. That January night, Didi Kinkaid considered Daniel Lute her personal savior. *Heading to town*, he said. *Need some medicine.*

She ditched the Apache less than a mile from the trailer, and slid into Daniel's El Camino. She told him: *One drink, that's all, three kids home alone*; and Daniel said, *No problem.*

If Didi learned to work with love, nothing like this could ever happen again. She had small hands and a good

eye for the eye of the needle, a mother's gifts, both curse
and blessing. Self-pity led to betrayal. Any work done with
dignity might become holy. Sometimes, as you sewed a frail
woman into her favorite lavender dress, as you stitched the
seams to fit close where she'd shrunken, you touched her
skin and felt all the hands of all the people who had ever
loved her.

After Didi Kinkaid came home to the children she'd
abandoned, she saw every filthy, furious, half-starved stray
who rose out of The Child Dump as her own. Their mothers
had failed to love them enough, and now they hated themselves with bitter vengeance.

Mine, she thought, *each one. I was that careless.*

When she cut gum out of Holly's hair, or bandaged
Meribeth's thin wrist, or touched the sharp blades of Evan's
narrow shoulders, she couldn't believe she'd done what
she had done; she didn't know how she'd survived one day
without them. No man could save her now. No tub was
deep enough to tempt her. She sewed with faith. She loved
her children. She never stayed out till dawn. She kept these
promises. She offered herself to the strays, and the ritual of
love made her really love them.

VII.   THE ROAD TO PRISON

Between March 1989 and early April 1990, Didi borrowed
her cousin Harlan Dekker's white van three times to de-
liver bicycles to Beau Cryder, who agreed to meet her just
south of Evaro. For testimony against her, Beau walked

free. *Flesh peddling,* the lawyers called it, not in court but to each other.

Nobody wanted Cryder, twenty-five and still a kid, a bad-luck boy, out of work seven months, with a pregnant eighteen-year-old wife and a two-year-old son. Nobody wanted to trace the bikes to Liam Jolley, Beau's uncle, a once-upon-a-time hero in Vietnam and now just a crippled ex-cop in Missoula. Nobody ever wanted to hear how Liam's devoted daughter Gwyneth had ferried the bikes—sometimes whole and sometimes in pieces—to dealers in Butte, Boise, Anaconda, and Bozeman.

They were the victims of Didi's crimes. Her body could be exchanged for theirs, her breath for their freedom. Nobody in or out of court objected.

When Didi learned the value of Merle Tremble's bikes, she understood she'd been both betrayed and cheated. Beau paid 200 the set, 320 for the load: at the time, it seemed a fortune. Didi planned to stop in Kalispell on her way home. She wanted to buy her raggedy band of thieves two buckets of fried chicken and a tub of buttery mashed potatoes. They needed brushes and toothpaste, calamine for poison ivy, gauze to wrap their cuts and burns, arnica for bruises. She intended to bring gallons of ice cream: *Fudge Ecstasy, Banana Blast, Strawberry Heaven.* She wanted the children to know there was enough: They could eat themselves sick tonight and still eat again tomorrow. Sooner or later, she'd spend everything she'd earned on them. She didn't care about her profit.

Didi took Evan on her last trip, to help her load the bikes, to help her deal with Cryder. She promised to pay him fifty. *My best boyfriend*, she said, *my partner.* In truth, she'd made him her accomplice.

They might have gone free for lack of evidence, but Beau Cryder refused to take Angel Donner's Dynamo and a cheap BMX with popped spokes and a bent axle. Didi headed back across reservation land, through Ravalli, Dixon, Perma. She thought she was safe here, outside whiteman's law, protected by the Kootenai and Salish. She planned to dump the bikes before she got to Elmo.

They stopped at Wild Horse Hot Springs, *to celebrate*, she said, and they left the bikes in the van while they soaked for an hour, naked together in one room, immersed in hot mineral water.

She never figured on a raid. Never contemplated the possibility that Travis Poole might become a snitch, might want to go home, might tell his father, who would tell the police, who would tip bounty hunters—two trackers who lived outside the laws of any nation, who were free to bust down the door of a private room and drag a kicking woman and her biting boy from sacred water. The men shoved Didi and Evan out the door barefoot and naked, wrapped them in stiff wool blankets, bound them, gagged them, and stuffed them face-down in the backseat of their beat-to-hell black Cadillac.

At precisely 3:26, back on whiteman's time, the fearless hunters delivered two fugitives and their stolen bicycles to the proper authorities in Kalispell.

VIII. THE KINGDOM ON EARTH

Didi never caught a break for good behavior. If a guard spat words, she spat back. She was disrespectful. She stashed contraband: twenty-seven unauthorized aspirin, ten nips of tequila, and one shiny gold tube of coral lamé lipstick. Lipstick inspired vanity and theft, dangerous trades and retribution. Twice denied parole, Didi Kinkaid served every minute of her 3,653-day sentence.

Now, four years free, she sews clothes for the living and the dead in Helena. She could start a new life with a new name and a grateful lover in Vermont or Texas. But she stays here, close enough to visit Evan once a week in Deer Lodge. Her boy lives in a cell, down for fifty-five, hard time, attempted murder.

Evan was twenty years old and out of the Pine Hills School for Boys just thirteen months when he hit the headlines. A weird tale: hunting with a forbidden friend, Gil Ransom, thirty-nine and on parole, a known felon—dusk, out of season—Gil's idea, *just a little adventure.* They fired from the windows of the car—dumb beyond dumb and highly illegal. Any shadow that moved was fair game: deer, dog, rat, chicken. They smoked some weed. They split a six-pack. Evan saw trees walk like men through the forest.

An off-duty cop who recognized the roar of Gil's Wrangler followed them up a logging road, bumped them into the ditch, and tried to arrest them. Gil shot Tobias Revell three times: *Just to slow him down, nothing serious.* They left him crawling in the snow, wounded in the leg and neck and shoulder. He could have bled to death. He could have died of shock or hypothermia. But he was too pissed off to die. He lived to speak. He lived to bring those men to justice.

Justice? Evan learned that it didn't matter who pulled the trigger. For the abandonment of Tobias Revell, for the failure to send someone out that night to save him, Evan Kinkaid shared Gil's crime: the gun, the hand, the thought, the bullets.

Meribeth does not visit her brother. She teaches in a three-room school and lives without husband or children in a two-room shack up a canyon west of Lolo. I picture her as she was: flat-chested and gangly. She speaks softly. She walks swiftly. She never looks anybody straight in the eyes, but she never looks away either. She seems humble and kind, dignified even when she wears a dress sewn from an old checkered tablecloth. Meribeth Kinkaid, a princess in rags, mysteriously moving among peasants who scorn her.

Meribeth's worst fear is that one day her mother and brother and sister will knock at the door of her secret cottage in the canyon. Meribeth's deepest desire is that Evan and Holly and Didi will one day sit at her table to share a meal of bread and fish and wine and olives, that they will all sleep that night and every night thereafter in one bed in the living room, on three mattresses laid out on the floor and pushed close together, breathing as one body breathes, heart inside of heart, holy and whole, miraculously healed.

Eight months after she was adopted, Holly Kinkaid escaped Reverend Cassolay and his good wife, Alicia. She didn't want to be saved. She'd been baptized by fire. If she couldn't live with her brother and sister, if the trailer was burned to rubble and gone forever, Holly wanted to live alone in a junked car or a tree or a culvert.

I am a mother now, an orphan, and a widow.

Sometimes in the early dark of winter I feel Holly at my window watching my daughters and me as we eat our dinner. She won't come in. The cold no longer feels cold to her. The cold to her is familiar.

This morning—a deep gray November morning, woods full of damp snow, light drizzle falling—I followed the school bus to town, twenty-three miles. My daughters Lilla and Faye, nine and six, sat in the far backseat of the bus to flap their hands and wave furiously, to smash their lips and noses flat against smudged glass. Their terrible faces scared me.

Isabelle, my youngest, my baby, slept in her car seat. I heard every wet sound: wipers in the rain, melting snow, dripping trees, the murmuring woods closing around us.

I saw flowers in the rain: boys in blue and girls in yellow, a tiny child in a pink fur coat, and another dressed in bright red stockings—all the pretty children waiting for the bus in bright pairs and shimmering clusters. Sometimes a mother stood in the center to shelter them beneath her wide umbrella.

In this rain, in this dark becoming light, I began to see the ones who won't come out of the woods. *Griffin, Bix, Wanda, Wendy.* They wear olive green and brown and khaki, coats the color of fallen leaves, jeans stained with blood, boots always muddy. They steal the skins of wolves and wings of falcons. The red fur of the fox swirls down Tianna's spine, and her teeth are long but broken.

Hansel, Heidi, Micah, LaFlora. They never grow up or old. They starve forever. Cleo Kruse, who vanished without a trace, who could never be just one thing or another, has the body of a lynx and the eyes of a hoot owl, the legs of a mule deer, and the hands of a child.

Faith, Bliss, Trevor, Nova.

Vince Lavadour, who betrayed Didi Kinkaid, who testified against her, has lost his arms and legs, has found instead his fins and tail. The boy slips free at last, a rainbow trout, gloriously striped and speckled.

Nate, Ray, Grace, Laurel.

Angel's skin bursts with thirty thousand barbed quills. Bold in his new body, Angel says, *Only fire will kill me.*

Dustin, Rose, Lulu, Chloë—Georgia, Sheree, Travis, Devon.

Rooster knows that if he eats as the coyote eats, he will live forever. And so he does eat: snakes, eggs, plastic, rubber, sheep, tomatoes, rusted metal, dead horses by the road, dead salmon at the river.

Simone, Nuke, Duncan, Daisy.

Last summer, Sufi flung herself fifty feet into the air at twilight. Flying heart, vesper sparrow, she sang as if one ecstatic cry could save the world. Now she lies broken under dead leaves. She smells only of the woods—pine under snow, damp moss, a swirl of gold tamarack needles. Her wish comes true at last: she is one with God, one with mud and air and water. But if Didi called her name tonight, from death to life she might recover.

Naomi, Quinn, Madeleine, Skeeter—Rhonda, JoJo, Neville, Ezekiel—Finn, Scarla, Luke, Jewell.

How quickly the night comes!

I am home at dusk, so many hours later, my three girls safe this night in the house their father built before he left us. Birds cry from the yard, and I go to them, a mother alone in the gathering dark. A flock of crows whirls into the gray sky. *Didi, there must be ninety-nine, there must be three hundred dark birds rising on their dark wings.* When they land, the crows fill a single tree, every branch of a stripped maple.

Your children are my children. They are dangerous. They are in danger.

One by one, each black-eyed bird falls to the ground, brittle and breakable, terrible and human.

Oh, my children, all my little children, I knew you before you were in the womb. Love is the Kingdom on Earth. As we fall to earth this day, let us love, let us love one another.

Confession for Raymond Good Bird

RAYMOND, I REMEMBER EVERYTHING about the day: the heat, the rain, the cold wind after. I remember Danny was sick, bloated up like a toad and moaning on the cot, so I took the call alone, which never happens on TV, but can happen twice a week out on Rocky Boy Reservation.

The situation didn't sound extreme: one forty-four-year-old man down on the floor in his sister's kitchen. Drunk, I thought. Heat and alcohol, a bad combination. I was simple that way, prejudiced against my own people.

I figured I'd cool you down with rags and ice, take you to the river for a reservation baptism. It was Fourth of July, almost. People had been celebrating or mourning three days now. If things were worse than I thought, we'd have a rough ride, the rocky roads of Rocky Boy to the hospital in Havre, where the medicine men use masks, but not the kind we know.

Doctors in town never appear as Owl or Coyote. They don't chant or smoke to heal your heart or sing the spirit back to your body. They carry drills and knives: they want to look inside; they need to open you. Doctors in green cut and cleave, suture and staple—they have miles of gauze to bind your wounds, respirators to help you breathe, electric paddles to jump you off the table.

If you swallow twenty-seven Darvocets with a pint of gin like Arla Blue Cloud, they pump your stomach dry, but they won't love you back to life—that's not part of the treaty. No hospital doctor ever pressed his ear to the flesh of Arla's womb to hear the bones of her lost children shatter.

Three months later, Arla chopped a hole in the ice and went down naked. In a dream, I'm swimming after her, and I can't breathe, and I'm so cold I'm cold forever, but I don't care because Arla Blue Cloud is quick as a pike and laughing like an otter; Arla is blue and green, beautiful as ice and water, and I think I can see—but I can't see—straight through her.

Nothing like that was going to happen to you and me, Ray. When I got the call from your sister Marilee, she didn't whisper, *No breath, no heartbeat.*

Danny Kite, my partner, my driver, tried to sit up, but his belly bulged with poison gas, something stuck deep in the bowel—roasted squirrel or kidney pie, blue cornbread and fried okra—something he ate two nights before, harmless once, and now gone rancid.

The woman on the phone, Marilee Dancy, older sister of Caleb and Raymond Good Bird, mother of Roshelle and grandmother of baby Jeanne, cousin of Thomas Kimmel, and granddaughter of Safiya Whirling Thunder, said, *Six of us here, seven, counting Raymond.*

I told Danny plenty of people to help me lift the man, carry him to the bed, the river, the white station wagon we called our ambulance.

Whatever seemed right.

Whatever proved necessary.

I don't know why I didn't feel you, Ray, sticky as the sticky heat, already here, already gone, already breathing down my lungs, already deep inside me. I told Danny: *Sit, lie down, stay*, and like the sick little dog he was, Danny Kite obeyed me.

We're not real EMTs, not even Woofers, WFRs, Wilderness First Responders, but we did get a crash course, five hours one day in Missoula, three pink-skinned dummies to rescue and resuscitate, 1982, nine summers ago, the year we started fighting fires.

We go every year we can—Arizona, Utah, Idaho, Wyoming. *Summer vacation*, Danny says. Stomping flames and plowing firebreaks is good work for a hungry Indian. We don't throw firecrackers in the grass. We don't torch timber. We're hungry, yes, but not that crazy. We've seen our own forests blaze—Mount Sentinel, Lost Canyon. We're Chippewa-Cree, some cloudy mix with French and Oglala. We've been wandering half our lives, dazed and unemployed for a century. When the smoke signals rise, when the fire is somewhere else, we give thanks for strange mercies.

Back home on Rocky Boy, we run the ambulance, our magically rebuilt Falcon Futura. We answer anybody's call, any day, any hour. We come when the dispatcher in Havre won't answer, when there's no money and no insurance to ferry the half-dead in a real ambulance with trained medical technicians and a pulsing siren.

Maybe Nadine Hard Heart slips us two dollars for gas.

Maybe her husband Kip who almost choked on a bone asks us to sit down, share their dinner: two little ducks, canned peas, a heap of instant mashed potatoes. Mostly we don't get paid, and it doesn't matter. Five terrified, not-so-hard-hearted children breathe their silent praise, and we feel lucky. Seven months later, one of those skinny kids appears at the door with three pounds of elk steak to sustain us on our journeys. Luisa Hard Heart's offering means her father survived, lived to hunt again, met the elk face-to-face high on a ridge in the Bear Paw Mountains. Now there's food to spare: this flesh, his flesh, our flesh, a miracle.

Danny and I don't keep track. It isn't necessary. We do this for us, all of us, our people, because we learned one day with pale dummies how to breathe into another man's body, how to slow the blood from a severed artery, how to pump a child's heart with our hands, how to count and not stop and keep our faith, the old one. We don't have a choice: things you know but don't use eat you inside out, starved weasels biting hard, furious in your belly.

Saving you is saving me. It's not a good deed: it's my own body.

Looking at Danny rolling on the cot, I thought I'd have to resuscitate him before helping you. *Stay*, I said. *Trust me*, I said, like a fool.

We were boys together, Danny Kite and me, one mother and one father between us. We'd rescued each other plenty of times. I rolled him home in a wheelbarrow the day he flew off Wendy Wissler's roof and broke his ankle. Six-year-old Danny pulled my head out of a pail the morning I passed out proving how long I could stay underwater. In a summer storm, we scrambled into the highest branches of a ponderosa pine to let the wind thrash us side to side; to spin, to heave, to be the storm, to think like wind and rain, to be that wild. Danny's father Earl had to climb the tree twice to save us.

One January night, my father drank six shots of tequila and walked out into the snow barefoot and naked. He wanted to prove that the real world is beyond this one, that everything here is only a shadow, that fire could not scar and ice would not burn him. We found the man two days later, the blue shadow of him, and it was true: nothing before or after seemed real.

Danny's mother lived in Billings, in prison, sixteen years for forging a hundred-dollar check. Joella Kite wanted bourbon and cigarettes, a pink blouse embroidered with white daisies. She brought us banana cream pie and frozen Cool Whip, Orange Crush and spicy tortilla chips. I remember thinking nobody on Rocky Boy had ever been this happy.

Then Joella was gone, but between our houses, we had a whole family, and so it was: Danny Kite and I loved each other as brothers.

Trust me, I said when your sister Marilee called. Trust was all we had. Trust and luck and some kind of weird, hopeful vision.

My mother Pauline died of a toothache. *Abscess*, the doctor told us. *If she'd come to town in time, we could have taken the tooth, drained the hole, given her antibiotics.* I suppose he meant to comfort us with knowledge. In Pauline's little house on Rocky Boy, bacteria spilled into her blood and brain. My mother's feet and hands and ears turned black before Hector Slow Child found her. She said, *I don't think we'll make it. Please,* she said, *just lie down here beside me.*

Danny's father died of old age at forty-seven. Earl Kite drowned in his own bed, wheezing with emphysema, rattled by double pneumonia. *It's a good day,* he said. *I'm tired.* Joella Kite got out but went back and got out again and drove into a semi.

Now we were orphans.

Raymond, I see your face, a dark brown Chippewa face, pocked and pitted deep, like lava that bubbled up from the center of the earth to cool rough and ravaged on the surface. Raymond Good Bird, scarred by acne or disease, scorched like the earth itself, a face that revealed the suffering of a thousand homeless Indians or the aftermath of some spooky chemical explosion—like the trees of Vietnam, you'd erupted.

Yours was a face to love: without love, there was no way to look at you.

Marilee's kitchen steamed. Your sister had been simmering beans all day, frying bread and onions. She'd boiled up two sad, sorry reservation chickens to shred the meat and make fajitas, a family feast to welcome you home, Raymond Good Bird, their soldier returned from the jungle war, then lost again, twenty-two years, working tugboats, hauling garbage, killing rats and roaches, grinding fat and flesh to stuff sausages, hosing hogs, plucking cherries, lying down drunk in the street and waking up half-frozen in jail—losing three toes, losing two fingers—Raymond found, Raymond recovered, Raymond come home at last only to lie down and die in the heat of your sister's kitchen.

You were skinny as a skinny chicken yourself, blistered from childhood and all the diseases of all our ancestors, wounded three times in the war, three times before, four times after it: firecracker, hand grenade, white boy's BB gun, brother's arrow—fishing knife, M-16, electric drill, broken bottle—shrapnel in the thigh, straightedge razor across the belly.

Raymond Good Bird, cut up inside every hour of every day from the war you'd fought and the wars that killed you, sliced for forty-four years and sewn back together with invisible thread, invisible sinew of the last white buffalo.

You had no alcohol in your blood today, nothing to preserve you, only the homemade root beer you'd been drinking with your big sister Marilee and your blind, toothless grandmother Safiya. Your brother Caleb and cousin Thomas snuck nips out back and pretended nobody noticed, but you stayed straight to be with Marilee and your niece Roshelle. You stayed sober to hold Roshelle's baby Jeanne, eight months old and already speaking some secret language.

I see you eating chilies from a jar, ten green jalapeños and seven fiery orange habaneros. The buzz was quick, but the burn lingered. Thomas and Caleb swallowed their peppers whole, a wild Raymond-Good-Bird-welcome-home contest.

You cradled wide-eyed, wonderful baby Jeanne against your wounded chest, and Roshelle, too beautiful for whiteman's words, Marilee's I've-come-to-break-your-heart daughter, gazed at you as if you were the child's long-lost belovéd father.

Roshelle was just a baby herself the last time you saw her, round baby Roshelle two years old when you dressed up as a soldier boy and said good-bye forever. She kissed you on the mouth this morning and swore she remembered. She kissed you on each pitted cheek. *Uncle Ray.* She held you tight—scrawny, pocked you—and you felt whole and young, pressed up that way against her just-turned-into-a-woman, just-became-a-mother body.

Lovely she was, your niece, long and lovely, smooth, as tall as you and much stronger, like Marilee before she swelled, soft and warm to touch like your mother Minnie before cancer curved her spine and turned her skin yellow.

In the light of Roshelle Dancy, in her body reflecting morning light, *this* morning's light before the heat grew terrible, in the sweet golden light spilling through worn-thin-as-gauze curtains, in the radiant love of Roshelle, your whole family came alive, the long-dead and unborn. All your wandering people filled the house and yard, and their voices surged, a song inside you.

That was morning, Ray, and now it was afternoon, getting on toward evening, and you rocked baby Jeanne to sleep, and you handed her back to her mother, and the silly boys came inside, not drunk, not quite, not really, and you swallowed jalapeños and habaneros, and the peppers made your head hum, and you said, *I need to sit down,* but you didn't make it.

You collapsed on the kitchen floor, and you stayed there till I found you. Now, in the thick glaze of afternoon, everything looked filthy. Bubbling beans and sizzling onions splattered; the smell of boiled chicken filled the house; orange cheese melted.

And it was hot, so hot, and I stood in the doorway, and I couldn't move: I didn't even try to help you. I've knelt over three dummies and twenty-seven real live human beings and thumped their chests to get their lungs heaving, but I saw you on the floor, and I saw something yellow above you in the terrible heat, a cloud of smoky yellow dust like the puff off a mushroom; I smelled something underneath the smell of boiled-to-smithereens chicken. Something a hundred times hotter than red chili dust seared my nostrils; and a voice that sounded like God's if God had died with the Ghost Dancers, if God had been shoveled into a pit in the snow and buried, if God had lain dry in the dry earth for more than a century, *that* crackling voice said, *Too late, little brother.*

It could have been you, Ray, or the pinto pony at the window over the sink, or the little black dog with one white ear and one white paw that wouldn't stop yapping.

I think now it was the wind, the hot wind, the useless fan beating hot air into the hot kitchen. This voice from the whirlwind said, *Who are you?* And the voice inside my chest said, *You can't.* And the dry silence from your body said, *Don't bother.*

Maybe it's all an excuse, something I imagined after. I was scared, it's true. I don't know why you scared me.

I can still feel Roshelle's fist hammering my back, can still hear Marilee whisper, *Do something.* The frenzied dog ripped the cloth of my pants and sank her sharp teeth into my ankle, and the little spotted horse put her whole head through the open window by the sink, and I looked at the faces of all your people—Caleb, Marilee, Roshelle, Thomas, Jeanne, Safiya—and I thought if they loved you so much, why couldn't they save you?

Once upon a time you tried to come home, but you couldn't live in peace among us. Every dark-eyed boy was one you'd killed, every child a gook, every woman your enemy. A thin teenage mother at the grocery store in Havre propped her plump baby on one hip and stared at you with unmitigated rage or benevolent wonder, her look as impenetrable as the gaze of the wounded Vietnamese mother bleeding out, five holes: chest, thigh, belly. She held her child in one arm on one hip—yes, like this—and with miraculous grace, the tiny Vietnamese woman slit her son's throat, clean and deep through the vein: so he wouldn't starve when she died, so he couldn't be spared, so you would not shoot him.

Your platoon lost thirteen men in nine days to booby traps and sniper fire. You burned the first village you found, unnamed on your lieutenant's map, just a cluster of huts at a slow bend of the Cua Viet River. You shot the people as they ran. You killed their pigs and dogs and chickens. Later, you found three women and two boys bleeding into the water. You knew these people, five slender Cheyenne cut breast to bowel and trampled at the banks of Washita,

slaughtered to the joyful noise of bugles and gunfire. The
ones whose thick blood swirled into the muddy Cua Viet
were Pocatello's stunned Shoshone, five of the four hundred
forty-three slain at Bear River. These five were Nez Percé in
flight, awakened to die, skulls crushed by the boot heels and
gun butts of drunken soldiers at the Big Hole.

If you opened their bodies, would you find your last word,
a curse spat out and long forgotten? What did it matter?
You fired. Their blood spilled. You witnessed. You'd mur-
dered them all: brothers, sisters, ancestors, grandchildren.

You didn't want forgiveness. You wanted the wounded
Vietnamese mother to take you in her arms as her own
child—to comfort, and to kill you.

For twenty-two years you lived without faith, without
love or the hope of it. *Bozeman, Coeur d'Alene, Walla Walla,
Wenatchee.* You thought if you moved fast enough the dead
might lose your scent and stop following.

You dangled sixty feet in the air, washing windows,
downtown Boise. You met yourself face-to-face, the blue-
skinned man hanging in dark glass, flesh pocked by soap
and water. You hauled thirty-seven dead sheep down a hill-
side west of Helena. They'd died as one, skulls fractured by
lightning, the head of each sheep resting tenderly on the
rump of another. They were filthy now, their gray wool
rain-soaked, their shocked bodies bloated. Flies swarmed
you and them. Crows and hawks and kestrels circled. You
lifted them by their broken legs, you and two Colombian
men who called themselves Jesús and Eduardo, who jab-
bered as they worked, quick Spanish words muffled by

bandannas. You tore your own rag from your mouth and nose to be with the dead, to know their smell, to breathe their bodies. The Colombian brothers laughed when they heard you choking. *Estúpido.* Even then you didn't hide your face. You heaved the pitiful animals into the bed of the rancher's truck. You saw that each face was distinct, with a certain space between the eyes, a soft curve of the mouth, a singular tilt of nose and forehead. Each one of them—and you, and Jesús, and Eduardo—secretly made, silently belovéd. Why were you whole? Why were they shattered?

You left that night. *Issaquah, Butte, Aberdeen, Seattle.* You slept in the woods, in a cardboard box, in a barn with a whiteman's cow, in a bed of leaves under a freeway. You dove in dumpsters for bruised fruit, half-eaten buffalo wings, cold biscuits and gravy. You snatched three perfect blue eggs from the nest of a robin. The birds woke you for a hundred nights, beaks sharp as barbs in your lungs and liver. You stole corn from pigs and a gnawed bone from an old wolfhound. He rose on his crippled hips to tug his chain, too sick and slow to nip you. A goat gave you her milk, and for this offering you praised her.

North of Spokane, you walked up a dirt road to a weather-wracked farmhouse. You meant to ask for work mucking stalls in exchange for one meal. Nobody answered your knock, but you touched the doorknob and it turned. You breathed, and the door opened. The sweet smell of cherries sucked you inside, pulled you in a dream down a long passage to a sun-dazzled kitchen.

There it was, all for you, a cherry pie with a lattice crust, cooling on the table. In the freezer, a half-gallon tub of vanilla ice cream waited—untouched, perfectly white, unbelievably creamy.

You thought, *Just one piece or maybe a quarter.* The pie vanished. Who could blame you? You tried to stop, but you couldn't do it. In your swollen stomach, seven scoops of ice cream swirled.

Your head throbbed. You felt hot and cold at the same time, stunned by bliss and suddenly so tired. You staggered to the living room, but the couch was old, too short, too lumpy. Somehow you gathered the strength to climb the stairs. You opened three doors before you found the room you wanted, cool and dark with a wide bed and a down comforter.

You were afraid to sleep, but a voice that was your own voice gone mad and mocking said, *Why stop now? Why resist this last pleasure?* You knew you might die in this bed, victim of your own delight and a farmer's righteous fury. You woke to a woman's voice, insistent and gentle. *Mister, you best get up now, go down those stairs, and keep walking.* She was white-haired but not old—thin, but not frail. A farmer's wife, yes, without the farmer. The widow cradled an unraised rifle. She was kind: she wanted you to go, but she didn't want to scare you.

That night it rained and you slept in a child's tree house. You crept out hours before dawn. If the boy came with his BB gun, he'd aim for your right eye and kill you.

Raymond Good Bird, twenty-two years gone. You walked

close to death every hour, but somehow you survived, and then one day you came home to rest, and I let you die in your sister's kitchen.

Yesterday, Thomas said he wouldn't believe you were home till he touched you with his own hands. But he didn't touch: seeing was enough, too much in fact—Thomas wouldn't look you in the eye. *The light,* he said, *I can't do it.* Late last night, in the shelter of darkness, your delicate, almost pretty cousin Thomas picked you up, lifted you a foot off the ground and held you high to dance you in a circle dance. Your grandmother felt your face and skull, traced your chest and ribs to see you whole with her fingertips. Long after, when the others had fallen asleep on the couch and floor and single bed, your big brother pulled you close and breathed you in. Caleb, like a mother and a father now: wide shoulders, soft breasts. You were twenty-two years lost again. Rocking in his arms, you thought, *I'm him.*

Now you lay on the floor, and I heard you say, *Let the dead stay dead.*

Your brother and sister rolled you onto a wool blanket. These two, and blind Safiya, and doubting Thomas lifted you by four corners. You swung in their grip, a man in a hammock. Roshelle cradled baby Jeanne to follow behind you.

Marilee's turquoise Catalina sat on cement blocks in the yard, its rusted engine propped against a stump, its hood torn off, crumpled in some junkyard. Sunflowers and thistle grew high and wild in all its open spaces. Your people slid you, most belovéd one, into the back of my white Falcon. Roshelle gave the baby to Thomas so that she could lie down with you, *Uncle Ray*, close, and hold you tight, *my love*, and keep you from rolling.

I resisted no one. Caleb took my keys and left me to walk seven miles. What did he care? Your people drove you to town, the dead man, the wounded-ten-times, the resurrected-and-returned-home and now dead-for-true Raymond Good Bird. They delivered you to the hospital in Havre, as if some man of faith might call you out of the cave of yourself, punch a hole in your vein or throat, split your chest, and work his miracle—as if some scrubbed nurse might forget her latex gloves, just this once, and lay her naked hands on your heart to close these last wounds, the wounds that saved, the wounds that healed you.

By then the rain had started, soft at first and still hot, more like dust than water falling, then hard and cold until the whole sky filled, a wailing, weeping rain of river.

I stood in your sister's yard, *estúpido*, cut by icy rain, jolted each time a drop hit me. At least you didn't die alone, foolish as our fathers, mine playing Crazy Horse in the snow, yours failing to jump a freight train east of Fargo. I didn't want to die today, another frozen Indian. I pictured my wife Delilah at our doorway, face blown open by the storm, long hair loose and dangerous, a tangled net whipping around her. I conjured Lulu, thin and dark, already too wise, strange and silent, old at seven. I heard tinkling Kristabelle, just three, our child of joy who burst into the world laughing.

That laughter fell from the sky, arrows of rain, sharp enough to pierce me. I dreamed myself home and safe, though I knew I didn't deserve it.

The wind spun, as if it wanted to speak, as if it were trying to become a person. I hoped to make it to Hector Slow Child's house, prayed that the man who loved my mother might let me sleep in his bed for a few hours, but I was barely a mile up the road, stung by rain, already staggering. I thought I'd fall, die here in a rut, drown in three inches of water.

God roared behind me. In a rush of breath, *his* breath, two angels thundered out of the storm, Luc Falling Bear and Leroy Enneas, my saviors, Luc driving Leroy's once-shiny-green-now-mostly-gray Torino. They didn't know yet what I'd failed to do, how I refused to kneel, refused even to try to help you. They didn't sense I was a ghost, gone like you, a dead man walking. They'd been drinking rum and Mountain Dew all day. To Luc and Leroy, I was still visible.

They were thoughtful drunks: I tried to slip in back, but they cried *no* in unison. They wanted me up front, soaked and shivering between them. They offered rum, straight from the bottle. I don't remember anything on earth for which I ever felt more grateful.

They ate corn chips with extra salt. *To stay thirsty,* Luc said. *You think drinking all day is easy?*

They were polite, the way Indians are polite. They didn't ask where I'd been or wonder aloud why I was walking. They didn't make jokes about my ambulance. They didn't mention my father.

They waited for me to speak or not speak. They lived on reservation time. They had forever.

I couldn't go home. Lulu and Kristabelle would grab my legs to pull me down on all fours and ride me like a pony. Delilah would say, *Let him go. Your father's cold and tired.* But somehow I'd find the strength to carry them, *my sweethearts, my darlings.* I'd buck and whinny. I'd be myself again, whole, Jimi Shay Don't Walk, father, husband, wet mustang. I wasn't ready for that much love. I thought the weight of it, of them, might crush me.

I must have said, *Drop me at Danny's,* because suddenly I was there, trembling in my brother's doorway. Without Luc and Leroy close, my skin hardly held my bones together. There he was, Danny the betrayed who didn't know it, Danny Boy curled up like a baby, smiling in his sleep, soothed by the sound of rain, back inside his mother's body.

Danny Kite was his thin self again, and I could smell the stink coming from the toilet, his bowels clean at last, the dam burst wide open. My Danny woke all sweet and groggy. He said, *Sorry, brother,* and, *How did it go?* And I said, *Fine, everything's fine.* I said, *Everything happened just the way it was supposed to happen.*

Let him sleep in peace, I thought. *Let the story find him.*

There are stories I like to tell, things I believe though I can't prove them. Sometimes I think Hector Slow Child is my real father, that he came to my mother as starlight falling through an open window, a constellation broken on her bed, the Great Bear, the White Buffalo.

My wife tells another story, how her mother died with Delilah inside her. Nona Windy Boy skidded on ice, side-swiped Martin Cendesie's truck, and rolled fifty feet down a gully. *Brain dead*, the doctor told her husband Joseph. *Fractured ribs—fractured feet, femurs, pelvis. No hope*, he whispered. *Fractured skull, massive hemorrhage.*

Somehow Delilah lived. Delilah, unborn, rocked herself to sleep in a windy cradle. The doctor stood amazed, listening to her heart beat. Softly he said, *We should take the baby now while we can save her.*

Joseph saw tiny flecks of his wife's blood spattered on the young man's glasses. Joseph said, *Let the child stay inside as long as her mother wants her.*

Nona's mother and Auntie Bea chanted thirteen days and thirteen nights without ceasing. I tell you now: on the fourteenth day, Nona Windy Boy breathed again, no respirator. She lived thirty-four more days, and the child came in her own time of her own will, and the mother with her own breath released her.

Delilah says, *I'm my father's bitter miracle.*

Delilah says, *My mother turned herself into a trout and swam down into her own womb and swallowed me and kept me safe for seven weeks until I got too big to hold and then my mother writhed three times and spat me out to live in the world without her.*

Nona never opened one eye to see her child. Auntie Bea swore she laughed when the baby howled, but the nurse who witnessed said, *The poor woman was finally choking.*

Tonight, when I lie in Delilah's arms, when we lie entwined, her long arms and long legs wrapped around me, when I tell her our story in the dark, the story of Raymond

Good Bird and Jimi Shay Don't Walk, my wife will say, *Not everybody wants to be saved. Not every body can bear it.*

Raymond, three months ago you took a real job, the first you wanted to keep, as a janitor, a custodian at Lewis & Clark Elementary School in Missoula. The urinals set to a child's height, the little desks, the low mirrors, the windows decorated with butterflies and birds broke your heart, and you let them. You wanted to hurt, and the hurt was love, and love roared back into you. You stole children's drawings from the walls and took them home to your motel, the River's Edge, a run-down dive where you paid by the week to live among prostitutes and addicts, where you shared bread and beans with bewildered half-bloods.

A little girl named Tania colored a family of bright angels—mother, father, sister, brother—even the purple dog had a halo. Max and Arturo drew a house on fire and a galaxy exploding. Coral painted a child in a garden where red tulips grew taller than she was. Darnell Lasiloo saw seventeen Appaloosas from the sky, as if he were God, as if he were White Bird in flight over the Bear Paws. The spotted horses lay on their sides, all sixty-eight legs splayed, all sixty-eight legs visible. The ponies seemed to float along a trail of tears beside a winding river. You taped the pictures to your walls and door and mirror. So many children alive to love! The miracle was endless. The dead whispered through the radiators. *Don't forget us.* They wished you no harm. They were hungry, like the rest of us. You saved six dollars the first week and nineteen the week after. You thought someday soon you'd send all your extra money and a child's vision home to Roshelle and your sister.

One night in a whiteman's bar, a half-Kootenai, half-Mexican woman danced you across the room, and you thought this was the end of hope, your last possibility. She asked you to come home with her, to her trailer up a rutted road north of Evaro. She was twenty-seven years older and fifty pounds heavier than you, but still, in your eyes, beautiful. You refused. Refused even to kiss, though her mouth looked soft as a girl's mouth. Her face was scarred, it's true, pocked as yours, but her lips bloomed full and ready. *No, please.* You thought if you kissed her once, you'd never stop kissing.

Fear made you unkind, and for this you were sorry.

The heads of elk curving out from the walls, the big-horn sheep, the pronghorn antelopes all watched you drink your beer and crack your nuts and keep your silence. The big Kootenai woman, Magdalena Avalos, drifted away to dance alone, and then to spin with a one-armed man by the jukebox. Three whitemen in the booth behind you bragged about the ducks they'd slaughtered last autumn. The creatures made a terrifying sound, mallards and pin-tails hissing and chewing. The first three shots cleared a path: dozens lay strewn, wounded and dying. The others rose, a jabbering cloud. The men fired again, three more shots, then another three—that was all it took—the sky opened. They stood stupid in a rain of ducks, stunned by a storm of feathers. A hundred and eight birds dropped dead between them. They laughed now, remembering the crime, ninety-nine ducks past the limit. The men spent all day gutting and plucking.

You tried to be Tonto, one of those two-syllable wooden Indians, but your thoughts roared, and the men must have heard them. You looked into the eyes of the auburn bear whose head and skin hung from the ceiling, and you meant to whisper only to him, but your heart betrayed you.

Father, you cried. *Father, forgive them.*

Then you laughed a wild Indian laugh and you whooped one last wild whoop and the three white hunters lifted you high and danced you out into the alley, not in a tender way, not soft like Magdalena. They pushed you to your knees. They wanted you to be sorry.

You were sorry: for the ducks and the elk and the bear and the children, for the sheep on the hill and a black man in Florida, electrocuted twice because the first time the chair sparked and fizzled and he didn't die: only his hair and slippers caught fire. His picture in the paper last week looked so familiar, so much like you, you taped it on your mirror, beneath the bright angel family.

The men wanted you to pray, and you wanted this too, wanted to believe in a god that hears, and comes, and loves in mercy. Your pants were torn, your knees scraped, your palms full of grit and bloody. You felt the first kick and the second, and the blow to the back of your head, and you closed your eyes, and the god who answers in mysterious ways spared you all joy and pain, all desire, all language.

You woke in the moonlight, facedown on the rocks by the Bitterroot River. They must have dumped you here, and

you thought, *This is fine*, and you saw ponies swimming
and a dog with a halo. When you woke again, Magdalena
Avalos and her one-armed friend Gideon Daro were rolling you up in a tarp and carrying you to her Chevy. They
were strong, these two, despite age and afflictions. Gideon
had a story like yours, an arm of his own left back in the
jungle.

In her trailer, in her bed, Magdalena splinted your broken fingers with sticks and bandaged your slashed belly
with rags torn from a child's Superman pajamas. *Try not to
move*, she said. *You're leaking.*

Twenty-two years you'd waited for this. You loved your
own precious life. You couldn't help it. You wanted to stay
alive—one more hour, one more day—to lie here like this
while a woman who wasn't afraid touched you.

When you were strong enough to kiss, you kissed. When
you could dance, you danced Magdalena Avalos out under
the stars. She wore a heavy shawl, sewn with acorns and
shells and juniper berries. It opened and closed, violet and
green, one great wing whirling around you. It sang with its
thousand bells, this shawl with a voice like no other. You fell
in the tall grass. You thought you had fallen forever.

But Magdalena wouldn't let you stay. She said, *If you
have a home, go home. If anybody wants to love you, let them.*

Twenty-two years, and then you were home, holding
baby Jeanne in your sister's kitchen. Blesséd was the God
who hears, who had kept you alive and sustained you and
delivered you whole to this moment. Blesséd was Roshelle's
kiss full and wet on your sweet mouth in the soft light of

morning. Blessèd was the child you held, the child reborn, the one come to save you.

Your people thought you'd stay for days and years to come.

The living, the left behind, the bereft think of all the days unlived—tomorrow and tomorrow. But you thought only of today, each holy moment. Blessèd was this God who belonged to no one, who was the spark in all things, in everyone, everywhere. Blessèd was this life, not held, not in you alone, not contained in one body: *this* life, *this* God, moving here as breath, as light, as love between you.

The wounded Vietnamese mother took you in her arms at last, Raymond Good Bird, her own, her most belovèd child. Blessèd was the mother of God. You and she knew only comfort.

Tu B'Shvat:

for the drowned and the saved

THE GIRL WAS RADIANT. I saw her in the shower naked. Glistening with water, she seemed lit from inside, a woman illuminated. I tried not to stare, then simply surrendered.

Alone, I tried not to look in the mirror, tried not to hear my mother: *The old are more naked than the young.* Before the camp, she had never seen an old woman naked.

One day last week the slender girl flickered beneath me. Three lengths she swam, seventy-five yards underwater. She had strength and desire, the discipline to stay down even if her lungs were bursting.

There are others like me at the pool, not that old, but already too fat or too thin, trying to stay fit, but already withered. There are others with scars: the woman with one breast, the man who leaves his left leg, his prosthesis, at the edge of the water.

The long, green-eyed girl gave us hope, a vision of a human being perfected.

My mother weighed seventy-two pounds the last time I dared to weigh her. I fed her puréed peas, strained carrots, tiny spoonfuls of mashed potatoes. I was always afraid. I thought her thin bones might snap as I bathed her.

She no longer spoke out loud, but the voice inside us said: *Love is stronger than death. Trust me.*

Yesterday, Mother and I bought figs and apples. She was strong, yes, five months dead and still walking. She squeezed a plum. *These aren't ripe*, she said. And, *Who will have pomegranates?*

She wanted carob, coconut, grapes, olives—chestnuts, cherries, pears, almonds—all the fruits of Tu B'Shvat, the new year of the trees, God's Rosh Hashanah. My father said, *God seeks us, this day above all others.*

In Israel, cold winter rains turned to drizzle; sap flowed through myrtle and cedar. Here in Salt Lake City, I woke to see new snow on white aspen, the whole world in pink morning light fractured. I envied my mother, the ease with which she moved, free of her body. She waited for me. She said, *This is something.*

By noon, sun shattered off snow, the day suddenly fierce, the blue sky unbearable. Mother opened her eyes wide, loving the light, able at last to take everything inside her. Only thirty-five degrees, but I was hot in my down coat, sweltering. I believed, yes: in this rage of light, the Tree of Life, *all* life, might be reawakening.

I told myself: *Rejoice.*

I whispered: *For your mother's sake, be thankful.*

And so I was—but more grateful to come home and close the blinds and close my eyes and let my mother go and lie perfectly still in perfect silence until Davia and Seth returned from school, until I heard Davia in the living room, lightly playing one phrase at a time on piano, then turning to the chair to invent an answer with her cello. She plays as she moves, graceful as water flowing, a girl who sees a mirage of herself shimmering across the desert: as soon as she reaches the place she appeared, she is already changing. My Davia learned piano sitting on my lap, hands resting on my hands, five years old, her whole body trembling. When I put her to bed that night, she lay quivering, near tears, unable to tell me why, unwilling to take comfort. Too much, too soon, a mistake, I was sorry. But the next morning, the trill of the piano woke me, Davia running her fingers up the keys—a ripple of light, the body becoming light, blood clear as rain—then down to the lowest notes, the mind a waterfall plunging. She had moved the bench to walk the full range, to touch every key, to feel the hammers strike wires inside her—Davia finding her first song, Davia in rapture.

Now she plays piano, zither, cello—Gipsy love songs, Bob Dylan, Arvo Pärt, Ludwig van Beethoven. Now she serenades a doll; now the snow is dancing. She conjures the carnival of Saint-Saëns: kangaroos and tortoise, wild asses, people with long ears—pianists, fossils. She plays the songs Dvořák's mother taught him, the cello strand of "Transfigured Night," Leonard Cohen's "Hallelujah."

She loves the cello because it vibrates through her bones, and its voice is almost human. She loves piano because it came first, that night, that morning. She loves the zither because even the wind knows how to play it—as if her gift is not her gift, only the breath passing through her. She lies on her bed in the dark, headphones on, sound searing straight into her skull—she's safe for all time, sheltered by *The Protecting Veil*, the voice of the Mother of God in a cello, Yo-Yo Ma playing Tavener. She turns the volume down lower and lower, until sound stops, until she becomes its lingering vibration. Davia, seventeen, and good enough for Juilliard, but she wants to live in the wild, meet the snow leopard face-to-face, hear its still, small voice high in the Himalayas—she wants to follow caribou across mountains and tundra, record the sounds they hear on their way to the edge of the world—Davia wants to sing as elephants sing when they visit the bones of their ancestors.

Seth already knows he'll be a fireman and a cantor. I see him now, my thin boy with narrow shoulders, small for his age, climbing the ropes at school, proving himself, faster than the other boys and able to squeeze his skinny hips through tight spaces, Seth Betos, unafraid of smoke-filled tunnels—our beautiful savior, bright hazel eyes ablaze with desire, eleven years old, my boy, singing the Kaddish, walking into the flames, healing the wailing mothers with a song as he lifts their babies from the embers.

My children! Let the night begin; let your father come home; let the dead stop speaking.

My mother died with a crumbling spine, bones too brittle to hold her. *Starvation*, Doctor Lavater said, *all those years ago.* Isaac Lavater, a smart and serious man with blue eyes and soft white hair—my husband's friend—he didn't mean to be cruel. When I bathed my mother, I imagined her as she was, Éva Spier, sixteen years old, thirty-one kilos, my mother in another life, already an orphan though she didn't believe it, an emaciated child stiff and bald as an old woman—Éva, a girl, younger than my daughter—Éva Spier standing thigh deep in the Vistula River with seventy other women just like her, *to even the banks, January 1945, the war lost, our final task, sublime madness.*

The camp sat wedged between the Vistula and the Soła, a swamp, a land of floods, soil impervious to rain and melting snow, marl two hundred feet thick, crumbling clay, impossible to drain and farm—but the Nazis still believed they could make everything in the world useful. Day by day for four years, they sent the women to the fields—hundreds, thousands—marched them five by five out the gate while the band played the rousing "March of Triumph" from *Aida*, marched them for hours, for miles, past deserted houses and evacuated villages, set them to work uprooting stumps or digging ditches, building roads, dredging fish ponds to spread the muck with their own muck as fertilizer. If a stone was too heavy to lift, a root too deep to dig, your shovel too dull, the clay too resistant—if you stopped, if you staggered, if you reeled, dizzy from hunger, the kapo beat you with a stick and you found the strength or died there.

In the end, my mother's captors contented themselves with one simple project: to move the stones, to even the banks, to make the river straight, to force the Vistula to flow more smoothly.

I see her bones, all their bones, glowing white through

their skin, washing away in frigid water. *Soup was God*, Éva said. *Thin as He was, God sustained me.* My mother lived because she was strong for her size and not too pretty, because she stood straight, because she believed her sister or her father or one cousin lived as she lived, by faith and will, by chance, somewhere. She lived because life itself was proof of rebellion. One day she collapsed and lay in the cold unconscious. When the whistle blew, she did not rise, and two other women whose faces she did not recall, whose names she never knew, who whispered to her in Czech or Polish, used the last of their strength, their love, to drag her back to the camp between them. My mother lived because the river ran cold, because frostbite, because fever, because too weak to march as the Russians approached, because left to die and instead liberated.

Éva Spier became Éva Lok and bore one daughter: my mother lived fifty-eight years after the war, twenty-three without my father—tiny Éva, one more survivor who never recovered, whose bones carried an irrevocable message: she couldn't walk and then she couldn't sit; one stroke took her desire to eat; another stole her voice in every language.

Night after night, my mother lives and dies. I touch her bones. I smell her. I breathe when she breathes. I count. If I don't stop, she won't stop. Am I awake or dreaming? There are things I know that my mother did not tell me, words I hear in the voice of her violin, Bach's "Chaconne" playing on barbed wire. *When you cried with hunger, I felt my own hunger. I praised God for your noise, your flesh, your fat—for fear I could soothe with a song, and hunger I could satisfy with my body*. Night after night, my husband lies beside me in this unstable darkness. He sleeps as children sleep, in complete surrender. He sleeps blessed, because he deserves comfort. I wake and wake again, and though I know it is unjust, each time I wake, I blame him.

My brilliant husband is famous: famously kind, famously patient. Doctor Liam Betos knows how to slip titanium ribs into the bodies of children with scoliosis so that they can breathe and walk, free of oxygen tanks and wheelchairs. He is not vain. *A man had to build a titanium bike before anyone thought to put ribs in a human.* Liam's children teach one another to do somersaults and cartwheels. They hang by their knees from the monkey bars at school, roll down grassy hills in the park, then charge to the top again, laughing.

If Doctor Betos sleeps in peace, he has earned it.

This morning I kissed them all good-bye, Seth and Davia and Liam, and I forgave him, my good husband, and I was unafraid, calm in the lavender light, no need to shield myself against it.

I walked to the pool alone, but not lonely. Mother comes when she comes. I cannot choose the day or the hour. Birds flew tree to tree, gathering twigs and hair, fur and feathers, hopeful and foolish they were, everywhere building. From a dense hedge, a hundred hidden sparrows sang, and I felt the sound, all their bodies in my body trembling. I smelled damp earth beneath melting snow and heard every seed, shells ready to split, green shoots quivering.

God, here, in all things: the birds, the song, the silence, the seeds—the snow, the coral clouds, the space between—the old terrier tugging at his chain, the hand with which I touch and soothe him. God immanent, God humble, God who offers Himself as olive, wine, wheat, carob—as the pomegranate we found at last—as sweet pears and nuts and apples. God who restores Himself through us each time we eat with holy intention. Tu B'Shvat, today, tonight, we celebrate this endless wonder.

I slipped, I almost fell, bedazzled by the thought, as if hearing God's Word, the seed in my heart, rupture for the first time. Mother came, light as light. She caught my arm. She laughed. She said, *Forty-four years old, and still you'd fall on your face without me.*

Yes, forty-four and so tired, and too weak to walk seven blocks, and fumbling in my body without you.

I was glad to see the green-eyed girl at the pool. She restored me. Her beauty seemed simple today, almost clear, not hers, merely the glass for God's reflection. I knew her name now, Helen Kinderman. Sweetly she'd given it to me last week when I asked her. She spoke softly, strangely shy, like a child; and though she stood five inches taller than I, though she glowed, blond and pale, a Nordic queen, she looked suddenly small and bewildered.

I loved her for this, the absence of all arrogance.

Today, everyone looked perfect. One leg, one breast—no fat, no hair—what did it matter? Carl Ancelet pulled hard with his left arm to compensate, and his right leg, his one extraordinary leg, kicked up and down and side to side, as he glided down the pool. A dark-skinned woman swam on her back, pregnant and joyful, frighteningly lush, buoyantly healthy, pink suit clinging to swollen nipples and navel, tight pink cloth exposing her, leaving her more naked.

Louise Doren appeared with two bald women, ones whose hair had fallen out in the grip of chemotherapy, ones healing now with her, their guide, their hope, because she had lost a breast at thirty-three and was not afraid, because she gave them a vision of how they might reclaim their strength in water—Louise, still alive at thirty-seven, and now her hair grew long and wavy, pale blond, shot with silver.

A tall boy with rippled muscles, one who'd shaved himself on purpose, stroked his smooth head, suddenly ashamed of this indulgence.

We were whole, each one of us, and all of us together.

I remembered my father's blessings: for lightning and thunder, for the beautiful ones, a narrow road through red maples, green dragonflies and white tulips, for lovely girls and strange-looking creatures: *Baruch ata Adonai Eloheinu Melech ha'olam mishaneh hab'riyot.* Blesséd are You, Adonai our God, Ruler of the Universe, who makes the creatures different.

Kristina Everly spoke to her deaf twins from across the pool, hands leaping in light, voice blessedly silent. How lucky they were to speak this way! I watched Ricky and Ryan dive deep to tell secrets underwater. Idris emerged from the tunnel of the dressing room, white towel wrapped like a skirt around him. One day after my mother's first stroke and before her second, Idris gave me a tiny cup of espresso at his coffee shop—warm and delicious it was, bitter and sweet as melted chocolate. I told him I would never need anything again, and he nodded; he understood; he believed me. *But come back,* he said. *Free for you, anytime, really.*

I didn't come. I was afraid of him, his beauty and his kindness, the way he said my name, *Margalit,* so lightly, as if it were not my name at all, but the word for his favorite dance, *the Margalit,* and as he spoke, he spun me—*yes,* Margalit whirled with Idris, a sleek Persian man as perfect as Helen Kinderman, elegant and smooth skinned, but her complete opposite: dark where she was bright, hair black, skin olive. We met only at the pool—he seemed to know why—but I was always glad on days like today when Idris chose the lane beside me.

Two more appeared, the last to join us, Samuel Killian pushing his wife, Violette, in her wheelchair. I loved to see him: stooped old man, thin skin speckled with dark bruises— dear, faithful husband, delicate and determined, every knot of his sternum visible. Fragile as he might seem, Samuel had the will to wheel his tiny, white-haired wife to the edge of the pool, lift her out of the chair, and ease her down to the water.

I thought what a blessing it was to swim with them, what a gift that they would allow it.

My father taught me to swim before I learned to say *no,* before I knew fear in any language. He could teach anybody to swim: little girls crippled by polio, soldiers with stumps

instead of legs, old women terrified of water. My father said:
Why be afraid of the thing that holds us? My father said: *I'm
right here; I'll walk in the water beside you.*

When Helen swam below me today, I found her foolish and splendid, extravagant in her strength, but not vain,
not driven. I loved her blond ponytail, long as a mermaid's
hair flowing. When she slowed, when she lay still on the
bottom, I thought: some new challenge, some watery medi-
tation, the mind making the body heavy so that she could
stay down without a flutter, as if floating. It made no sense,
floating twelve feet under, *floating on the bottom*, but this is
what I saw, and in my mind how I said it.

I confess: I grew vaguely irritated. She stayed too close
to the edge. Despite her depth, she distracted me, and so I
blamed her when I missed my flip turn. I forgot how lucky
I was, how privileged to swim with these people. I forgot
about coconuts and pears and olives, all the fruit at home,
waiting to be cracked and sliced, the endless gifts waiting
to be opened. I forgot about God as wine and swallowed a
mouthful of water. He left me sputtering, separate from all
things, trapped in myself, pitifully human.

My awe for the girl grew hard, a pit of shame sharp in
my belly.

I swam over her three times before I thought to go down,
before I felt her as I'd felt the birds, before my mother said,
She needs you.

A trick, I thought, this voice in water. I did not believe.
I did not trust her.

Dive, she said, and I obeyed, but the breath I took was

quick and shallow. I had to rise again and gasp, and dive again to reach her. I thought I'd find Helen, green eyes open, that we would speak in sign, in bliss, that there would be no struggle.

But I touched her arm and I knew; I knew then already.

Limp, the girl, water-logged, heavy, no breath in the lungs and so she floated on the bottom. I took Helen Kinderman in my arms; I wrapped my arms around her. I kicked hard, and we rose like this, not joyfully, together.

Then the others came, *so fast,* as if they'd felt my grief move through the water: Idris, the closest one, already on the deck, taking her in his arms, lifting Helen away from me; Kristina waving furiously at the lifeguard, trying to make that flushed boy comprehend the wild silence of her language; then another guard, a girl with a whistle, blowing hard, a short, thick, red-headed girl with powerful thighs like one of those miniature gymnasts; and Louise Doren touching Helen's feet, believing the one who'd almost died could heal the one not living.

The flustered boy yelled, commanding us to step back, me and Kristina, Louise and Samuel, as if we had no part in it, no place or purpose here, no desire—running now, the guards, telling Idris to set her down, *gently, gently;* scolding us with their voices, not the words themselves, but the tone, the inflection, the implication we'd done her harm, the insinuation our touch was violent.

They knelt beside her—the boy, the girl, these two, these children. The fierce little gymnast pumped Helen's chest, and we saw her: Helen Kinderman exposed, pale skin blotched and blue, supple legs weirdly bloated. *Stop*. I wanted someone to stop this. But nothing stopped. In her chest, tiny bones cracked; from her mouth and nose, water spurted. Then the boy had his mouth on Helen's mouth, and the girl pressed hard with the heels of her hands, and Helen's bones broke and her body surrendered and there was hope the lungs might heave, the heart clench, the love of life return, the delicate pulse throb in her neck again.

Where was the manager?

Out back, smoking a cigarette?

On the phone, scolding her befuddled father?

What did it matter where or why, legitimate or foolish? She'd left us in the care of two teenagers who had done the drill ninety-nine times but never resuscitated an actual not-living, not-breathing person. *Too late, my fault, I'm the one, I saw her.* Or maybe it was Helen's fault for swimming underwater so many times, for teaching me, Idris, the rippled boy, Samuel Killian, the buoyant woman—all of us— how strong she was, how ridiculous we were to worry. I wanted to rage at Helen, God, the manager. *Where are you now? What are you doing that's more important?*

Two firemen and a paramedic descended, dark birds in black jackets, fast and graceful, called by God, terribly efficient. Helen belonged to them now. They had paddles to jolt her heart and a syringe full of epinephrine. Her body rose and shuddered and stopped, and rose and shuddered and stopped, and rose and shuddered and stopped, and then these three raised her on their wheeled cot and took her away from us.

Gone, our beautiful girl, gone all the way over, already on the other shore—I knew it as soon as I touched her.

Now the jittery manager and her quick guards herded us to the locker rooms, told us not to shower. *Dress and go home. Pool closed for the day. Come back tomorrow.* Tomorrow, and tomorrow, and tomorrow. Violette sat in her chair, cap curled up like a crown, damp red towel like a cape around her. Crippled queen! I wanted to kneel before her.

We didn't go home. We clustered outside, though the day had gone dark, though the wind whipped icy snow into dancing funnels. The pregnant woman sobbed, blaming herself. *I saw her,* she said. *I didn't even try to go down.* She touched her huge belly. *I can't. I'm too buoyant.* Then she laughed, a high yip that made her gasp until Idris put his arm around her.

She wanted to touch me because I'd touched Helen, because she thought I was good, because she believed I'd tried to save her.

I let her believe; I let them all believe what they wanted.

Carl looked in my direction, but his focus went far beyond, to the trees, to the snow on the mountains behind us. Louise and her two friends pressed up against me, and only then did I realize how weak I was, that I had almost fallen. I whispered, *She'd be alive if I'd gone sooner.* And Louise said, *It could have been me or Joan or Hannah. It could have been Kristina or Samuel or Violette.* She touched the place where her left breast once was to remind me: anyone can drown or save or fail. *Or you,* she said, *you might have been the one on the bottom, Idris the one who dove too late, Idris the one who waited.*

She meant to be kind, but her words pierced me.

She drove me home. She unlocked my door. *The guards,* she said, *their job.*

I nodded. *But we were there, with Helen, in the water.* I didn't say it.

She wrote her phone number on a little scrap of paper. *Call me if you need something later.*

I thought God was here, in this room, still alive but unable to help us, revealing Himself to me in Louise Doren. I couldn't bear Him, His grief, His terrible need, pomegranates and grapes, three fat pears, a jar of black olives, all that fruit, *His* fruit, in my kitchen.

And then Louise closed my door, and I was alone, completely, and everything in the house scared me: fruit uncut, wine unopened, Mother's white tablecloth rolled tight, Mother's white-on-white scroll, the Tree of Life embroidered in satin stitches, a wedding gift from Datiel, her cousin, Mother's blessed cloth, never once creased, never once folded.

I smelled Helen Kinderman in me—soot of adrenaline, burn of chlorine—we shared this: one scorched body. I wanted to wash her away, the smell, the memory, the thing that had happened but couldn't be, and I tried to climb the stairs, but I was too weak to stand, too light in the head, and I was afraid of the water, my father there, dead of a heart attack at fifty-seven, Leonard Lok crumpled in the shower, alone, two hours—my father who might have survived if Mother had been home, if Mother had heard a cry, if he hadn't hit his head so hard on the tile. Even now,

today, he might live—if only I could climb the stairs, if only
I could reach him.

How can this be?

My mother's sister Edith died because she was too ripe,
too beautiful, because her hazel eyes were almost gold, because she scared them. The doctors thought if they could
sterilize a girl like this, they could sterilize anyone. Cut
without anesthesia, burned with acid, she died barren,
bearing only their secrets.

Any day you might be the one, or the one of a thousand
chosen. *Because you resisted, because you stumbled, because
one cell grew wild, because you spat blood, because you held
your breath, because you chose to stay under.* For two hours
the water ran cold over my father's cold body. *You died because you were exceptionally kind; you lived because you were
spectacularly cruel—because you were wise, because you were
foolish—because you didn't hide in time, because you didn't
believe, because you couldn't imagine.*

How can this be?

My mother said, *Our neighbors turned us out. Our good
Christian friends delivered us to the soldiers. The midwife who
brought me safe into the world probed me now, deep inside
every opening, searching for stashed gold, luminous pearls, glit-
tering rubies. My own mother wept, watching.* "Please, she's
just a girl, be careful." *But Katarina's fingers pushed hard.
Katarina Szabó pierced me. As if I were nothing to her—goat,
dog, Jew, stranger—as if my aunt Lilike had not baked the
three-tiered wedding cake for Katarina's daughter, as if my*

*mother had not sewn the white dress and stitched a hundred
and twelve glass beads into the bodice.*

How can this be?

*The family jewels were inside, it's true, but not in my body—
four gold rings, wedding bands, all we'd ever had between us, four
thin rings hidden deep in the belly of the doll my father brought
me oh-so-long-ago from Budapest. Hidden: as if we would return, as if our house would be our house, the doll uncrushed,
Mother's china cups unshattered. Anastasia had porcelain teeth,
a red tongue, tiny dimples; she looked ready to speak, thin pink
lips lightly parted, the princess Anastasia sweetly smiling. I
stared at her on the shelf, and all the while Katarina probed, red-
tongued Anastasia kept her silence.*

How can this be?

*She had golden hair, silky hair, human hair curled in ring-
lets. I would crush her now myself to stop remembering.*

My mother's uncle Tamás died because his neck was
thin, his beard long, his only gift teaching Hebrew. Her
father lived seven months, longer than most, because he
was a carver, a craftsman, because for a time, a short time,
Bertók Spier's clever hands proved useful. Long ago, he'd
carved an altar for a synagogue in Vienna. He carved
headboards with vines and flowers, cradles that never
tipped, caskets without nails. In silence, in delight, he
carved nutcrackers and puppets. Bertók Spier carved the
delicate legs of chairs and tables. In Sárvár on the Rába
River, no one asked, no one cared, if these legs belonged to
Jews or Gentiles. For his son and daughters and nieces and

nephews, he carved tiny bats with folded wings, slender does, sweet-smiling camels. Once he carved a tiny whale, a fine filigree of myrtle with a little man inside, a man you could see, a man with a dove, a miniature Yonah.

How can this be?

Even Bertók the carver couldn't explain how he'd done it.

In the camp, he extracted gold from the mouths of the dead, found emeralds stashed in the bowel, sapphires the soul didn't need, diamonds his neighbors had swallowed.

My mother's mother, Amiela, died because she carried Tavi, three years old and always hungry. *Efron, Jozsua, Tzili, Judit.* Her cousin Datiel lived because the sun struck his face and he looked stronger than he was: older, taller, almost fair, almost pale, enough like them, almost a soldier. He wheeled carts of the dead and almost dead. He heaved them into ovens. *On Rosh Hashanah it is written, on Yom Kippur it is sealed: who shall be tranquil and who shall be troubled.* Datiel survived the war and hung himself twenty-six years later.

They arrived at night on the train. Work would make them free—if they were quick, if the wolf dogs didn't kill them. Somewhere in the eerie fog, an orchestra played Hungarian Rhapsodies to soothe them.

Are you mad? Is this possible?

And then they began to see, yes, a piano and a cello, a violin dancing in the air, in the mist, and a woman with a baton, standing very straight, and then forty other women, female shapes shifting behind solid instruments, ghosts gathering themselves from smoke, from soot, from that

weird black dust everywhere falling. Music muted the cries
of children, and they thought: *If the music doesn't stop,
anything—anything at all—is bearable.*

My mother's grandmothers died because they were old;
her grandfather because he hobbled behind them. Aunt
Lilike took the hand of a child, a little boy lost, a waif abandoned. Lilike and the son of a stranger died together. *You
lived because your shoes almost fit and you found a piece of
wire to close them, because you stole a spoon from a dead man,
because you tore his shirt to wrap your feet, and your feet didn't
freeze and swell and blister, and the sores didn't cripple you;
because you pulled the straw from the dead one's pants to stuff
your own pants, because you weren't afraid, because the dead
were dead and couldn't hurt you.*

*You died because you failed to button your tunic to the top,
because you failed to make your bed flat and tuck the corner, because you failed to stand three hours in the freezing rain as the
guards called your ridiculous numbers, as their dogs searched
for the ones who didn't answer, the ones who failed to rise, the
ones whose hearts and minds had failed them.*

One day my mother thought she would run into the
buzzing fence and end it. A song, it was, electricity in wire,
a sweet, high hum, the *Mephisto Waltz* tenderly tempting.
She didn't care about her own life or the fifty women the
guards might shoot in retribution. *I dared God to accuse
me of murder.* But she stepped outside the barracks into
the light and the sun on her bare arm felt warm, and the
sun on her skin saved her. Another day, later, near the
end though she didn't know it, my mother moving rocks

in the river thought, *So easy to go down, so cold, so sweet to slip under,* but twilight came and the sky turned pink and lavender beyond the trees, and a prayer began to pass among the women, a whispered song between them, as if in a single breath they'd all remembered the day, the hour, *Shabbat,* the holy night, the queen, the bride already here, radiant among them. They had one choice: to live as long as possible, to let God hold them in the river. *Hungarian, Greek, Czech, Polish—Lithuanian, French, German, Italian— suddenly we spoke as one; suddenly we knew one language: Shalom aleichem malachei hasharet malachei elyon mi melech malchei hamlachim Hakadosh Baruch Hu. And the angels came and hovered there, close, though we worked, though we couldn't stop working, and God gave us each an extra soul, a holy spirit for the Sabbath—He gave us five souls; He gave us fifty; He gave us all the dead swirling down this river. Did we sing aloud or only dream this dream together? The guards would have killed us if they'd heard, wounded us one by one, left us facedown in the water, silent women, floating Jews, free at last, saved, delivered, but the wind in the trees and the water over rocks were the prayer and the song, and the river and the night and the wind saved us.*

How can this be?

You lived because your bones heard *Aida* in your sleep, and the beat of the drums kept your heart beating.

My father said, *Even Moses didn't want to die. Old as he was, Moses feared the Angel of Death. When he climbed Mount Nebo at last, Moses asked God to kiss his mouth and eyelids.*

Father, did you wait for God? Did He kiss you as you fell?
Did you die afraid, or surrender in wonder?

Helen, I confess, I kissed you: as Idris lifted you out of my
arms, I pressed my lips to your leg—to taste, to know, to love you.

I do love you.

Two hours gone since we lost her. Is love fiercer than
death? *Mother, are you with me?* I thought of Helen's mother,
the words she might hear, her husband the first to know, the
one to tell her, the terrible sound she might make as slowly
she understood him. Do the dead die when they die, or only
when we believe it? My father lay dead nine hours before I
knew it, and all that time, if I imagined him at all, I imagined him walking in the water, in the world, beside me.

The police found Helen's father first, Peter Kinderman,
a pharmacist downtown, and when he saw them, he was
afraid, but not for Helen—he never thought, *It's her, she's*
gone, my beautiful daughter. He thought accidental overdose,
a mistake in a prescription, a stranger dead somewhere
or in a coma, his fault, or the fault of one of his technicians. He made the stuttering policeman say it three times.
Drowned, today, this morning, Helen. He walked from the
drugstore to the library, thirteen blocks in the cold without
hat or gloves, and the wind bit and he liked it, the small
hurt, the swirling snow, the distraction, the drifting in and
out, the seconds when it was still untrue, a terrible mistake,
someone else's drowned child, but not his, not Helen, not
possible.

How Helen would suffer when she heard it!

She'd hold him, her distraught father, while he wept in

relief and terror, grieving now for another man, feeling him, the one he didn't know, the father of a child missing. *Oh, Helen!* She was always the most sensitive of his children, the quiet one, Helen who came from the womb with her eyes wide open, just a few minutes old and already watching. She would understand his sorrow, the hours of pain when she didn't come home, when he began to take it in, when he couldn't breathe, when he had to invent words to tell his wife and somehow find his other children.

Peter Kinderman climbed the winding stairs to the fourth floor of the library because even the glass elevator looked too small, the air inside too close, too much like water—the fourth floor where you can see paintings by Fra Angelico or read the words of Mahatma Gandhi—where you can visit Saigon, Machu Picchu, Wounded Knee—where you can climb Denali. The copy of John James Audubon's *Birds of America* lies in a glass case, protected. If you took it out, it would stand three feet high and be too heavy to steal. Sixty pounds! *Oh, how Helen loved it.*

Clare Kinderman saw her husband and thought, *What a lovely surprise, not my birthday, not our anniversary, and here he is in the middle of the day, Peter looking handsome and sad, cold and disheveled, but surely he's not sad because he's come in time for lunch, like the days when we were first married, before the children, before Vonda Jean and Helen, before Jay and Karin and Juli, when the day was too long to be apart, when he had to come, sometimes three times a day, just to look, just to see that I was still here, still his, still real.*

He took her outside to say it, so she could wail into the

wind, so she wouldn't have to hold it in her body as he held it, so the cry wouldn't splinter her ribs the way his ribs were splintering.

I was not there; I did not hear the sound my mother made when she found my father in the shower, when she understood she'd lost him too, her one, her only one, her love, her Leonard.

A Sunday morning, late summer, and Mother had gone to the hospital to play her violin for the children. Leonard Lok slipped free of his body fast to follow her, to hear her play, to see Éva swaying to the songs inside her—*one more time, my love, my darling*—before his spirit dispersed, before his holy sparks scattered. She stood with her back to the windows, face in shadow, bright glass blazing behind her—Éva Lok playing her violin for the children, giving them her wild joy, the miracle of survival in these strings, an endless hymn of praise, a vision of their own perfection— Éva playing Kodály's *Dances of Galánta* and *Marosszék*, each one a fusion, a rondo and a rhapsody, playing with her beloved Zoltán, imagining him, the teacher who visited her school, who believed every child could sing, who said every child *must* sing whenever possible. *Hum if you don't have breath; let your body feel it.* And so in his spirit, in his name, Éva taught a simple song to these children in wheelchairs, the ones without hair, the ones without fingers, the ones with fluttery hearts and failing kidneys, the burned boy with a patchwork face, skin sewn from the skin of others. He'd made a collage of himself, a picture pasted together: right ear of a pig and tail of a peacock, open eyes of an owl, closed mouth of a seal. He offered it to my mother when she came, a gift, and she saw who it was before he said it, and she touched his left ear, the ear that was really his, the soft ear, the ear that could still hear and flush and feel, and she said, *It's beautiful, you're beautiful, thank you.*

How can this be?

Because the boy's mother fell asleep, and the boy and his sister torched the drapes, because they wanted to see a wall of fire, because the sister furled herself inside, and the brother tried to save her.

My father blazed in the window behind Éva. As light, he fell on bare heads and throats; as light, he warmed naked legs and shoulders; as light, he transfigured all these shattered faces. My mother saw, and almost understood, but couldn't believe it.

And then a cloud passed, and as light leaves, he left them.

How can a man die so swiftly, without resistance, without a witness? How can anyone die in her own bed, or his own shower? How can a twenty-two-year-old girl who learned to swim before she walked drown in a pool? How can you survive the worst and not live forever?

Helen, I can't make sense of it.

Last week, three deer stood still on our back porch, transfixed by their own reflections. The next day, I saw one struck by a van, and I knew her, I remembered her, lighter and smaller than the other two, hungry like them because of the snow, desperate, and so they'd come down from the hills into the city. She leaped away, a miracle, unharmed

by the van, alive in the moment. But later, I was sure I felt
her in the snow, hidden in the park by the river. I looked
for her; I don't know what I meant to do—lie down with
her, as I lay with my mother, float away at last, give myself
to water? I was certain she would die that night, that inside her starved body ruptured organs bled, weak muscles
quivered.

How can this be? Even now, I hear Helen's mother softly
say it.

My mother who lost everyone she loved rocked me in
her thin arms one day and said, *I have you and Liam and
Seth and Davia.* My mother whispered, *My life for this, God
has mercy.*

My father and his sister Antje lived because their
mother had a cousin of a cousin in America, a man with a
farm and a wife but no children. Miklós Zedek agreed to
take these two if they could learn to milk cows and pluck
chickens, if they weren't afraid to twist a neck and break
it, if they promised to love mucking stalls, shoveling snow,
heaving thirty-pound pumpkins.

His mother said, *We'll come soon; we'll come after.* She
meant when they'd saved enough to travel, enough to bribe,
enough to secure visas. She packed their finest clothes:
Antje's lace blouse with feather stitching, her velvet skirt,
Leonard's black wool jacket with sapphire silk lining.
Worthless, she knew: they weren't going to wear silk and
lace on a farm outside Buffalo. *Buffalo: what did it mean,
and where was it?* She ironed Leonard's trousers and hand-
kerchiefs though Antje begged her to stop, though Antje

said: *On the boat, everything you've packed will crumple.* She darned their socks, toes and heels, saving her children's lives with tiny knots and stitches. Their mother sang as she worked, peculiar melodies known only to her, giddy and bright, then suddenly mournful. Ironing was perfect bliss, folding her children's clothes the piercing joy she'd keep forever.

Their father wrote: *There's been an unexpected delay.*

Their mother added: *Just a few more months. Be good, my darlings.*

And they were good, very good, and they slept in one room, in one bed, at the back of the house where the rain came through the roof, and the heat never reached them. Their father wrote: *The American Consulate has not approved our applications to immigrate. We'll try again in four months. Keep your faith in us. We'll be there.* His scrawled note at the bottom of the page sounded like a whisper, a secret sputtered at the last moment before he could scratch it out or regret it: *Better we have to wait. Your mother's been sick, nothing serious, just some fluid in her lungs—she'll be well again when she sees blue sky and the weather's warmer. She sends her love. She says don't worry.*

Their mother died on the train. Their father died in Dachau.

Soon, after, delay, don't worry.

You died because you kept your faith. You lived because you lost it. You sang when you heard how your mother died, because even if God was deaf, you wanted your mother to hear you.

My father carried three photographs to America: Greta and Hevel Lok six days after they married, a clear alpine lake and snow-covered mountains in the distance; Hevel as a child in short pants, a boy holding a butterfly on his finger; Greta Erhmann walking through a field of poppies, a hopeful girl, conceiving two children in her mind, dreaming her life to come: *I did; I saw you*. Hand-tinted, singular and precious—this photograph held their whole lives: together, apart, before, after. The artist had flushed the girl's lips and shoulders, had revealed heat rising beneath the skin of cheeks and fingers. The poppies glowed, lit from inside, translucent yellow.

Vivid as these pictures were, they were not as strong as the visions in his mind, the last days, the last hours, Mother ironing perfect creases in his trousers, Mother holding Antje's cape, dancing without music, swirling the long gray cape into a person. My father remembered his father on his knees the day the blond boys of Vienna became Nazi accomplices. They wore swastikas on their armbands and flicked their little dog whips. They wanted Hevel Lok to scrub the street, to wash away the Austrian cross some rebel nationals had painted. The doctor had known these three in their mothers' wombs, had felt Dieter's appendix before it burst and saved him, set Emil's fractured legs after he leaped from the tree house, listened to Hendrik's heart and lungs, laid his naked ear on the little boy's bare chest when he had whooping cough—because the stethoscope was too cold, because he didn't want to hurt him. *Dieter, Emil, Hendrik!* Hevel Lok wanted to say their names, to call them out of themselves, to remind them who he was, the one they knew, the man who loved them.

My father's mother loved her children enough to let

them go, to believe, to trust, to lie: *One day soon we will all be together.*

My father the Austrian orphan became an American soldier, a liberator of Mauthausen who saw the dead—in pits, in the quarry, ones forced to leap, ones half-burned, ten thousand in one grave, hundreds never buried. He saw how hungry they were, the dead, limbs bent back, impossible angles, humans so thin their spines jabbed up through their bellies. Even now they cried and wasted. *So hungry!* The dead wanted my father to feed them. Each one was his own mother. His broken father lay in the pit, whispering the Kaddish ten thousand times, then starting over. Leonard Lok stared across the open grave and saw his unborn child on the other side, his daughter ready to leap, Margalit silently wailing.

He had never loved like this. He thought love might kill him.

How could he go home, and where was it?

Antje wrote: *121 inches of snow in Buffalo this winter and still snowing.* He wanted to be there, under the snow, with her, with them, to sleep without dreams and not be dead but never wake from it. He stayed behind to work in displaced-persons camps in Austria, then Germany. To his sister Antje he wrote: *I think I can be useful.*

He meant nothing else makes sense. Nothing else matters.

Antje wrote: *People go over Niagara Falls in barrels, to say they did, to prove it's possible.* He hated these foolish men who risked their lives on purpose.

The ones returned from the dead told him stories. They lived by chance, by grace, the sacrifice of another. *Because I lied when they asked if I could play accordion; because the orchestra needed a cellist; because someone else had died in the night; because I spoke German; because I pricked my finger and rubbed blood on my lips and cheeks to look rosy; because I was a chemist; because God filled my lungs and I sang "Un bel di" and this pleased an officer, and he chose me to watch over his children, because his wife was too tired after the baby, and I scrubbed their pots, and I scoured their toilets, and they weren't unkind in their house, and I couldn't hate them, and sometimes I stole the baby's bottle, sometimes I sucked milk pumped from the breast of his mother, and I was always afraid, but she never saw and she never killed me.*

They told of the ones set free who died anyway, hundreds a day, thousands in every camp, because the soldiers, the good ones, their liberators, gave them meat and chocolate and wine and cigarettes, and they ate too much, too fast, and their bowels twisted, and the food that promised life became the poison that killed them.

Sometimes he sat with the children while they ate, teaching them to take a little at a time, to trust that there was more: chicken soup and bread and oranges, carrots and peas and milk and potatoes. And then one day she was there, Éva Spier, an orphan just like him but not destroyed, Éva, a girl who still loved her life, the thin thread of it, who weighed thirty-four kilos, nine pounds more than the day she was liberated, Éva who gave bread to the birds, who said, *Enough to scatter on the ground, enough to share, imagine.* The crumbs on the ground and the birds at this girl's feet were life, all of it, all he needed forever and ever. If she could choose life, who was he to deny it? When the bread was gone, the birds pecked her bare feet, and she laughed, and he laughed with her, these two, these mother-less children.

Imagine a love like this, here, after, in this place—imagine a life where laughter is possible.

To Antje he wrote: *I'll never leave her.*

But he did leave one bright Sunday morning while Éva played her violin, while light fell on the stunned faces of fifteen children, ones outside of time, ones caught in the rapture. Light was all the weight they could bear, light the only touch tender enough not to hurt them.

If my father had lived, he might have taught some of these children to float, to swim, to walk in water when their legs were too weak to stand, when their frail bones wouldn't hold them. Children like these saved him every day, and every day he needed saving.

How the body loves life! How the body wants to heal!

On the last day of my mother's life, I saw the sores on her feet closing.

How can this be?

I was glad when my mother died. I don't deny it. I thought now she and I can rest, now we can stop hurting. But it doesn't stop. You might be ten or sixteen or ninety, you might be a hundred and twenty, old as Moses, and still be afraid to leave this earth, still cling to your precious body. At the top of the mountain, you might insist God kiss your eyelids. You might surrender, yes—you might forgive the one who gave you life to lose—but still weep, still wish to touch the body, the face, the mouth of every one taken before you.

Four hours gone, and even I who held Helen Kinderman in my arms can't believe it. She was radiant. Last week, I saw her in the shower naked. Today, she floated on the bottom. She distracted me. I started my flip turn too soon, and my feet missed the wall—no push, no glide, no rest for the weary—and I saw her again, the second time, just moments after the first, and I blamed her. I didn't love her then, not enough to sense despair or know her sudden weakness in that moment. I swam to the shallow end and back, and I was slow, too slow, because I was tired, and I saw her the third time, right where I'd left her, twelve feet down, twelve feet under, and I think I was afraid, but I didn't want to be afraid, so I was angry instead and I sputtered, and my mother said, *Dive*, and my mother said, *She needs you*. And I did dive; I held her in my arms, and I understood how it was, how it will be, and I kissed her leg as she rose, as Idris lifted her away from me, and I loved her as God loves—in helpless grief, in terrible pity—and then the others came, *so fast*: Louise and Violette, the firemen and paramedic, the shaved boy, the swollen woman, the one-legged man, the unborn child—and I loved them too, and I knew that what had happened to Helen had happened to all of us, and forever.

How can this be?

There are a thousand ways to die, any day, any hour—yet

one child lives, one little girl devoured by the wolf cuts herself free of his bowel and walks out of the woods into the sunlight. One woman in a pit moves, and another one says, *Can anybody hear me?* A wife pulls her husband from the shower in time, and a doctor makes an incision just big enough to slip his fingers inside, and this man, this doctor, this human being, holds the heart of another man in his hand while he repairs it.

Arise, my darling, my beautiful one, my daughter. You have seen God face-to-face. Now all suffering is over. Now it is time to forgive. Now it is time to surrender. Love is fiercer than death. I set myself as a seal upon your heart. Trust me. And so I rose. I did as my mother asked. I did every-thing she'd taught me. *You lived because a woman hungrier than you, one too sick to swallow, gave you her soup and bread, and you saw that she was God, offering herself to you even as she lay dying.* I unrolled the white tablecloth with its white satin stitches, and my mother and father appeared, smell-ing of rosewater and myrtle, shimmering behind lush white leaves, then hiding themselves again so that I could see dove and goat, lamb and lion, wolf and weasel, snake and tiger— three fish swimming under roots, one tiny bear growling in the distance—owl and elephant, ram and raven: life every-where, life abundant.

Now, this is the hour.

I imagined Davia walking from Rowland Hall to the McGillis School, five steep blocks, to wait for Seth and then walk two miles home, together. Every day she goes.

They could take a bus, but never do. *Time to think,* she says, *and besides, I miss him.* She will not say she's afraid. I know she can't explain it. A child doesn't need to hear a story to feel it. The story is there, trembling in the body and the blood, in the wind through the pines, over rocks in the river. The violin lies in its case, but the zither plays itself, and the song swells unspoken.

Let me speak now, my children. Let me tell you.

I saw Karin and Juli Kinderman coming home too, on the same bus, but not together, a kind of agreement they have, to pretend to be strangers, Juli a freshman at West High, Karin a senior. They'll find their parents in the living room, and they'll know their loss before they hear it. All their lives, Helen's sisters will wonder why their father let them stay in school today, why he let Juli dress in drag to play Hamlet, why he let Karin learn to pose questions in Italian. *Are you afraid? Are you hungry? Who is your favorite saint? Shall we go to the opera?* They'll rage. How could their mother allow Karin to eat her lunch in peace while little Juli, Prince of Denmark, sneaked outside to lie in the bed of a truck, to get buzzed on cigarettes and blow smoke into the mouths of her two boyfriends? Forever and a day, Karin and Juli will blame their parents for these terrible hours, macaroni and cheese, hot ash, complete ignorance.

Peter Kinderman has found Vonda Jean, has called her home from her honeymoon in Hawaii. When she heard her father's voice, she thought: *He knows about the black-footed albatross and the black sand beaches, the orange amaryllis growing so fast I heard it, the pink hibiscus. He knows about the first day, a waterfall with three rainbows, scarlet 'apapane birds blazing through a forest so green it scared me. He knows the sea is bluer than the sky, the world upside down, heaven underwater. My father who loves me too much knows about the tequila and ginger I used to ease the sting of sunburn, the mango daiquiris last night, the flaming sambuccas after dinner.*

And perhaps she is right—perhaps he imagines the tiny red bathing suit she wore, the strapless dress, her near nakedness at this moment, but the words he speaks are soft, and in the breath before the cry, all transgressions past and still to come are by a sister's death forgiven.

Helen, I don't know why it was our time. I don't know why I didn't save you.

Eight hours gone and Jay Kinderman, serving his mission in Hermosillo, walks a dusty road at the edge of the city, hoping to save one soul today, hoping to win one convert. He does not know. He cannot imagine a world, a life, a day without his four sisters. He hears Helen's mocking voice above the others, Helen, three years older, calling him *Elder Kinderman*, and he laughs at himself, at his white shirt, stained with sweat, filthy from dust blowing. He laughs and she's there, watching, his Helen. He loosens his tie at last, as if she has whispered: *It's okay. Do it.* His companion is sick today—heaving, dehydrated, afraid to leave his bed, afraid to drink the water. If Jay liked Elder Mattea better, would they be more successful? Something to overcome—in time, if possible—part of the test, part of the challenge: surrendering to love long before you feel it.

He is forbidden to work alone. All day, he has been

disobedient. Not one crime, but a crime committed moment by moment, street to street, hour by hour. It would
have been right to stay with Jared, good to care for him
today, to watch over him as he slept, change the sheets a
third time, fetch the bedpan or a doctor—it would have
been generous and just to boil water clean and sit with
Elder Mattea as he sipped it. But there will be other days
to learn this kindness. Today has been a gift, time apart,
his opportunity. All day, he has failed, but now, as twilight
comes, he feels calm again and strengthened—and he is
not alone: Helen has come to walk this scrap of earth beside him.

He sees a small Indian woman moving toward him,
slowly gathering herself out of the dust until she becomes
a shape he recognizes. He counts, he tries to count, all her
skinny dogs, all her skinny-legged children, all the mottled
chickens that lead this strange procession.

And he thinks, *Now, today, this is the hour,* and for once
he won't preach, won't try so hard, won't provoke himself
with language. Helen is here. Helen has revealed his mistakes to him, the failure of practiced words, the hopeless-
ness of his precise Spanish.

He knows what his sister would do, knows she would
walk in silence with this woman and her seven skinny children and her six scrawny dogs and her multiplying chickens, knows Helen would walk side by side along the tracks
to the Rio Sonora. His throat is too parched to speak of
God and salvation. Even the chickens refuse to squawk.
It is better to go home with the woman and her children,

to offer the rice and beans and corn he always carries, to drink their water unafraid, to trust, to keep his faith, to help them cook this food over an open pit, to sit, to eat, to share this meal.

Jay Kinderman knows he will do this—for Helen, with Helen. He will dance with enchanted legs. He will learn every song the children want to teach him.

And he will be the one swayed; he will be the one converted.

My children! Let the night begin! May you all forgive me!

Davia opened the door, and here they were, alive, both of them, home, my precious ones, to help me slice pears and crack coconuts. I touched their faces, and they understood everything had changed, though I dared not tell them what had happened. I imagined how it would be if Helen were their sister, if she'd died today, but they didn't know it, if they'd been conjugating verbs in French or memorizing the names of tribes, learning to spell, to say, to imagine *Hohokam, Tutsi, Zapotec, Yaqui, Eyak, Gwich'in, Kuna, Maasai, Malagasy*—if they'd been watching a film about birds: snow geese in flight, dancing cranes, emperor penguins emerging from the ocean. Oh, if they heard now, how foolish and blessed it would seem, this life, all of it!

Liam returned to us, just in time, just before dusk, in the hour of twilight. We blessed the wine of every season: white, pink, rose, red. We drank it down, the year to come, the year behind us. We blessed each fruit. We ate because God needed us—our human love, our frail bodies—to restore Him, the Tree of Life, to give God life in the world.

Everything I have is yours! How slow we are to learn it. We ate pomegranates with shells because on this perilous earth we need protection; we ate dates, plums, olives—fruit with pits—because fear makes a stone, sharp in the belly. We ate figs and grapes—we devoured them whole because God longs to enter us whole, to become one with us.

We sang as trees sing: *Ehyeh asher ehyeh, I am what I am becoming.* And the silence between words, our breath, was the fruit of God unseen, too sweet to taste, the fruit of life, ethereal. Three deer came to the back porch and stared inside and were not afraid of us.

Later, our children passed some secret sign between them. Davia rose and Seth followed. Our daughter began to play the piano, low and soft, in a rhythm impossible to repeat, moonlight through fluttering leaves—the wind, and then the water. I was hearing notes, but Davia was listening to the space between them, hearing the song inside her song, the first words of unborn children. Davia was waiting for the one word, the note before the note where she might join them. I was afraid to lose her, but she trembled with pure joy, the bliss of finally going. And then it came. I don't know how she did it. A single bell rang clear and high as one by one the low notes faded. Davia dove. Davia concealed herself as water.

Imagine the song you would sing if you loved silt, weeds, rocks rippling you. Imagine your joy if you reflected stars, then swallowed them. Imagine if you had no choice as creeks entered you, if you wound slowly through silent woods, then with delight roared down a narrow canyon—imagine the wonder of it all, how you'd laugh and leap as you ceased to be, as you emptied yourself into the ocean. *Never again, never again I, never will I on this world be walking.* This was Davia's voice, life beyond hope and fear, proof of love, God unfathomable. Seth brought his fingers to the keys in a jubilation of sound, three times Davia's speed, but with astonishing lightness.

Rain, brilliant rain, water bouncing off water.

I looked at my husband's hands, the hand that holds the knife, the hand that slips a rib into a child. I felt them here, the children whose lives he'd saved—Sophie, Joseph, Daniel, Remy—Nina, Dorothy, Matthew, Eric—I saw each one of them and all their children; I saw fathers and mothers spared, sisters and brothers not abandoned.

You lived because you chopped fallen trees in a nearby forest. One day you prayed as you walked: Please come, please come. You meant God, death, your mother, your father. But instead you saw blue butterflies, a quick fox, three rabbits; instead, white flowers bloomed along the path, white, with scarlet anthers. Everything here seemed kind. Nothing here wanted to kill you. This was how wind through pine answered: If the butterfly survived the night, why can't you live one more day, one more hour? If the clouds are part of God and part of you, why can't they be good? Why can't they be sentient?

Thirteen hours gone, and Jay Kinderman is learning Yaqui Deer Songs from the children, songs to carry them from here to over there, from this world to the flower universe.

The deer looks at a flower.

The bush is sitting under a tree and singing.
With a cluster of flowers in my antlers I walk.
This is the truth you asked for.
Dressed in flowers, I am going.
Never again I, never will I on this world be walking.

Somehow he has to get back to Hermosillo. Surely Elder Mattea has exposed the depth of his betrayal. How will he explain what he saw here in the wilderness?

I have ears to the wilderness, as I am walking.

Whether I turn to the right or to the left, I hear a voice behind me saying, This is the way, walk in it.

Is this the truth they've asked for?

Here in the wilderness, I am killed and taken.

The four boys who have all become little deer brothers laugh at him, his stiff attempts to dance as deer dance. There is a song for his failure: *You who do not have enchanted legs, what are you looking for?* There is sorrow: *The fawn will not make flowers.* There is consolation: *White butterflies in a row are flying.*

Helen, if the butterflies survived the night, why can't we live one more day, one more hour?

My children climbed the stairs, and their enchanted father followed. But the music did not cease. The song surged through wood and wire, a wild river of blood, the throbbing pulse in my skull and pelvis.

I had to rise, or die there.

I came to Seth and Davia in their dark rooms to kiss their mouths and eyelids. They allowed it; they indulged me, my generous ones, my children who are not mine, who do not belong to me, these two who belong to God and rain and river, who saved me with a song, who found the secret chord, who held me even now, floating on the surface of their music.

I kissed them, and I left them; I let them go, my darlings.

I came to my own room, the room where my husband lay on the bed, not undressed, not sleeping. I opened the window to feel snow fall: everywhere, snow—six inches since morning, feathery and light, merciful snow, silent snow, snow that would be fast to melt, snow that in the dark seemed endless. Liam rose and stood behind me, and I leaned back; I let my weight fall against him; I let my husband gently rock me. And in the hour that came at last, in the new day just beginning, I began to speak, and he began to hear me.

My mother was alive again today, but dying, and my father fell as light on the tree where Datiel is hanging. Edith, Efron, Tzili, Judit. Helen drowned today with Seth and Davia, and I couldn't climb the stairs to save you in the shower. Then you all came home with Amiela and Éva, and three deer stared inside to bless us. Davia played cello and piano while the wind played violin and zither. Seth sang Hallelujah as he walked into the fire. Children with metal ribs climbed trees and leaped to the ground without breaking. Samuel eased Violette into the water, and my father walked in the water beside them. God appeared as Louise Doren. God appeared as hidden sparrows. God appeared as a starving woman who offered her soup and bread to my mother. God became wine, and we drank Him.

Edith Spier became herself and bore three children. She called them El Shaddai, El Olom, El Khai. Bertók Spier made a coffin for himself without wood or grief or nails. Lilike saved the son of a stranger, and Juli Kinderman crowned herself Prince of Denmark. Karin answered every question: I'm not afraid; I'm not hungry. We ate pomegranates and plums and apples, and God as fruit sustained us. Karin said, Cecilia is my favorite saint. My mother played her violin while a burned boy slipped free of flayed skin to emerge as owl, and pig, and peacock. Vonda Jean lay down naked on a black sand beach so hot her whole body melted, and the 'apapane birds sang her name and the dark-eyed man ate fire. Peter Kinderman saw Clare as she was before she knew, before she imagined, and their daughter Helen came home with open eyes to comfort them. Hevel Lok pressed his ear to a child's chest and heard the boy's blood roaring. All the hungry birds of Europe landed at Éva Spier's feet, and she fed them, and she laughed, and my father swore he'd never leave, and then he left us. My mother's bones washed away in an icy river, but we were not afraid because the twilight came, and the song, and the angels, and we had survived; we had lived through it, and the doll named Anastasia split her own skull to spill her secrets. Our children heard the first word and laughed like God as they became water. They held me, they gave me strength, and I took Helen Kinderman in my arms, and I kissed her leg as she rose, and all her people, all their love and grief, poured into me.

Now, even now, Jay Kinderman begins his long walk back to Hermosillo. *With a cluster of flowers in my antlers I walk.*

I hear the wilderness as I am walking. Late, so late. There will be repercussions and restrictions, the ritual of repentance or even a return home—depending. And if that, how will he explain and who will understand him? Only Helen. He was called to go, and made to follow, and the children taught him a song, and the woman built a fire, and the food they shared gave life to God inside them, and they danced with enchanted legs, deer with flowers in their antlers. Helen will understand when he says: *Nobody wants to die, but sometimes little deer brother offers himself to the people. In the wilderness, I am killed and taken. I am not afraid. I am joyful. The bush under the tree is singing. There is no such thing as "I." Oh, sweet sister! This is the truth you asked for.*

Please note: the translations of lines from Yaqui Deer Songs appear in *Yaqui Deer Songs,* by Larry Evers and Felipe S. Molina, and come from numerous songs. The phrases have been rearranged and juxtaposed (and occasionally altered) in Jay Kinderman's mind to create his own deer song, a prayer of praise and wonder. He hears the words of the prophet Isaiah, too, strikingly in tone with the deer songs.

Acknowledgments

I am grateful to the Lannan Foundation for providing
sanctuary and support in Marfa, Texas. I am also grateful
to the National Endowment for the Arts; the Mrs. Giles
Whiting Foundation; Corby Skinner and the Writer's
Voice Project in Billings, Montana; Bob Goldberg and
the Tanner Humanities Center; the University of Utah,
especially Dean Robert Newman and the College of
Humanities; the New York Foundation for the Arts; The
Ohio State University; the Utah Arts Council; the St.
Botolph Club Foundation of Boston; the Massachusetts
Artists Foundation; the Ohio Arts Council; and the
Centrum Arts and Creative Education Residency Program
in Port Townsend, Washington. The faith of these individuals and the support of these institutions have made my
work possible. The Avery and Jule Hopwood Award and
the Virginia L. Voss Memorial Award at the University of
Michigan gave me the courage to begin and the will to con-
tinue. Thank you.

I thank my family for their unwavering belief, their extraordinary contributions to research, their joyful reading, and

patient listening. Dear Gary, Glenna, Laurie, Wendy, Tom, Melinda, Kelsey, Chris, Mike, Sam, Brad, Hayley—Dear Mom, dear Father even now—Dear Cleora, Randy, Alicia, Valerie, Kimmer, Kristi—Dear Jan and John: without your love, there are no stories. Thank you.

To my students who shatter all opinions and challenge all assumptions, thank you.

The blessing of my agent Irene Skolnick's friendship and dedication has upheld me for twenty-five years. I am also indebted to Erin Harris for her generosity and commitment. Thank you.

To the editors of the journals where these stories first appeared—*Antioch Review, Agni, Paris Review, Antaeus, Granta, Ontario Review, Bomb, Story, Southern Review, Hudson Review*, and *Drumlummon Views*—thank you.

I am grateful to my friend and editor, Fiona McCrae, to Steve Woodward, and to the entire staff at Graywolf Press. Thank you.

Many friends have sustained me through the journeys of these stories. Kate Coles, Christine Flanagan, Caz Phillips, Mary Pinard, Miles Coiner, Antje Lühl, Matthew Archibald, Eric Shapiro, Don Engelman, Janet Kaufman, Diedre Kindsfather, Leigh Gilmore, Lauren Abramson, Michael Anne Sullivan, Alice Lichtenstein, Andre Dubus,

ACKNOWLEGMENTS

Michael Martone, Vonnie Mahugh Day, Glenn and Ginnie Walters, Georgina Kleege, Nick Howe, John Vaillant, Erin McGraw, Roy Tompkins, George Lord, Margot Rogers Calabrese, Bruce Hilliard, Ruth Anderson, Annea Lockwood, Sheila Moss, Diana Joseph, Beth Domholdt, Margaret Himley, Jane Marie Law, David Gewanter, Dev Lerman, Reesie Johnson, Barbara Painter, Mark Robbins, Mary Tabor, Betsy Burton, Matthew and Jenae Batt, Bruce Machart, Randy Schwickert, Larry Cooper, Halina Duraj, Katy Ryan, David McGlynn, Stephanie Matlak, Matthew Pelikan, Ken Miller, Jill Patterson, Megan Sexton, Joel Long, Lance and Andi Olsen: dear friends, for your love and companionship, inspiration and insight, for reading with joy and contributing to research, I thank you.

Melanie Rae Thon is the author of two collections of stories, *First, Body* and *Girls in the Grass,* and four novels. She was named a Best Young American Novelist by *Granta,* and has received a Whiting Writers' Award, two fellowships from the National Endowment for the Arts, and a Writing Residency from the Lannan Foundation. She teaches at the University of Utah.

Book design by Connie Kuhnz.
Composition by BookMobile Design and Publishing
Services, Minneapolis, Minnesota.
Manufactured by Versa Press on acid-free 30 percent
postconsumer wastepaper.